Block Party

True 2 Life Street Series

Part II

Block Party

Al–Saadiq Banks

True 2 Life Productions

Block Party

For information contact:
True 2 Life Productions
P.O. Box 8722
Newark, NJ 07108
E-mail: True2lifeproductions@verizon.net
Website: www.True2LifeProductions.com
Author's E-mail: Alsaadiqbanks@aol.com

ISBN: 0-9740610-1-8

Printed in Canada

Introduction

Today is my first day home. The last time I saw the streets was August of "93" when the judge sentenced me to 108 months in federal prison.

I was released about 26 months before my time was up. I'm the first one from my crew to make it home. In total, seven of us were busted. They charged us with everything including organized crime, money laundering, and tax evasion. You name it, we were charged with it.

Being that I had no prior convictions and they didn't have any recorded phone conversations with me on them, I got off the easiest. At the time of my departure, I was 28 years old. The others ranged from 31 to 38 years old. We were nabbed through our cellular phones. The leader, the eldest member of the crew, ignorantly started doing business with a federal agent. He was welcomed with open arms. We fully trusted him, and we were thrilled that he sold kilos to us so cheap. That was the bait he used to reel us in. At that particular time, kilos were going for $21,000 a pop; we were getting them at $14,000 a piece. Greed made us accept him without a doubt.

He knew everything about all of us. He knew where everyone lived, and he even knew each of our girlfriends personally. Everything was fine until he supposedly came across a cellular phone connection and gave every member of the crew a phone.

We never did business with him directly. The only two who did business with him were Big Jake and Ab. They're never coming home. The feds have them on tape negotiating a deal consisting of 50 kilos.

Big Jake and Ab were the leaders. They bought the work and distributed it to me and the other four guys. Each of us controlled our designated part of the city. Jake and Ab were selling kilos all over the planet. Never did I imagine how much money they were making until we were on trial and all the evidence was brought up.

One thing Ab always told us was to mind our own business and only worry about what we were doing. His saying was "Never look in a man's mouth while he's eating." I always took heed; besides, I had too much on my own plate. I was only a baby in the game, and I was already getting major loot. Ab always told me how much love they had for me. They admired the way I handled my business and stayed out of theirs.

I learned so much from those guys. They taught me all kinds of money getting tactics and strategies. But now it's over. They're never coming home. No more Jake and no more Ab. Just me, "Cashmere," and I'm going to make it to the top one way or another.

Just watch me!

CHAPTER 1

June 2000

"Baby, are you ready?" Love asks as she hurries to the door.

"Yeah, here I come," I reply. "Where are my car keys?"

"On the top of the refrigerator," Love answers.

Love is my wife. We got married while I was in prison four years ago. Don't ask me why such a beautiful person would marry a prisoner. At times I ask myself that same question. She has so much going for her. She has beauty and brains, not to mention that she has the cutest little shape- petite but sexy. She's built sort of like a ballerina. She only stands about 5 feet 4 inches.

Love is an English teacher at a high school. I met her when she was in college. We would hang out every now and then, but it was nothing serious. Back then I had too many women to take one seriously. Shit, I was only 20 years old, and I was already ghetto rich.

For the entire first year that I was away all my chicks came to visit me, and they wrote to me faithfully. But eventually, they all faded- all except Love.

When I was upstate, she would visit me every weekend for years. I was totally shocked when she proposed to me. I mean, I felt the same way for her, but I didn't want to play myself by proposing to her and getting rejected. I accepted, and she's been holding me down ever since. That's why I promised her a big wedding and the biggest ring I could afford, just to show her my gratitude.

"Damn baby, you look good this morning," I compliment.

"Thank you," she replies, blushing from ear to ear.

She does look good this morning. She's so beautiful. Like I told you earlier, she is 5 feet 4 inches and she only weighs 105 pounds. She is very petite, but she fills out in all the right places. She has hair well past shoulder length. Her complexion is a reddish-Indian colored tone. She has big brown eyes and the prettiest smile you could ever see. She is so attractive. She doesn't have to wear tight clothes to get attention. Her natural beauty alone turns the heads of everyone in her presence.

"Give me a kiss," I suggest. **(Smooch) "Give me another one,"** I demand.

"No, come on. I'm going to be late," she says as she opens the front door. **"Come on!"**

Sniff! *Aghh! This ghetto air sure smells good. This is one of the things I missed the most. Spending seven years cooped up in prison made me realize how ungrateful I was. I mean, it's a blessing just to be able to walk out to your porch and take a big sniff of this polluted air. I wouldn't give it up for the world.*

I couldn't have come home at a better time. Today is such a beautiful day. Today is the first day of summer. The temperature is perfect; it's not too hot. It's only about 76 degrees, with a nice breeze.

As we reach the porch, I notice a junkie all huddled up on my bottom step.

"Pardon me, are you waiting for someone?" I ask.
"Huh?"
"I said, are you waiting for someone?"
"Nah," he answers quickly.
"Well, I would appreciate it if you don't block my porch."
"The Mayor instructed me to sit here," he replies.
"What?" I ask.
"The Mayor, he told me to sit here and watch over the block."
"The Mayor?" I ask. **"Who the fuck is the Mayor? Listen, the Mayor don't own this house, I do. I bought this**

house for my grandmother nine years ago for $160,000 cash. Me, not the Mayor, not the fucking president. Now get the fuck off my stoop."

"Calm down honey," Love insists.

"Nah, fuck that!"

"Whoa, whoa, I don't want any trouble with you. I'm getting up," shouts the man as he rises and starts crossing the street. "You'll have to settle this with the Mayor."

"Fuck the Mayor! Tell him I said it. My name is Cashmere."

"All right, I'll tell him," he replies arrogantly.

"Baby, baby, calm down," Love whispers as we walk through the alleyway toward the garage.

This is my first time in my car in seven years. It's a 1993 S-500 Mercedes Benz with a walnut colored interior. I bought it brand spanking new. Back then it cost me $70,000 cash. It doesn't look quite the way I remember it, with seven years of dirt covering it.

As I get out to jump my battery with my wife's car, I notice the filthy rims. Never would I have let my rims get this dirty. I still remember the exact day I bought them. At that time, Lorinsers were going for $2,500 a tire. I was so in love with this car. I used to hand wash and wax it myself every morning.

"Baby, try to start it up now," I shout. "There we go. Rev it up a little bit." (Vroom, Vroom!) *As I sit behind the wheel letting the car warm up, I go back in time. I envision Love and me back when we were just dating. You couldn't tell me nothing, riding around the town in a brand new Mercedes. I was just barely 20 years old. Niggas was hating, but they couldn't do anything. They knew better than to cross anybody from our crew. Big Jake didn't play. He was the muscle. He loved to put in work.*

"Come on Donald. I'm going to be late!" *Love interrupts my thoughts. Oh yeah, Donald is my government name-Donald Pierson. Cashmere is my nickname.*

9

As we bounce down the avenue, I turn on the cassette. You wouldn't believe what came out of the speakers- Miss. Jones singing on Ron G's back- to- school- mix tape. Whoa, that definitely takes me back. My favorite tape is still in the tape player.

Love laughs. **"I haven't heard that song in a long time."**

"Word up," I agree.

"I was so tired of you and that tape," she admits. "Every time you came to pick me up, you always had that same tape playing."

"Yeah, this was my favorite joint."

"Pull over right here," says Love. (Smooch) "Bye baby. I'll see you at this exit at 3 o'clock."

"All right," I confirm. *As I watch her walk through the door, I realize how lucky I am to have a wife like her. For seven years she has held me down, and she also took care of my grandmother while she was sick. After Big Ma died, Love kept the house up. Big Ma died from throat cancer my first year into my bid. She loved to smoke cigarettes.*

Big Ma raised me. My mother and father are both strung out on drugs somewhere in who knows where. Actually, who cares? I haven't seen either of them since I was about 5 years old. I probably wouldn't recognize them if they were right in my face. After they walked out of my life, Big Ma took all the pictures she had of my mother off the wall. It was like she never existed. As for my father's side of the family, I don't know any of them.

As I get closer to the house where my kids live, I get nervous. I haven't seen them in three years. We lost contact once I left from upstate. Prior to that, my sister always brought them to visit me. From there, they shipped me off to Indiana. You know, I didn't get a single visit while I was out there.

What will I say to them? Will they remember me? We have a lot of catching up to do.

I have two boys. Ahmir is the older one. He's nine, and

Ahmad is eight. The mother, well that's another story. Her name is Desire. She's a money- grubbing weed head, whom I spent most of my time and money with. I couldn't shake her. Everywhere I went, she always ended up too until my last day on the street. I haven't seen or heard from her since I've been away. Any dealings that I had with my two boys were through my sister.

Desire had a baby by some cat that everyone called Rah-Base, who later turned out to be Rah-Base head. Now he's a straight crackhead. I've heard he's running around here smoked out, weighing about 125 pounds. He was a big nigga, about 185 pounds solid. He's from across town. He supposedly was big time. I don't know him. He wasn't big time when I was home. The only niggas who were moving out was us, and if you weren't with us, you couldn't eat. There were no stragglers; Jake made sure of that.

As I pull up in front of the house, I notice a black Denali with big rims parked in the driveway. It's fully loaded. It has televisions, running boards, chrome pipes- the works.

My heart is pounding so hard as I walk up the stairs. Before I can ring the bell, the door opens up.

"What's up Big Time? Bang Man! They finally let your ass go, huh?"

This is Desire's father. He's my man. He's a junkie has-been. At one time, he was the shit. Back in his day, he really had it going on. He had more money than you could imagine. In the 70s, any drugs that came through this town came through him. The only problem was that he loved to shoot dope. After his wife left him, he went haywire. She always complained about his lifestyle, and then one day, she picked up and left him and Desire. Her whereabouts are unknown.

This guy knows everything. Anything you need to know, just ask him. He schooled me about these streets. Had I listened to him, I wouldn't have gotten cased up. He told me over and over again to stay away from Jake and Ab. He had known them ever since they were little kids, and had watched them grow up. He always told me their greed would be the cause of their downfall. He would say

11

"Boy you keep running around here with them, you're going to go to jail forever." I didn't want to hear it. I was living the life.

"Slim, what's up?" I ask.

"Bang Man, I'm so glad to see you!" he shouts back.

"I'm glad to see you too."

As I look Slim over, I notice that his hands and feet are much bigger than they were. They're also swollen from shooting dope. His feet are busting out of his sneakers. He cut slits in his sneakers so his feet could fit in them. And his hands, they look like 14-ounce-boxing gloves.

"Where are you headed?" I ask.

"Bang Man!" *That's how he starts the majority of his sentences. He says it's a habit. He's done that ever since I first met him.* **"I'm about to go down the hill and do me. I'm on E."** *E means he needs his morning dose of dope.* **"Let me get $10 Big Time," Slim begs. "I'm sick. If I don't get my medicine, I'm going to shit on myself."** *That's the effect the dope has on some people. If they can't get it, some will throw up or even shit on themselves. They can't function without it. The majority of them will just lay around, cramped up, suffering with aching bones until they get a hit.*

"Here you go," I offer. "Get two bags." *I hate to see Slim sick. He's done so much for me. Anything I can do to help him, I'll do it. I know giving him dope isn't really helping him, but if I don't give it to him, he'll be in a world of pain. What am I supposed to do?*

"Bang Man, thanks. I didn't know how I was going to get off E. I might have had to pull my razor on a motherfucker, he admits with a smile. *He's smiling, but he's serious. A dope fiend can get violent if you have what he needs and won't help him. I've seen it done a million times. Dope isn't pleasure; it's a necessity. Users have to have it by any means. Never forget that.*

"When are we getting back in business?" Slim asks as he limps down the stairs.

"I don't know yet, but I got big plans," I reply.

12

"Bang Man, that's what I'm talking about!" he shouts. "Big Time, let me give you a word for the wise. No more cocaine. The dope game done took over."

"Yeah?"

"Yeah," he answers. "Did I ever steer you wrong?"

"You know I don't know nothing about the dope game," I admit. "All I ever fucked with was that powder."

"What do you think I'm here for?" he asks. "I know all about it."

"All right Slim. We'll kick it later. Are my boys in there?"

"Yeah, they're in the back. Desire is in the room with some little chump. This is his truck right here. I'm glad you're home; maybe you can knock some sense into her head. She's out of control. She won't listen to me. She's a damn go-go dancer now."

"Yeah?" I question as if I didn't already know.

"Yeah, little gold-digging hoochie. I take the blame though. It's all my fault. I gave her too much. I spoiled her. Back when I was rich, I gave her whatever she wanted. She was only six years old, wearing mink coats and riding in the back of Cadillacs. She's used to the finer things in life. Then you came along and added more fuel to the fire. She never had to work for anything. All she knows how to do is put on a sad face when she wants something. But the game has changed. These young boys are a lot smarter than ya'll was, Big Time. You gotta fuck and suck these young niggas before you get a soda out of them. Ain't shit free!"

"I hear that," I agree.

"Bang Man, let me get moving before I pass out right here," Slim says.

"All right, later Slim."

I thought about what Slim just said. It was partly my fault; I did help spoil her. Instead of pushing her to do something with her life, I just gave her money to tear up the mall. Now she's almost 40

*years old with three kids and no skills. She's resorted to shaking
her ass for a living and letting niggas stick their dirty fingers in her
pussy for one lousy- ass dollar.*

*I had heard about her. My sister told me back when she first
started dancing.*

(Knock! Knock!) *No one answers.* **(Knock! Knock!)**
The door opens slowly. It's my older boy, Ahmir. **"Daddy!" he
screams.** *He jumps into my arms. Then Ahmad, who was sitting
in the middle of the room playing video games, slams the controller
down and runs over to me. Both of them together almost knock me
off my feet. It feels so good to know the love is still here.*

"Owwww! Owww! Stop boy!" screams a female voice.
"Ahmir! Ahmad! Help Mommy!" *When I look into the kitchen,
I see Desire rolling around on the floor play- fighting with some
nigga.*

"Mommy! Mommy! Daddy's home!" Ahmir yells.
*When she looks up and finally sees me, I can see the embarrassment
in her face. She's laying there with her hair all wild, and she has
it dyed honey-blond. I must admit it looks pretty good on her. All
she's wearing is a sports bra that's about two sizes too small for her
and some tight coochie shorts.*

*They both hurry to their feet. The giggling stops. Desire
walks over to me while the young boy takes a seat at the kitchen
table.*

*Desire's shorts are so small you can see the blackness on the
bottom of her ass cheeks. Her ass is the darkest part of her body.
She has a pretty, dark- chocolate complexion, but her behind is so
black it looks blue. Back in the day, I would tease her about that.
She hated that.*

*She definitely has her weight up. I can tell she's been
working out. Shit, she has to, being that she's a dancer. She has to
stay fit. Her body is her meal ticket now.*

*Her thighs are so tight and strong looking, like the legs of
a track runner. The sweat all over her body makes her chocolate
skin glisten. All of the wrestling around must have made her horny,*

because her big hard nipples are ripping right through her bra.

"What's up?" she asks with the dumbest look on her face. "When you came home?" she questions.

"Last night," I reply. *The kid starts walking from the kitchen. He can barely look me in the eyes as he passes me. I can't help but notice his big, baggy jeans. He's wearing about size 40 jeans when his waist can't be any bigger than a size 30. His pants are sagging damn near to the floor, showing his boxers.*

"Ma, I'm out. Hit me later," he whispers as he diddy bops. *He's walking like he's the coolest motherfucker in the world. I have never seen a motherfucker this cool.*

"All right later," Desire replies. *Ahmad closes the door behind him.*

"Were you baby-sitting?" I ask sarcastically.

"Huh?" Desire responds with a confused look on her face.

"Are you his baby- sitter, or is he one of the kids' classmates?"

"Stop playing boy!"

"Na, I'm serious. Why are you rolling around on the floor play- fighting with their little schoolmates?"

He isn't that young looking, but he does look too young for Desire. He doesn't even have any facial hair. He appears to be about 16 years old. One thing I learned as a youngster is, that when you push up on an older woman when you're 18 and broke, you're just plain 18. You're too young. But when you're 18 with money, it's all right. It seems like the cash evens everything out. It adds five to ten years on to your age.

"Go ahead Cash."

"Na, for real, how old is he?" I ask.

"Why?"

"I just want to know."

"Why do you want to know?" she questions.

Pssst! *I suck my teeth in frustration.* "How old is the

damn boy?"

"Do it matter?" Desire asks.

"Hell yeah, it matters! I want to know what kind of niggas you got my boys around. For all I know he could be a blood or crip, gangbanging and shit. I don't want my boys around that madness!" I shout.

"Your boys are all right."

"Don't change the subject! How old is he?"

"Oh boy!" Desire shouts. "Nineteen Cash, damn!"

"Nineteen? Girl, you almost 35 years old and you fucking with teenagers. You crazy as hell!"

"That's my business!" she replies. "I ain't asking you about Love, am I?"

"Don't ask about Love," I reply.

"I ain't! Fuck Love!" she screams.

"Fuck you!" I shout defensively.

"No fuck you!" she yells back.

I don't want to get into this with her. I knew she would start as soon as I got here. Ughh, Aghh. I take a deep breath to calm myself down, and then I walk over to the little raggedy, worn- out, black leather sofa and take a seat. My boys jump on my back, and we start to play-fight.

This is the day I've been looking forward to.

After wrestling with my boys, we play video games for about three hours. They beat me at every game. Before I know it, it's 12 in the afternoon, and time for me to leave.

As I stand up and start to give my little men the Peace, Desire calls out. "Cash!"

"What?"

"Come here before you leave," she demands.

"Where are you?"

"Back here," she yells. *I know what she's calling me for. She wants to beg me for some money. I'm just getting home, and she's already going to ask me for money.*

When I enter the kitchen, I don't see her. Then she calls

me again. **"Cash!"** *Her voice is coming from the direction of the bathroom. I walk over there. To my surprise, she's standing in the middle of the bathroom floor, butt naked. Soapsuds cover her entire body. The shower is running boiling- hot water, so the room is completely foggy.*

"What?" I ask.

"Come here," she whispers.

"For what?"

"Just come here," she demands. "I want to ask you something." *Judging by the look on her face, I know what she wants to ask me. She has her horny face on. I remember that face.*

"Ask me what?"

"Come in here. I don't want the boys to hear me." *When I step into the bathroom, she quickly kicks her leg up and closes the door with her foot. She rests her foot on the doorknob as if she is securing it so no one can get in and I can't get out.*

There she stands directly in front of me. She has me pinned against the wall. Her legs are wide open. She is so clean-shaven I can't help but see the pinkness of the inside of her pussy. Her clit is peeking out from between her tiny dark lips.

Oh boy! I swallow the lump that forms in my throat.

"Huh? What do you want to ask me?" I inquire with a high- pitched squeaky voice.

"Come on," she begs.

"Come on what?"

"Let's do it," she whispers in a low, sexy voice as she rubs my chest.

"Chill Desire."

"Don't you miss this pussy?" she asks as she gently strokes herself. "I miss that," she whispers.

Before I know it, she grabs a handful of my dick and starts groping it. I push her off.

"Chill, Desire."

"Chill what?" she asks.

"Cool out Dee!"

17

Now she's leaning on me with all of her weight. She starts humping on me. I struggle to push her off. As I push her, she falls to her knees. She starts to tease me by gently nibbling my dick through my jeans. The more she nibbles, the more excited I become. I 'm getting weak. I'm almost ready to give in. Finally, I manage to lift her up. She turns around and backs up on me. She starts rubbing her soft ass against me, then bends over and grabs her ankles. After she's fully bent over, she starts grinding her butt in a slow, circular motion. Her heavy breathing is beginning to turn me on. Finally, I squirm to the side and push her away. She stumbles to the sink. I quickly grab the door and open it.

As I step into the hall, she speaks. **"Oh, it's like that? All right. It's like that. I see. I see."**

"You see what?" I ask.

"Cash, I can't get none?"

"Go ahead with that shit Desire."

"Oh, I see. You don't want to cheat on your wife, huh? Get your punk ass out of here."

She's furious. She slowly bends over to pick up her shorts from the floor. Before rising, she pauses for a second, allowing me to see her big ass spread open. She peeks at me from between her legs. I guess she thinks I'll change my mind.

"Later girl."

"Fuck you," she shouts.

I then walk back into the living room, hug my boys, and bounce.

On my way home, I turn the air conditioner on full blast to cool off. Desire definitely had my temperature up. A little more grinding ain't no telling how things might have turned out.

What was she thinking? Did she think I would smash her? I don't know. I can't blame her for trying though. Look at me, my first day home. I ain't fucked nothing in all these years. I got my weight all up, skin looking good. I got the just- coming- home-glow. No, no! Ah, ah! She probably thought she could give me some and have me running around here all strung out over her again, spending all my money on her. I know her. Her biggest fear is probably me getting an asshole full of money and her not being able to get any of it.

When I pull into my driveway, I notice a small group of people forming on my stoop. I zoom up the alleyway. As I quickly walk to the front, I'm steaming with fury. I step to the group. I take notice of a man standing in the middle of the group. He hands everyone around him something while a frail, dirty woman collects the money.

"Block party! Block party!" she yells *at the top of her lungs.* **"Hand me the money, get the dope, and keep it moving!"** she instructs. **"No hanging around! Clear it up! Clear it up!"**

After all the customers are served and the crowd clears out, I can finally see the face of the man who's handing out the work. It's the same guy who was out here this morning.

"Yo, what the fuck did I tell you?" I ask. *He doesn't respond. He just looks me in the eyes as if I haven't said a word. I hate to be ignored. I grab him by his neck and push him down. One hand is on his collar, and the other is pointed in his face.*
"I see you're a hardheaded motherfucker! If I catch you on my stoop again, I'm going to pop you. Do you hear me?" *I shake him by the collar. He still doesn't respond. He's sitting there like a deaf mute who can't understand a word of what I'm saying. Then he nods his head to someone behind me as if he's signaling the person. When I turn around to see who he's looking at, I see one man crossing the street toward us. He's dressed in all black. I can't see his eyes because he has a skullcap pulled down to the bridge of his nose. Then appear two more men, with hoods on their heads. The hoods are drawn tight. They're coming from each direction, and they have their hands tucked in their pockets. I'm not a fool. I realize what's going on. I let the man's collar go, and I back up against my porch so I can watch all of them.*

As they approach me, one of them draws his gun and points it at my chest. My heart is racing. I'm scared to death, but I refuse to let them sense it. I stand there face to face with the gunman. Out of the corner of my eye, I can see a blue Intrepid pull up and stop in the middle of the street. The windows are so dark that it's impossible to see who's driving. One thing I do notice is the out- of- state- license plates.

"I told you that you would have to settle this with the Mayor," **the man brags.** *I still don't say a word; I just give him a cold stare. The gunman grabs me by the collar and tries to snatch me closer to him. I push him back and try to position myself away from the wall. The other men simultaneously draw their guns. The Intrepid's driver- side window slowly begins to roll down.*

"Hold up. Hold up. Let him go," **the driver shouts.** *The men then back up, but they still have their guns aimed at me.* **"Put the guns up,"** **the driver instructs.** **"Cash! What's happening?"** *I glance over at the car, still trying to keep an eye on the gunmen. I don't have a clue who this guy is. He's a young, long- faced kid with chinky eyes. He has diamond earrings in his ear that are the size of nickels. He appears to be about 19 or 20 years old.*

"Who are you?" **I ask.**

"You don't remember me?" **he asks with a big smile.**

"No, not at all," **I admit.** *The more I stare, the more I realize I don't know this kid from a can of paint.*

"Dre's little brother!" **he shouts.**

"Junebug? Are you Junebug?" **I ask him.**

The kid then pulls over to the curb and parks, and the gunmen get into the car. As the kid steps out, all I can see is his long, skinny legs. It seems like his long ass is never going to make it out of the little car.

This kid has definitely grown. The last time I saw him, he was about 11 years old. A little guy, now he's standing over me. I'm 6 feet 2 inches; this kid has to be about 6 feet 6 inches. He looks like an NBA ball player. His jewelry is crazy. He has platinum everything. His watch is fluttered with so many diamonds you can't even see the face. Not those cloudy ghetto diamonds you normally see in the hood; these are good- quality diamonds, clean and sparkling. Each time he moves, you can see the rainbow reflection bouncing everywhere. The glare alone can blind you.

He has on big baggy jeans, sagging well below his waist. As a matter of fact, he has on the same kind of jeans Desire's little friend had on- Omavi. That must be the latest designer. Times have changed. When I left Polo was the shit. I guess Omavi has taken over.

He has on a tight tank top that shows off his little muscles. You can tell he hits the gym regularly. He is slim framed, but he's ripped up. He sort of looks like a statue of one of those Greek gods. His upper body is covered with tattoos. One of his tattoos especially stands out. It takes up his entire arm. It's a picture of a tombstone, and it reads **R.I.P. CHARLES.** *The tombstone has teardrops coming from the bottom of it. Right next to it is a geographical sketch of Italy, broken into little pieces, with blood dripping from them.*

Charles was their father. He was a number runner for some Italian mob men. More than ten years ago police found his body in a lake at the park. Rumor has it that the Italians murdered him because he cut a side deal with another family.

Junebug's hair is faded with big curls on top. This is my man Dre's little brother. The more I look at him, the more I can see the resemblance, especially with his hair cut like that. They're mixed. Their mother is from the Philippines, and their father was black. The ladies loved Dre. He was a straight pretty boy. Growing up, we had to take the girls he didn't want. He always got first pick on every chick. Dre is one of the dudes that caught the fed beef with us. I haven't heard from him in two years. We were keeping in touch, but somehow the letters went from once a week to once a month to no letters at all. After five years in the joint, you start running out of shit to talk about. It's the same thing over and over, day in and day out.

"What's up nigga?" **Junebug asks.**

"You," **I reply.**

"When did you get home?"

"Last night. What's up with Dre?" I ask.

"He's cooling. He's in Florida right now."

"How long has he been there?"

"About three months," Junebug replies.

"He should be short, right?"

"Yeah, he should be coming home in 2004. Yo, don't mind that shit that just happened. They told me somebody was around here mouthing off. I didn't know it was you," he claims.

"Nah, the man was blocking my stoop this morning. Me and my wife couldn't even get past," I explain. "I told him to get up, and he started telling me some shit about some Mayor. I told him, fuck the Mayor." *Junebug chuckles with a cheesy grin. Before I can spit the words from my lips, a dopehead lady walks by.* "What's up Mayor?"

I stand motionless for a moment.

"They call you the Mayor?" I ask.

"Yeah," he answers blushing from ear to ear.

"Mayor? How did you get that title?"

"Well, for the past few years I've been holding everything together around here."

"Yeah?"

"So what do you think about the block?" he asks. "I've made a lot of changes out here since you left."

"I see. What's up with that blowcaine money?" I ask.

"I don't really fuck around with that cocaine too much. Every now and then I'll buy a bird or two and let my little niggas pump it with my dope. I'm killing them with the dope," he says.

"Yeah, I can tell," I admit. "I see the crowd."

"Yeah, that's that Block Party! I named it Block Party because any given day that you come out here, there are so many customers out here it looks like we're having a block party," he brags. "I'm doing 100 bricks a day out here." *(A brick consists of 50 bags of dope. Each bag costs $10.)*

"Damn, the block amped up like that?" I ask.

"Hell yeah!" he shouts.

"What's that, like $50,000 a day?" I calculate.

"Yeah. I pay them junkies $50 off each brick. I step off with about $15,000 profit a day."

"How many of ya'll out here?"

"What do you mean?"

"How many other crews are out here?" I ask.

"Out here?" he questions sarcastically. "Ain't no other crews out here, or nowhere near me," he replies. "Are you crazy? I ain't having that! I wish a nigga would sell some dope around here; my young goons will tear his ass up. My young jacks don't play," he says confidently as he points to the five *dudes in the car.* "Them boys wild. They don't care about nothing. The oldest one is only 18 years old. That's my first-born. My baby ain't but 15 years old. He'll pull the trigger faster than any one of them. None of them don't have a problem mirking (murdering) a nigga," he claims.

His arrogance is starting to piss me off. I guess he's telling me this to warn me about trying to get my old block back. I don't have plans of coming back to the streets, but if push comes to shove, him and his young goons will have to pack it up. Especially now that those young boys just disrespected me like that.

"So Cash, what are your plans?"

"I'm not sure yet," I reply. "I got a few things brewing, but I'm not sure if I'm ready yet. I don't want to jump out there yet. I'm just going to sit back and take baby steps," I explain. "I met a Mexican boy upstate. He was real big on me. He gave me his brother's phone number and told me to call him as soon as I touch down. My man got four more years to do. They got a connection out of this world. I mean, unlimited kilos of blow. It's just a matter of when and where I want to put my hat down. You know how the old song goes, "wherever I lay my hat is my home," I sing. *I have to tell him that just to let him know I'm Cashmere, and I can get money anywhere in this town. I paid dues around here. I pioneered this block. That'll be the day when I let some young punks tell me where I can put my thing down.*

"I feel you," he claims. "Do you need anything?"

"Nah, I'm straight," I reply. "Everything is in order."

"Are you sure? You don't have to be modest."

"Nah, seriously, I'm all right, but good looking out though."

"No problem," he replies. "Anything I can help you with, just holler. Later Cash, I'm out."

"Alright later," I reply.

After shaking hands, he starts walking toward the car and I begin walking up the steps.

"Just holler if you need me!" he yells as he opens the car door.

I go inside the house and plop onto the couch. I'm furious. These young jacks just played me, and on top of that, this little punk motherfucker, who I used to stop motherfuckers from chasing home, in so many words just told me I can't come back out here. Never in all my years on the street have I been disrespected like this. Ten years ago, this never would have happened. I guess the game has changed.

CHAPTER 2

A couple of days pass. They're not working from my stoop anymore. They moved about seven houses down. The block stays so crowded. It's nothing like the way I used to have it. I mean, I sold a lot of cocaine out here, but it was a little more discreet. These young niggas act like this shit is legal. I guess there's no quiet way to sell 100 bricks a day.

As for the Mayor, I'm really getting tired of him. I see him every morning before dropping Love off to work. Every morning, he has a slicker remark than the day before. That money has really gone to his head. He thinks he's untouchable, and he truly thinks his young goons are ready for war.

"Listen baby, I'm driving my own car today," says Love.

"That's cool. I have a few things to handle anyway."

"Let's go out the back door," Love insists.

We proceed out the back door and get into our separate cars. Love pulls out of the yard first. As she slowly drives down the alleyway, I can't help but notice the rust spot that's beginning to form on the trunk of her 1986 Honda Accord. As soon as I start back rolling, I'm going to buy her a brand new car of her choice.

When I get to the end of the driveway, the first thing I see is the blue Intrepid. Please let him keep on going, But unfortunately, he stops and rolls down his window. He then gestures me to roll my window down.

Here we are, blocking up the street as the cars behind us are blowing their horns. As I look into his car, me and the passenger lock eyes. He just sits there nodding his head up and down with a crooked- tooth grin. This kid is ugly. If it weren't for his big pop eyes and his raggedy yellow teeth, you wouldn't be able to see him. His skin is pitch black, and his big bald head makes him look like an alien.

"Yo, pull the fuck over! Ya'll blocking the motherfucking street up!" *Yells a man in the car behind Junebug.*

Before I know it, the Intrepid's back door flies open. A short kid jumps out with a 44 magnum in his hand. All the horn blowing stops.

"What the fuck did you just say?" the gunman asks as he points the gun at the driver.

The driver is shook. He's trying to speak, but he's tongue-tied. **"I, I, I," he stutters.**

"Shut the fuck up, punk!" the young kid yells. "Do you know who the fuck is driving that car up there?" he asks while pointing to the Intrepid.

"N, n, no," the man stutters.

"That's the motherfucking Mayor! Don't ever yell at him! Do you hear me?" *The driver doesn't respond. This makes the gunman furious.* **"Motherfucker, do you hear me?" he asks.** *He then grabs the door handle of the Lincoln Continental, opens the door, and drags the man out.*

This is an older man, about 50 years old. The gunman appears to be about 17 years old. The man is old enough to be the kid's grandfather.

"Go up there and apologize to the Mayor!" the kid shouts.

The man nervously walks to Junebug's car. He keeps his eyes on the gun- toting teenager the whole time. **"I apologize," he mumbles.** *You can see the embarrassment in his face, but it's the fear in his heart that makes him swallow his pride and do what he has to do to make it out of this situation.*

"What do you want me to do to him?" the teenager asks. "Nothing. Let him live," June bug replies. "Pop, watch your mouth when you come through here!" Junebug yells as the man walks back to his car and sits patiently.

I feel sorry for the man. These kids have no respect. They really think they own this town.

"What's up Cash?" Junebug asks.

"Nothing much," I reply.

Junebug can tell by the sound of my voice that I'm not too happy about what just happened.

"Let me get out of here before my goons hurt something," he laughs. "I'll kick it with you later!"

" Alright later," I reply.

As we're pulling off, he yells out the window. "You need to get out of that dinosaur!"

"What?"

"That dinosaur," he repeats. "That old ass Benz you're in! They changed the shape. That's not a good look for you!"

All the passengers laugh as Junebug takes off.

These guys are really getting under my skin. It takes a lot for me not to say something to them. Mainly I think it's the respect I have for Dre, but I don't know how long that's going to last. My patience is really getting thin. I've only been home for a few days, and I'm already fed up with them.

I decide to spend the entire day with my boys. When I pull in front of Desire's house, I notice Slim sitting on the porch. As I'm parking, he limps over to the car and sticks his head in the window. He has tears in his eyes, and his mouth is white like he's dehydrated.

"Your boys not here, man," his voice drags. "They left with Desire."

"Where did they go?"

"I don't know man. They left over 20 minutes ago. I think they went school shopping," he adds.

"What's the matter Slim?"

"Bang Man, Pop fucked up man. I'm sick. I need my medicine. Please look out for me, Big Time," Slim begs.

"Damn Slim, she getting the best of you."

"Getting? She already got the best of me," Slim admits.

Slim looks pitiful. His pain is showing in his face.

"Get in man! I'll take you there." *His eyes light up.*

Bang Man, thanks! I don't think I could have made it all the way over there. My bones are aching."

"Slim, you need to slow down. How many bags do you do a day?"

"In one day?" Slim asks. *The look in his eyes lets me know he's fumbling for an answer.*

"Yeah, one day," I reply sarcastically.

"Uh, uh, I ain't sure man," he answers foolishly.

"What do you mean, you're not sure? How many bags of dope do you use in one day?"

"Big Time, that's personal."

"Personal? I didn't know nothing was personal when it came to us. At least it wasn't when I left." *He just offended me. Back in the day, we never kept secrets.*

"Bang Man, you right." *He lowers his head in shame.* "I'm just embarrassed to tell you," he admits.

"How many?"

"Nine," he mumbles.

"Nine! Damn, Slim! You doing nine bags a day?"

"Yeah," he answers with shame.

"So you spend $630 a week on dope?" *He nods his head up and down.*

"I was doing more than that," he admits. "I was up to 12 bags a day. You see, I was working with some jitterbugs on the block. Being that I had access to all the dope, I was getting high just because. Before I knew it, I had a 12- bag- a- day habit."

"Turn right here," Slim instructs.

"So what block were you on?"

"I was across town," Slim replies.

"What happened? Why did you stop?"

"Oh, I got knocked off and them punks left me in jail stinking," he explains.

"Yeah?"

"Yeah! My bail wasn't nothing but $500. All the money I made them; they let me sit on that punk ass bail. They played

28

me like a dope fiend."

Like a dope fiend? He must not be aware of who he is right now.

"Make the right," he blurts out. *I then hand him $30.*
"Here, get three," I insist.
"Bang Man, good looking out, I owe you a million."
Slim jumps out and follows the small crowd into an alleyway. At least 20 other customers are forming a line at the beginning of the alleyway. Besides that, 50 others are swarming the block. As far as clientele goes, this block has to be running neck and neck with Dre's little brother's block. Cars are double-parked everywhere. Lookouts are standing on every corner. Every customer I watch go in comes right back out almost instantly- all except Slim.

I'm beginning to get nervous until five minutes later when I see Slim limping out of the alleyway of the house next door.

As he sits down in the seat, he's wiping his arm with his handkerchief. When he notices me watching, he quickly unrolls his sleeve. Slim always wears long-sleeved shirts no matter how hot it is. It could be 100 degrees and he still wouldn't wear his arms out. He has to hide the tracks that are all over his arms. Slim doesn't have a clean spot anywhere on his arms. He's been shooting dope ever since the early 70s.

He can't even look me in the face. I guess he's too embarrassed. The stupid look on his face reassures me that he has already shot his dose, not to mention him nodding. He can barely keep his eyes open.

"Yo fam, clear this up!" the young boy yells to me as I pull off.

"Shut the fuck up," I yell back to him. *The nerve of this nigga talking to me like I'm one of these dope fiend motherfuckers. I look over at Slim. He's in the middle of one the biggest nods ever.*

"Damn Slim! Is that shit that good?" I ask.

"Bang man, this the best shit around," he says slowly with a dry voice. *The dope is really starting to settle in.* **"This that**

29

Block Party. Ain't nothing touching this! On a scale of one to ten, this is an eight."

"Block Party?" I ask. "Don't they have that across town?"

"Yeah," he replies. "The kid got two spots."

"Oh, you know him?" I ask.

"Yeah, I know him!" Slim shouts. "Everybody knows the Mayor! I used to work with him."

"Yeah?"

"Yeah, I taught that boy everything he knows. I'm the one who told him to stop struggling with that coke and get some dope. The same thing I told you. Ask him; he'll tell you. Bang Man, that young boy blew up overnight! I used to go over to New York with him. Man, let me tell you, he wasn't picking up no more than 28 grams, and it would take him all week to sell it. That's when I told him, young blood you playing with this shit, you are wasting your time. If you get caught, you gonna get the same time as the big boys, so you might as well play like the big boys. Them crackers ain't playing; they giving out football numbers. Leave this coke alone. It ain't working for you."

"He started off buying seven dollar bags, you know, that tabletop shit. He'd buy the bags for seven dollars and sell them for ten dollars. Next thing you know, he hooked up with somebody. I don't know who, but Bang Man, that motherfucker blew up right before my eyes. He went from Dre's little brother to the Mayor!" Slim shouts.

"So you really do know him?" I ask.

"Yeah I know him!" Slim answers. "I even know where the stash house is, unless he moved it."

"So what's up with the kid? Is he cool?"

"Yeah, he's cool. If he wasn't cool, you know I wouldn't fuck with him," Slim adds. "He reminds me a lot of you when you were younger."

"Oh yeah?" *Shit, he ain't nothing like me!*

"Yeah! He's strictly business," says Slim.

"What about them niggas he be with?"

"Who, his goon squad?" Slim asks. "Them young boys crazy!"

"Are they really that wild or what?"

"Yeah, they definitely that wild!"

"Them motherfuckers know who to play that shit with," I shout.

"Nah, Big Time, them boys don't care about nobody. I never seen them back down from nobody, not even the police. The Mayor controls them boys' minds. All he does is point the finger and they do the rest. I seen them shoot motherfuckers broad daylight 2 o'clock in the afternoon in front of everybody-no mask or nothing. I remember he used to always tell them: Do whatever you want. I have enough bail money, to bail us out for the rest of our lives, and my lawyer can beat any case."

"So he thinks he's untouchable, huh?"

"Yeah," Slim replies. "As of right now, he hasn't been touched. Only one nigga had the balls to try him. Do you remember Crazy Rob?" Slim asks.

"Yeah, I remember him. He got killed a couple of years ago, right?"

"My point exactly," says Slim. "Bang Man, Crazy Rob had just come home. He came around there and tried to extort the Mayor. Word on the street is he told the Mayor he wanted $25,000 or else. He had a whole crew backing him, a bunch of killers. They set up a meeting place. When they met up, the Mayor had a surprise for them. One of them boys snuck up on him and shot him in the face eight times. Police found his body in the cemetery. He was laying there ass naked. Bang Man, them boys ruthless!"

"Did anybody get caught?"

"Yeah, they tried to charge two of them but they beat it. They got the toughest lawyer in the state. That's why them boys run around here like that. They think they're on top of the world."

"I just hope when I put my thing down, they just stay out of my way," I shout out.

"When are you coming back?" Slim asks.

"I'm not sure yet. Right now I'm just keeping my eyes open and my ears to the street."

"Bang Man, don't take too long. I'm ready to eat!"

"Slim, you know if I eat, you'll eat."

"Bang Man, I know you'll take care of me. You always do."

I pause before speaking again.

"Slim, I just want one more run. I'm not going to make a career out of this shit. Three months, that's it. Ninety days. Whatever I don't get in 90 days, I'm never going to get."

"Bang Man, now you're talking. I just hope you stick to the script."

"I will."

"Yeah, that's what your mouth say, but you know how it goes. Once you start getting that fast money, it's hard to stop," says Slim.

We both sit quietly, no music playing or anything. We're just riding with no destination. I don't know what Slim is thinking about, but I can tell he's deep in thought. I can tell by the way he's picking his raggedy teeth, the few he has left. He's missing the front four teeth in the top row and the bottom row. The ones he has left are brittle and brown from decay. He always picks his teeth when he has something on his mind.

Me, I'm reminiscing about back in the day, before I went away. If I hadn't gone to jail, I probably would be rich right now. I was making so much money, I didn't know what to do with it. I just wish I had someone in my corner to teach me how to manage my money and invest in something legal. Then I wouldn't have to hit the streets now. I would have been straight, out of the game. But you know the saying "You have to learn how to live with regrets."

Slim interrupts. "Bang Man, I'm sitting here thinking about the old days. It's all fucked up now! If I would have saved just one third of the money that done went through these hands," Slim says with a frustrated tone as he lifts his ashy, mitten- sized hands before his eyes and stares at them in disgust. "Boy, I was rich! But I was living the fast life. $2,500 suits, Alligator shoes, three Caddies at a time. Look at me now! I ain't got a pot to piss in." *He sits there nodding his head with tears forming in his eyes. I never seen this side of Slim. I guess he's living with regrets too.*

"Bang Man, whatever you do, don't end up like me. Do something with your money. Don't end up 60 years old and broke. Look at me. I'm broke! I'm too old to work! I can't collect Social Security, cause I ain't never worked nowhere. I'm fucked up. All the money I done made, I'm going to die broke. Huh! Huh!" he chuckles. Ain't that something?"

"Slim, don't worry, I got you. Just stick with me. We're going to blow. Just trust me. All you have to do is just ease up on the dope and I'll handle the rest." *Slim continues to pick his teeth. I know he has something serious on his mind. I know him too well. I can read him like a book.*

"What's up?" I ask. "What's on your mind?"

Slim doesn't say a word; he just looks me in the eyes. I see 60 years of pain, suffering and stress in his face. At 60 years old, he looks like he's 80. They say the streets will do that to you.

"Bang Man, I got something to tell you." *He pauses for half a minute. He doesn't look at me. He keeps his eyes straight ahead.* "Big Time, I'm fucked up," he whispers.

"Fucked up how?" I ask.

"I'm fucked up, fucked up."

"Slim, what the fuck are you talking about?"

He pauses again.

"Bang Man, I got that thang," he mumbles.

"That thing? What thing?"

"The monster. AIDS man," he admits.

My heart drops. AIDS? I don't know what to say to him. I fumble for words.

33

"Big Time, please don't look at me different," he begs.

"How can I look at you different?"

"You the first person I ever told this to. Desire don't even know. Promise me you won't tell her."

"Slim; don't ever disrespect me like that! Have I ever told any of our business? How long have you had it?"

"I found out a long time ago but it just started having an effect on me the past couple of years," he explains. "Bang Man, I'm a dead man walking. Do you know the worst part of it all?"

"What's that?"

"I passed that shit to Desire's momma."

"Yeah?" I ask. *This is a shock to me.*

"Yeah man, that's why she left me. She was too embarrassed. She didn't want her friends to find out. I destroyed that woman's life, man."

"Do you know where she's at?" I ask.

"Yeah, dead!" he shouts.

"Dead?"

"Yeah, she died four years ago. Desire don't know that either," he adds.

"How do you know then?"

"I ran into her brother sometime last year. He told me. He wanted to kill me. I had to beg for my life, man. He told me that after she left me, she moved with her aunt in Alabama, where she died."

"Damn Slim, when are you going to tell Desire?"

"Bang Man, I want to but I'm scared."

"Scared of what?"

"Scared that she'll hate me. Big Time, she's all I got. She hates her mother for leaving her. If I tell her why her mother left, I'm afraid she'll hate me too."

"Slim, you have to tell her."

"I know," he says as he slowly nods his head up and down.

"How did you get it?"

"I don't know if it was them dirty needles or them dirty hoes. It was probably both," he adds. "But I didn't really share needles. I mean, I might have slipped up a few times, but them hoes, I had to have them. When I look back, I can't figure it out. I had the baddest wife in this town, and I'm out tricking with them filthy hoes. The baddest wife," he repeats. "Desire's momma was something pretty. She was a model when I met her, but I begged her to stop modeling. I was so jealous; I didn't want anybody else to look at her. I made her put her dream on hold. How selfish was that? I talked her into putting everything on hold just to be a housewife. Can you believe, as beautiful as she was, I barely slept with her? I was so busy tricking them filthy bitches, I had a beautiful young wife at home who wasn't getting fucked. Sometimes I would go two months without fucking her. And when I did, it would only last about 30 seconds. I would only give her 30 seconds of this dirty, AIDS infested dick. Bang Man, I'm ready to die!" he shouts. "I want to die!" he screams even louder. "I want to die, so I can see Desire's momma and beg and plead for her to forgive me. I ain't happy here! I ain't gonna be happy till I die! How can I still live with myself, after I have killed the only woman I ever loved? Big Time, I'm a murderer! A damn murderer," Slim cries.

He starts banging his head onto the dashboard. After about four times, he screams out, "I want to die! I want to die!"

I've never seen Slim act like this. He's crying loud with no shame, just like a baby. Snot runs from his nose. I don't say a word. What can I say? I just continue to drive. I drive for about two hours before dropping him off.

As we approach his house, my two boys are in front throwing a basketball against the garage. When they see me, they haul ass toward the curb. "Daddy! Daddy!"

"What's up ya'll?" I ask.

"Nothing," they reply.

"I was here earlier. Where were ya'll?"

"We left with Mommy and Ice," Ahmir replies.

"Ice? Who's Ice?"

"Mommy's boyfriend!" Ahmad replies. "You know, the one with the black truck."

Damn, the thought of my boys chilling with this guy really crushes me. For a second, it feels like my sons crossed me.

"Daddy, does that truck cost more than your car?" Ahmad asks.

"Why Ahmad?"

"Cause Ice said your car ain't nothing!" he replies.

"Yeah, he said it's played out!" Ahmir adds.

"He said that?"

"Yeah, and he told me you ain't nothing. You broke," Ahmir states.

"Daddy, are you broke?" Ahmad asks.

I don't answer. I just chuckle. I'm smiling on the outside, but my insides are raging. Those words cut like a knife. This nigga is trying to belittle me to my boys. I'm like a superhero to them, and he's trying to make them think differently. I'm not going to let anyone come between me and my boys.

"Get the ball and get in," I demand trying to change the subject before I really get pissed.

As they run to get the ball, I pick up my car phone to call Desire. "Yo, the boys leaving with me."

"Whatever!" she replies sarcastically.

Stinking bitch! How can she allow this motherfucker to play me in front of my boys? "Let me tell you something bitch!"

"Your mother is a bitch!" she replies.

"You better tell that young motherfucker to keep my name out his mouth," I shout.

"You tell him!" she shouts.

"Listen bitch, if you love him, you better tell him before I put his ass to sleep."

"You ain't gonna do shit!" Desire shouts. "He ain't

scared of you!"

"He should be!"

"Cash, you ain't nobody! You still living off that old shit! Nobody ain't worried about you. Jake and Ab ain't here no more."

"What you just say, bitch?"

"You heard me!" she replies.

After hearing that, I'm at a loss for words. She has just totally disrespected me, like I'm nobody. Just to think, this is how she really sees me. She doesn't see me as a stand- up nigga. She sees me as a punk who needs Jake and Ab to handle my problems.

"Desire, you heard what I said! You better tell him to watch his mouth before I get at him! You dumb ass bitch!" *I hang up. That bitch just made me furious, acting as if I'm some punk motherfucker who won't finish that little nigga. Not only am I mad, I'm hurt. She hurt my pride. I have to straighten my face; my boys are on their way to the car.*

I take them to the park to give them some pointers on basketball. I can barely concentrate. That shit Desire said to me keeps sounding off in my head over and over. After about an hour of shooting around, I finally manage to put Desire in the back of my head. Watching my boys bounce that ball up and down the court helps me take my mind off of her. To my surprise, Ahmir, my older boy, his game is serious. He can handle that ball, and he can shoot from anywhere. Come to find out he's been playing on small- fry teams ever since he was four years old. I didn't even know. I've been away for too long.

CHAPTER 3

It's Saturday morning, Labor Day weekend, the last weekend of the summer. I think today is the hottest day of the summer. It's 98 degrees, hot and muggy.

I'm on my way to the car wash. I have to get the car cleaned. It's filthy. Today me and Love are going to spend the day together. We're going to New York to do a little shopping, eat, and maybe catch a movie.

As I'm in the bathroom washing up, I raise the window to let in some fresh air. **"Block Party! Block Party!"** is all I can hear. I'm so tired of hearing that. I hear that first thing in the morning, and then I hear it before I go to sleep and anytime in between that I happen to be around here.

When I pull out of the alleyway and drive to the corner, I notice that the streets are blocked off with orange cones. As I get out to move the cone so I can get past, a black Mercedes Benz pulls up. It's sparkling clean. The interior is lighter than mine. It's more like a bone white. The rims are so shiny the glare almost blinds me. The car has a temporary license plate on the front windshield. I can't see the driver because the temp tag is blocking my view.

While sliding the cone over, I cut my eye at the car. I don't want the driver to see me looking; he might think I'm sweating his car. As I glance, the only thing I can see are these big platinum earrings. **"Cash!"** It's Junebug. And here comes the Intrepid right behind him. His goons are in that. I can tell because the driver has the window down, blasting Tupac. **"Do you want to ride or die?"**

"What up Junebug?"

"Mayor!" he corrects, with a cold face.

"Yeah all right, stop playing with me boy," I holler **jokingly.**

38

"Nah, I'm serious. My name is the Mayor. I would never disrespect you by calling you Donald. You go by Cash; that's what I call you. Right or wrong?"

I don't respond. He's right, but I'll be damned if I call him Mayor. I'll call him anything but that.

"I see you got a new whip, huh?" I ask.

"Yeah, I saved up all the money you paid me for going to the store for you when I was a kid!" he says sarcastically with a smile on his face. *Him saying that reminded me of the times his mother would bring him to the corner store, where I was posted up. His mother would slap his face every time they came to the store. He would make her wait while he shook hands with everybody who stood on the corner. He just wanted to be down with the big boys; he couldn't have been older than six at the time. I used to watch him as his mom dragged him by his arm. The look in his eyes told me that one day he was sure to play the game. He used to watch all of us in admiration. He would look each of us up and down as he shook our hands.*

In his passenger seat sits one of the prettiest Chinese chicks you could ever see. They look like two movie stars sitting in there. They have on matching Cartier wood-frame shades. The wood from their eyeglasses complements the wood grain all over the interior of the car. If I didn't know him, I would have sworn he was a rapper or a ball player or something.

"Yo, if you ain't doing nothing later, come through! I'm having a Block Party out here, celebrating my 19th birthday," he says.

"Yeah?" I ask, as if I'm really concerned.

"Yeah, that's why I bought this car," he claims.

"Happy born day!"

"Thanks! So are you going to stop by or what?" he asks. "It's going to be real nice. I got a lot of big time rappers coming through to rock the M.I.C. Plus I got some cats from my label rocking. You know I got my own label right?"

Another motherfucker in the music business. Every young

39

nigga thinks he can rap. "Nah, I didn't know," I reply.

"Yeah, I had it for a while now. My goon squad, they'll be on the microphone. They all right; you need to check them out!"

"Nah, I won't be able to. I'm taking my wife out today. I'm on my way to the car wash now."

"Are you taking your wife out in that car?" he asks sarcastically. "Stop playing!" he shouts. "Don't make your wife suffer like that. She held you down all these years and this is how you're going to repay her? You're going to make her ride around in that old ass Benz. As a matter of fact, you don't call that a Benz. You call that old motherfucker a Mercedes. You riding around here looking like an old school rapper," he jokes. "Throw your hands in the air and wave them like you just don't care!" he sings as he waves his hands in the air from side to side. *The driver of the Intrepid is laughing loud and hard. The Chinese girl is looking shocked as if she can't believe he's talking to me like this. Right now I'm furious. He's going on and on.* "Here, take my car! I'll drive the Intrepid," he urges.

"Nah, I'm good."

"Here let's switch," he insists.

"Nah!" .

"You better not leave that old motherfucker with me; I'll run that big raggedy boat into a wall."

Now I'm enraged. It feels as if the whole world is laughing at me. I have to get him back. I have to say something slick.

"**Listen Junebug!**" *That catches his attention. Everyone stops laughing and gets quiet. His face turns red.* "**The shit you doing, I already done it. The places you thinking about going, I already been there. I'm Cashmere, a legend and an icon. You consider yourself the Mayor of this little ass town. I'm well respected here, New York, Indiana, Wyoming, Florida, and Nebraska. That's right, federal prison!**" I shout. "**Not Annandale, not Bordentown, Federal Prison! I've been federal material for a long time. You've just become! You're a rookie;**

I'm a veteran! Welcome to the Big League! I hope you're worthy. Any fool can make money, but it take a real nigga to hold onto it. I'm not impressed by how you ball out when shit rolling. I need to see how you ball when shit slow down. I've been away for almost ten years. You hear me? Shit been slow for me almost ten years now and I bet you I can still match you dollar for dollar. Stay in your lane little boy!"

I walk back to my car and exhale. That was a mouthful. "Later Mayor!" I yell sarcastically. *I then stare into the eyes of the driver of the Intrepid. Little ugly motherfucker, I think out loud.*

As I pass the car, I look at the numbers on the back. They read S500. It's the new version of mine. It costs about $85,000. I can't hate. That young boy is definitely going hard.

On my way to the car wash, I can't help but think about what he said about making my wife suffer. I wonder if she feels like that? Although she's never been one to care about materialistic shit, we're due for an upgrade. I mean I don't care who you are, everybody likes nice shit. Nah, I can't think like that. I can't let that young boy make me lose focus. I did that already. I'm on some new shit. I want get out the game money, so I can retire comfortably to my legitimate businesses. Fuck a car. I'm not about to compete with him. I'll get back in the game when I'm ready to get back in the game- not a minute before.

CHAPTER 4

It's Monday morning. I picked up Slim bright and early. He asked me to take him over to the spot so he can get off E. As we pull up, I notice that the block is crowded as usual. Before I can pull up to the alleyway where they're pitching (dealing) from, Slim jumps out. He doesn't even wait for me to stop. He jumps out while the car is still moving.

Slim is about the twentieth person in line, but the line is moving rapidly. When he gets to the front of the line, a tall, dirty dope fiend hands him the dope and he disappears into the alleyway, just like he always does.

As I'm sitting here, I see the Intrepid pull up on the opposite side of the street. The driver jumps out first and quickly glances over the entire block. Then he nods his head for the passengers to follow. The passengers jump out simultaneously. The smallest of the passengers dashes across the street like a track star. He's holding a big shopping bag in his hand. He runs right through the alleyway where they're hustling from. The driver stands on the curb.

The little kid comes back out in about two minutes flat with no shopping bag in his hand. The shopping bag must have been filled with dope.

The kid then walks over to the driver and they start conversing. The whole time they're standing there, me and the driver continuously take long stares at each other.

After about five minutes, Slim finally limps out of the alleyway. As he gets close to the curb, he stops. He then bends over, lifts his pants leg up, and begins scratching his leg. The scratching looks more like he's digging right through his skin. Something about heroin makes the user itch. The scratching session lasts about a good 30 seconds.

The driver looks over at Slim. He does a double take. Then he immediately runs over to Slim. By now Slim is stepping off the curb. I know the kid is about to do something. I can tell by the devilish look in his eyes.

I open the door and get out, but it's already too late. Slim is already in the air. The kid scoops him up and earth slams him onto the concrete. Slim lands on his back. Everyone stops and watches in amazement. It seems like it's taking me forever to get over there.

When I finally get there, the kid is standing over Slim. He's about to stomp him. His foot is in midair. Slim is laying there helplessly. His high has faded out, and fear has taken over. I push the kid before he can stomp Slim.

"Yo motherfucker!" I shout. *Slim quickly gets to his feet. The kid pushes me.* **"Nigga, don't put your hands on me, I'll kill you!"** he shouts. *I push him again. Now all the goons have surrounded us.*

"What the fuck did you slam him for?" I ask.

"Mind your business before I slam you!" he shouts back.

"Go ahead and slam me!" I challenge. **"I bet you, you can't slam me!"** I further challenge. *He starts to come at me, and then he stops and shakes his head.*

"Slim, you better give me my fucking money you owe me!" the kid shouts. **"I ain't bullshitting with you! If I don't get my money, I'm going to fuck your old ass up and nobody ain't going to be able to stop me. I don't care who you go get,"** he adds.

Slim doesn't respond he just stands there looking pitiful. One thing I do notice is that Slim already has his straight razor opened. The kid can run up on him if he wants to, but it would be a bloody sight.

"Slim, you owe this motherfucker some money?" I ask.

"Yeah," he answers slowly.

"Mind your business man!" the kid screams.

"Nigga, don't tell me what to do," I shout back.

43

"Alright, you can't say I didn't warn you," he whispers.

"Don't warn me! Just make your move," I shout. *By this time, out of the corner of my eye I see a dope fiend walk over and slide another kid a shiny chrome banger (gun). I don't let them know I saw the transaction.*

Right now they have the upper hand on me. I take my tone down a notch- not too much, just a little bit. I don't want them to think I'm backing down. That's all they need to see is a sign of fear and they'll really try to take advantage of the situation. But on the same token, I don't want to get them pissed off at me either.

"How much do you owe him?" I ask *in a low tone.*

Slim hesitated before answering.

"Four hundred and fifty dollars," he mumbles.

I then reach into my pocket and pull out my money. I have $500 even in my pocket. I peel the $50 bill off the top and hand the kid the rest. He snatches it out of my hand and starts to count it. Somehow the kid with the gun has eased behind us.

As we start to walk away, I glance over at the gunman just to make sure he's not making a move. He looks me straight in the eyes without blinking. "So that debt over with, right?" I ask the kid.

"If you say so," the kid replies, never once looking at me. *He just looks in the sky, shaking his head up and down with a satanic smile on his face.*

We ease to the car. I get in and sit down. Exhale! *Damn, for a minute I thought they were going to kill us right here. I wish I had my banger on me. Then again, maybe not. Shit might have gotten ugly. I got too much to lose right now. I look over at Slim. After he closes the door, he closes his razor.*

I can tell his pride is hurt. "Big Time, you didn't have to pay my debt."

"Slim, that nigga wanted to kill you out there. What do you owe him for anyway?"

He doesn't answer right away.

"Remember I told you I was working with some young boys and they let me sit in jail without bailing me out?" he asks.

"Yeah!" I reply. "It was them?"

"Yeah, it was them," he replies. "After I finally got out, I came back around and they put me back to work. As soon as they put me in the hole, I might have sold one bag, before I slipped through the backyard," he admits.

"You ran off?"

"Hell yeah!" he brags. "They owed me that!"

"How much did you run off with?"

"Three bricks!" (*One brick consists of 50 bags.*)

"So how do you only owe him $450?"

"Oh, the Mayor came to the house and told me just pay him for two bricks, being that I had to pay my own bail, or Desire paid it rather. I paid for one already, but I wasn't going to pay for that last one," he explains.

"So if you talked to Junebug already, what does that kid have to do with it?"

"Well, he was the one who gave me the work," Slim explains. "He had to pay for it out of his money because he was responsible for it."

I pull off slowly, watching all of them just in case they start shooting.

Neither of us say a word for about 20 minutes. Then Slim mumbles, "Big Time, I hope you're not looking at me different. Them boys played me. I was loyal to them. They could have bailed me out."

"Slim, I ain't looking at you different, but that ain't the way to do shit. You don't repay a motherfucker by stealing from him. That's snake shit! You know that ain't the man way to do shit."

Slim pauses for a moment, then mumbles. "Big Time, you're right."

"I know I'm right. You know how I know?" I ask.

"How?"

"Because you told me the exact same shit a long time ago. Remember the time I showed you five kilos and I told you Ab gave them to me?"

"Yeah."

"Do you remember telling me to treasure the fact that someone had that much trust in me. You told me at all cost to make sure I get that money back to him. You said a man with good credit is worth more than a man with all the money in the world. You have to practice what you preach."

Slim sits quietly for a minute. "So I guess I just fucked up my credit report?"

I don't answer him I just let him soak in it. Even though he's right, I don't want to let him know I agree with him. I don't want him to think stealing is acceptable in my eyes.

CHAPTER 5

Not five days have passed since the battle of words me and Junebug had before I call my Mexican boy's brother up. I try to make myself believe I'm doing this for me, but deep down inside, I know it's because of what Junebug said to me.

I'm supposed to meet with the Mexican dude this weekend in Connecticut. I guess me and Slim will take a ride up there.

Meanwhile, for the next three days I need to start putting some things in motion. I would hate to get hold of some work and not be able to move it. So basically I have to hit the streets and do a little groundwork. I need to know who is buying cocaine, who they are buying it from, and how much they are paying for it. Basically, my plan is to corner the market and beat any price out there, even if that means selling kilos for a half a point ($500) more than I pay for them. You see, in the cocaine business, it's not how much profit you make off of one bird; it's how many birds you can move.

This is going to take a lot of networking. Networking is the hardest part of the business, because you have to deal with too many egos, and some niggas' egos are bigger than their bank accounts. They want you to believe they're buying kilos when in all reality they're only buying ounces. These niggas are what you call fronting ass niggas. These dudes have everything: clothes, furs, jewelry, and expensive cars. But the money they have in their pockets is all they have to their name; it's the re- up money, the car note money, the rent money, and the boss's money all in one. They look good on the outside, but on the inside they're crying, struggling like a motherfucker. They don't know how they're going to pay the car note (they lie and tell everyone it's paid for), and they still live at home with their moms. This kind of dude is always on the scene, running his mouth about how he's doing this and how *he's doing that. In all actuality, all he's looking for is a handout. When his car finally gets repossessed, you won't see him anywhere. He'll hide out until he swindles enough money up to put $2,000 or $3,000 down on another $80,000 car. He's a dude with champagne taste, but he only has beer money.*

These are the guys I'm trying to avoid this go-round. You get too many problems dealing with these kinds of guys. You lose too much money. They always want consignment, knowing they can't pay you back. 'Just front me a kilo, I'll have your money in two days, is what he says', knowing he never even had a quarter of a kilo. Instead of just admitting to himself that a bird is too much work for him to handle, what does he do? He takes it. It takes him a month to finish it; he fucks up the profit and the money he owes you.

In order for me to do my networking, I have to be in the places where everybody is at. What's a better place than the go-go bar? Naked women are something everyone has in common. There you can find anyone: police, drug dealers, pimps, murderers, and stick- up kids. You name them, they're in there.

Me and Slim just pull up in front. As I'm parking, I notice all the exotic cars parked in front. I almost want to hide my old ass car down the block. Ever since Junebug said that slick shit to me, I've been kind of self-conscious about driving my car.

"Bang Man, it's a lot of money in here tonight!" Slim shouts. "Look at all these big cars out here. I can smell money!" *Slim smiles as he takes a sniff of the air. He isn't lying. All kinds of cars are out here. Some shit you've only seen in magazines. Judging by the type of cars that are out front, I think I may have picked the wrong night. These cars appear to belong to businessmen. But when I get inside, I don't see a nigga in here over 21. I ask myself if these guys are really getting money like that or are they fronting?*

The security guard meets us at the door and asks us for I.D. Can you imagine, he asked us for I.D? I'm almost 40, and Slim is 60 and some change. But these teenage kids are in here doing what they want. After the security guard frisks us, we immediately stand against the wall.

My attention is drawn to the center of the stage. Right in the middle of the stage there sits a big black bathtub. The entire tub is trimmed in gold. It's not really the tub that catches my attention; it's what's in the tub. Four ass naked women and some young kid are in the tub. Apparently, they picked the kid from the audience. How lucky is he? Two of the women are tearing the kid's clothes off of him. One of them is a petite black girl, and the other is a thick white girl with the fattest ass I've ever seen on a white girl. He stands there bashfully as they attack him like vultures. When they finally get his clothes off, they commence to lick his entire body. One is on his right leg and the other is on his left. They're on their knees. They reach his middle simultaneously. They both anxiously reach for his tool. They begin to fight for it playfully. While both of them are looking up at him, they tug back and forth on it. Each one takes a big lick before the other one snatches it out of her mouth. Finally, they begin to share him. They alternate, taking two licks apiece. At the end of the second lick, they passionately tongue kiss while the head of his dick is in both of their mouths. After the wet sloppy kiss they both take on separate jobs. The black girl continues to suck him off, while the white girl licks his balls.

The other two are Asian. They look like they could be twins. Both of them are extremely thin with enormous titties. They're putting on a show of their own. One is standing up showering. She has her legs slightly spread apart while the other one is on her knees submissively, licking her crazily. Her tiny body trembles uncontrollably as she reaches her climax. Beads of water drip down her tiny- framed body as the water sprays from the shower.

Finally, they sensually rub baby oil all over each other. They didn't miss a spot. Their sexy bodies glow as they lay there hugged up in each other's arms like they've fallen sound asleep. All five of them lay in the tub soaking wet.

"Whew! Yeah!" Clap! Clap! *The crowd is going wild.*

49

A tall, slender kid is approaching us. I don't know where he came from because I was so busy watching the show. He's all smiles for the entire walk. I can't place his face at first, but as he gets closer, he begins to look more familiar.

"Slim, do you know him?"

"Who?"

"The kid walking over here."

"Oh yeah, that's Wu," he whispers.

"Little Wu from around my way?"

"Yeah," Slim answers.

"I knew I know him, I just didn't know where from," I admit.

"Cashmere, what up!" Wu hollers, from five feet away.

"What up!" I reply.

"You don't even know who I am!"

"Come on man, I know who you are," I reply.

"Who?" he asks, trying to test me.

"Little Wu!"

"All right, I thought you was fronting," he admits. "When did you come home?"

"I checked in a couple of weeks ago," I reply. "What is your young ass doing in here?"

"Young, I ain't young. I'm 20 years old."

"Young like I said; you ain't 21. What's up with your father? Is he all right?" *His father was my man. He used to move out with us. He's locked up in Virginia. He caught his case two years before we got jammed up. I think he was sentenced to 20 years. He got caught with something small but they don't play in the down states. You'd be better off killing somebody down there than to get caught with drugs. What really hurt him was the transporting charge they hit him with.*

"Yeah, he all right. I take care of him," Wu answers.

"You take care of him? You can't even take care of yourself," I joke.

"Yeah, all right," he replies. "Oh, what up Slim?" *He*

finally acknowledges Slim.

"**What up, young blood?**" **Slim replies.**

I hate how everyone disrespects and overlooks Slim. If this were 30 years ago, they would be happy just to be in his presence. He was really a made man. But I guess they're too young to respect his gangster. These young boys don't care anything about what you used to do. They're only concerned with what you are doing now.

"**So what's up Cash?**" **he asks.**

"**Nothing, just chilling.**"

"**Yeah, whatever!**" **he shouts.** "**I ain't never known you to be just chilling. You can tell me. I ain't wired; I ain't no FED,**" **he laughs.**

"**Nah man, I doing nothing yet.**"

"**Yet, you said the magic word. What do you plan on doing?**"

"**I'm not sure yet. I'm trying to put some things together.**"

"**Well, when you put shit together, bring me in.**"

"**Bring you in, huh?**" **I ask.** "**What are you doing?**"

"**I'm fucking with that cook up** *(crack.)* **I'm tearing they ass up in the projects!**"

"**Oh yeah?**"

"**Hell yeah!**"

"**Are you cooking it yourself, or are you buying it cooked already?**" **I ask.**

"**Hell no, nobody ain't cooking shit for me. I'm cooking myself. That's how you really eat,**" **he explains.**

"**How are you doing with it?**"

"**Nigga, what did I just tell you?**" **he questions.** "**I told you I'm killing them. Slim, what's wrong with him? He must think it's a game,**" **he shouts with a big smile on his face.** *Slim just smiles and brushes him off.*

"**I go through about 200 grams a day out there. I got one whole side of the projects to myself. Everybody else selling that dope. I go through a half a joint** *(half a kilo)* **every two** days. I could do more than that, but I don't be having enough of that shit. If I had more, I could bang more. But my money ain't calling for that shit right now," Wu explains.

"Shit, if you're doing it like you say you are, you should be straight!" I shout.

"Yeah, I was straight but I've been taking too many losses," he answers. "Two weeks ago, police ran up in the court and knocked off three of my little men. Between the shit they found and their bail money, my dough funny as hell right now," he explains.

"Wu!" *A group of kids scream, as they're walking out the door.* "Yo, I'm out! Here, take my number!" *He begins to write his number down on a napkin. After he writes it down, he hurries to the door.* "Hit me!" he shouts.

"What's up with him?" I ask Slim as Wu runs through the door.

"I don't know what he doing but one thing I know is, they selling a lot of cook up in them projects," Slim answers.

"Yeah?" *I tuck his number in my pants pocket. That's one candidate.*

The way these guys are dressed, with all the jewelry and all the champagne they're popping, you would think we were at a video shoot. It seems like everyone is focusing on us; they're not even paying attention to the chicks. I guess we look out of place. We're the oldest guys in the bar. Even the owner of the bar is young. He's sitting behind the counter sipping champagne. He doesn't look much older than 23 or 24.

"Slim, what are you drinking?"

"Bang Man, let me get a Scotch," he replies.

I wave to get the barmaid's attention.

"Yes, may I help you?"

I'm standing here almost drooling. I can't even answer. I'm speechless. This chick has a set of titties I can't believe- big and round with thick, dark nipples. She's a smooth, honey complexioned chick with long, curly hair. Her jet-black hair falls well past her slim waistline. Streaks of blond highlight her hair. She has green eyes and pretty white teeth.

"Hello, may I take your order?" she asks again.

She speaks with an accent that sounds like she's Brazilian.

"Yeah, let me get a Scotch, for him and get me a cranberry juice."

"OK, give me a second."

As she's walking away, I can't help but notice her fat ass. It's so big, it swallows her thong, making it look as if she has nothing on. The thin string disappears into the crack of her ass.

She unsuspectingly turns around. We lock eyes. She stops in the middle of the floor. From the angle she's standing at, I can view her entire profile. Her ass protrudes so far from the rest of her body that it looks like you could set a drink on it, while she walks and not one drop would spill. She continues to the other side of the bar. As she mixes a drink for another customer, I watch her ass jiggle like Jell-O as she shakes the pina colada extra, extra fast. She knows she has my undivided attention. Right now she's just trying to tease me.

She walks over to me and places the drinks on the counter. **"Eight dollars, please!" she shouts over the loud music.** *I'm not looking her in the eyes; I can't take my attention off of those tits. I pass her a $10 bill, and she gives me back the change. As I try to pull my hand back, she grabs hold of both of my hands. One she places on her firm tit, and the other she slowly rubs over her clean-shaven pussy. I slide my finger in between her pussy lips searching for her clit. I roll her clit gently between my thumb and my pointer finger. She starts to grind on my hand slowly as she whispers the words of R. Kelly's "Bump and Grind," which is blasting through the speakers. I sneakily slide the tip of my index finger into her hot pussy. To my surprise, she does not pull away. Instead, she arches her back and begins to fuck my finger. She begins to pump faster. She applies more pressure as she grinds with short, deep pumps. I slide my finger further inside her. She's wet and deep. I*

53

slowly finger her as she grinds away. I have my index finger inside her while my thumb is firmly pressed against her clit. She's getting wetter and wetter. She closes her eyes and leans her head back. Suddenly she grabs my hand with a tight grip and slowly pulls my finger out of her. She puts my hand close to her face and kisses the palm of my hand. Then she begins licking my index finger from top to bottom. Finally, she places my hand onto her other tit. Her nipple expands two sizes right at the touch of my fingertip. She then leans over the counter and gestures for me to bring my head closer. I lean closer, just as she instructs. The sweet smell of Victoria's Secret's Strawberries and Crème fills the air. She begins to stroke my ear with her moist tongue. My dick is so hard it feels like it's going to bust through my jeans. **"You touched it, so tip it," she whispers.** *I clumsily dig into my pocket and peel off another $10 bill. Before I can get the money out, she slides her hand into my left pants pocket. She fumbles around before grabbing my balls. She gently squeezes them one by one, then slowly slides her index finger from my balls up to the head, teasing it with the tip of her fingernail. She grabs the head tightly before slowly jerking me. My dick is pulsating; she has such a tight grip, I'm about to bust!*

She stops suddenly. I then grab her by the hand and spin her around. She immediately bends over and wiggles her tail in the air, just like a cat in heat. Her tiny waist shifts from side to side. I spread my hands across both cheeks. Her muscles tighten up as she flexes each cheek alternately, causing them to jump up and down. She loosens up. I continue to massage her. Her ass is as soft as cotton. My hands aren't big enough to palm her perfectly rounded cheeks. I slowly drag the $10 bill up the crack of her ass. With my knuckle, I can feel the wetness soaking through her thong. After about three gentle strokes, I tie the bill in a knot around her tiny thong.

"Big Time! Calm down," Slim laughs. "You losing your cool. That was the horniest face I ever saw!" he jokes.

I snap back into reality. For a second, I almost forget about the crowd of young niggas in here who are all watching me like I'm a pervert or something.

I can see why this is the hot spot. There are some bad chicks in here- not the average trampy- type dancers either. I see some who are definitely wife material. I mean, if you met them on the street, you wouldn't have a clue what line of work they did in the wee hours of the night. And the way some of them look, I think the average dude would be willing to forget what her occupation is. The barmaids look just as good as the dancers. Each barmaid is topless, wearing only a thong and stilettos. All races of women are in here, Black, Asian, Spanish, Jamaican and White, - one big melting pot. The prettiest one of them all is this tall, Russian chick. She stands about 6 feet tall. She has long slender legs, blue eyes, and short blond hair. She has little doorknocker tits, but she has the biggest and tightest ass in the entire bar. She is so beautiful; these guys are tipping her without getting the slightest touch of her. Huh, that's funny. The sisters have to let a nigga damn near fuck them while getting a lap dance, just for them to give her a dollar bill, while all this white chick has to do is wiggle her no- rhythm- having ass to the beat as close as she can, and they're just throwing fives and tens onto the stage.

I notice the barmaid walking in our direction with a big bucket of ice with a bottle of Cristal in it. She stops right in front of me and places the bucket on the countertop. I don't know why she brought that over; I'm not paying $300 for no champagne. She must have me mixed up with these young boys. Yeah, she has me horny, but I'm not that damn horny.

"This is from the kid in the corner with the New York Yankees cap on," she says.

"For me?" I ask cluelessly.

"Yeah, for you!" she shouts sarcastically.

I look over in the direction she pointed to. I see a small crowd of kids with about six bottles of Cristal in front of them. They're bugging. They're spitting champagne on the dancers. They're pouring it all over the girls as they lay on the counters with their mouths wide open letting the champagne drip down their throats. One kid even pours champagne on one of the dancer's pussy and licks it dry. I squint so I can see exactly who the barmaid is talking about. But I don't see a Yankee baseball cap until a little frail kid stands up and waves at me with one finger in the air. I recognize him, but again I can't place his face. I wave back, but I'm trying to figure out where I know him from. Was I locked up with him? Was he one of my soldiers back in the day? I can't place him. I've been away for so long and through my travels I've met so many people, it's impossible for me to remember everyone.

The kid steps away from the crowd so I can get a better view of him. Now I know who he is. It's that nigga, Ice, Desire's little friend. I stop smiling instantly remembering what he told my two boys about me being broke. I slide the champagne away from me and shake my head no. He begins to walk toward me.

As he approaches us, he shakes Slim's hand first. The sight of him infuriates me. I'm about ready to get at him. As he gets closer, I can see the fear in his eyes. He extends his hand for a handshake. I hesitate until he says, **"Peace!"**

"Peace!" I return. *I wasn't going to acknowledge him until he stated he's coming in peace. That's one thing I respect is peace. If a cat comes to me using that word, I have to trust him but only to a certain degree. The majority of the time I can look in a joker's eyes and tell if he's coming in peace or not. His eyes tell me he doesn't want any trouble.*

"You know me, right?" he asks. "I'm Ice."

"Yeah, I know, and?" I ask sarcastically.

"Listen Cash, I don't want no trouble with you. I'm about getting paper, just like you about getting paper," he states. "Desire told me what you said. I ain't with that shit," he explains. "I don't have a problem with you."

"Then why did you tell my sons that bullshit? You don't know me to be playing with me," I state with a sharp tone. "I'm a grown ass man! When I left you were only a baby; you're too young to respect my gangster. That car shit, I been

there and done that. If I don't buy another car in my life, it won't matter to me because I've driven everything already. I was driving BMWs when I was 15 years old. Don't try to compare yourself to me!"

"Nah, it wasn't like that, Cash," he interrupts. "I know who you are! You used to mess with my big sister."

"Who is your sister?"

"Reyna."

"Reyna?"

"Yeah, a long time ago. I was like four years old. I remember you coming to pick her up in BMWs. I respect your gangster. I used to see you doing you. I wasn't trying to assassinate your character. I was playing with the kids. They were telling me your car is better than my truck and how you're rich and you have more money than me," he explains. "True indeed, I shouldn't have said what I said, but I was only bugging. Trust me, I know you ain't broke. I used to hear my sister tell her friends how she used to help you count money and how you had $100,00 stashed in her room back in the day."

"Oh, that Reyna?" I interrupt. "Double R!"

"Yeah. Reyna Richardson!"

"What's up with her?" I ask.

"Man, she's doing good. She's married and the whole shit. She married some Muslim dude from Philly. They got a big house out there and everything. She got her own beauty parlor."

"Yeah?"

"Yeah, the dude is supposed to be rich. You know, money in the millions. He sells a bunch of real estate out there."

"Yeah? That's all right! Reyna Richardson, that was my heart! I raised her. She was a good girl, but at that time I wasn't looking for good girls. I was busy trying to find me a skeezer to run up in." *Ice laughs.* "You know?" I ask.

"Yeah, I feel you."

"Yo, check this. I don't know what's up with you and

57

Desire. Actually, I don't care," I admit. "Our thing is over. I'm a married man. I'm not trying to be a threat to you. I'm not attracted to Desire. I have no feelings for Desire. But I do love those two boys. All I'm asking you is not to get in the way of me loving my two boys. That's the only way we'll have problems. You feel me?"

"Yeah, I feel you."

"Cool!" *We shake hands and hug. He goes back to his side, and I continue to do what I was doing.*

It seems like the crowd accepts me more after they see Ice and me kicking it. They even stopped staring at me. Judging by the way people make it their business to run over and shake his hand, he must be somebody. He also has his own VIP section. One of the dancers went over there and stayed for almost a half hour. He's tipping big, too.

It makes me feel good to know that this kid knows who I was. Finally, someone respects and remembers me. These young cats have really taken over, and I was starting to feel extinct like the dinosaur.

Me and Slim sip on the champagne. Normally, I don't drink. I'm not a drinker. I'm afraid to drink. Alcoholism runs in my family. My daddy was an alcoholic, my grandmother, and my great-grandmother, a whole family of drunks. I'm drinking in celebration. I'm finally home after seven long years.

The door opens real wide, and a big shadow covers the entrance. The security guard looks up as the darkness of the shadow gets closer and closer. I can tell that whoever is coming in must be huge. I can tell that by the way the security guard has to look up while talking to him. There must be controversy at the door because the security from the back is running to the front. I can hear someone yelling.

"I ain't got no fucking ID! Listen man, you better ask somebody in here about me! Move out my way Bro!"

Whoever it is has a deep voice. The crowd opens up for him as he backs in. He's pointing in the security guard's face. This dude is huge. His back is almost as wide as the doorway. His arms look like the arms of a wrestler. The sleeves of his bright white T-shirt are choking his biceps. The crazy part is his tiny waist; as big as he is up top, his waist can't be any bigger than a size 29.

The music goes low. The crowd becomes tense. The 6-feet3 inch monster turns around and stands in the middle of the aisle. I look him in the eyes from across the room. He looks back with the meanest stare. I stick both of my middle fingers up at him. He taps his chest as if to say, Who me? I shake my head yes and whisper "Fuck You." He reads my lips. He's furious. Now he's coming toward me. Slim looks at me like I'm crazy. **"Bang Man, what the fuck you doing, Big Time?"** *I don't respond. I take notice of Slim. He already has his straight razor open, concealing it in the palm of his hand and hiding it inside his cuff.*

As the Gorilla gets closer, I slide my drink away from the bar and grab an empty beer bottle. He's coming fast.

When he gets up to me, we stand face to face. **"What?"** **I ask.** *He cracks a rotten- tooth smile. He doesn't have any front teeth, and he has the flattest nose.*

"Oh shit! Oh shit!" he shouts. *He embraces me. He almost squeezes the life out of me as he picks me up off the ground like I'm as light as a feather. He twirls me around. Slim doesn't know what to do. He's dumbfounded. I wink at him and gesture for him to put his razor away.*

That's one thing about Slim; he doesn't go anywhere without his razor, and he'll cut a motherfucker in a heartbeat. Everybody in this town knows that much about him.

"Cashmere! When did you get home?"

"I've been home a couple of weeks," I reply.

"Damn, I ain't know who you was! I was ready to go up top on your ass!"

"Yeah right! My old head already had the drop on you. He already had his razor out and the whole shit. He would have cut your big ass too short to shit." *He looks Slim up and down before smiling at him.*

59

This is Mike Mittens, a.k.a. Puffy Paws. This nigga is no joke. His real name is Michael Jones. He got the nickname Mittens because of the size of his hands; they're huge, and he's deadly with them. He can box his ass off. He was a pro fighter, but being that he can't stay out of trouble, he was always going back and forth to prison. That ruined his career. When he's in prison, he's a trainer. That's how he survives in the joint. He trains the young jokers for a fee. When he's on the street, he survives by extorting the same young jokers that he trained in prison. No one plays with him.

In the ring, none of his fights go past 30 seconds. He's big, strong, and quick. His specialty is trick boxing. His moves are so creative. I've watched him totally embarrass guys on the street. One time I saw him flurry a guy, then he paused to let the guy throw a punch at him. He slipped it, bent down, and untied the guy's shoe laces. Then he rose back up and knocked the guy out.

Then there was the time another slick fighter called him out. He let the dude shoot an eight-piece combination at him. He slipped all eight punches, grabbed the guy by the elbow, spun him around, grabbed hold of his waist, and pumped on his butt like he was buttfucking the man. Then he spun him back around and hit him with a left uppercut, followed by a quick right hook. That finished him. The man fell over backwards. Mike let him sleep for 60 seconds as he counted the seconds out one by one. Then he further disrespected the dude as he stood over the man and pissed on him. The man woke up to a golden shower.

Everyone fears this guy in jail and on the streets; he's well aware of that. He uses that to his advantage. One thing about him is that if he likes you, you know, it and if he dislikes you, he'll definitely show you.

"What's going on Mike?"

"Nothing much, I just came home today," he replies.

"Yeah?" I question. **"How long were you away?"**

"Six months, parole violation. I knocked my punk ass parole officer out!"

"Mike you're still crazy!" *He laughs.*

"So what's up Cash? What are you doing?"

"I aint doing too much, I'm trying to put a plan together, but first I have to see what's going on, who doing what, you know how it goes."

"Yeah, yeah, I know. Let me brief you on what's going down. I know all the major players," says Mike. "It's only two major players in this town right now. You see the kid in the corner over there, with the Yankee hat?" *He 's pointing at Ice.*

"Yeah."

"That's Ice," says Mike. "He's in your line of business, that cocaine. He's heavy in it. He run a little block up the hill. They getting a bunch of money. All they sell is 20s. But his main thing is the weight. He tearing them up in the down states, Virginia, Carolina and Georgia. He killing them."

"Yeah?"

"Yeah," he replies. "You see that little truck he got? You see it has North Carolina plates on it right?" he asks. "He doesn't live up here. He was making so much money down there, he bought a house and moved his whole family down there; his mother, his grandmother, the dog, everybody. He's a pussy though. When I came home the first time, I didn't know him from a hole in the wall. He approached me on some punk ass scary shit and gave me $10,000. He told me to get right with that. Every time his punk ass sees me, he gives me a grand or two. That's why I came in here. I was on my way home and I saw his car out front," he admits. "Then on the dope tip, you got the Mayor. That young boy is rich."

"Yeah, I heard," I reply. "What's the deal with him? Is he soft or what?"

"Nah, he's a cool dude. He real. If he's feeling you, he'll look you out; if he ain't feeling you, he'll tell you 'fuck you' to your face. You have to respect that."

"True," I agree.

"He looks out for a lot of niggas, but he doesn't have to. He don't look out because of fear. He looks out cause he got a

good heart. He really don't have to fear nothing. His little crew
is serious. Them juveniles wild. I don't know where he got
them from or who raised them like that, but they really ain't to
be fucked with."

*Damn, Mike Mittens even sounds scared of these niggas.
This really discourages me. I sort of looked up to Mike ever since
I was a kid. He's one of the most treacherous, if not the most
treacherous old head around. Mike has to be at least 42 years old,
and he's been bringing the noise ever since I can remember.*

"That's about it right there. He got the coke and baby
boy got the dope. Are you still messing with the blow?" he asks.

"I ain't sure yet."

"Well, let me tell you like this. It's still a lot of coke
money to be made, but the dope is rocking right now. If you get
the right food, you can do you," he adds.

"I'm thinking of fucking with what I know," I interrupt.
"I know powder; I don't know shit about heroin. If I did I
would say 'Fuck Junebug' and do me!" I shout.

"Nah, you can't say fuck the Mayor," says Mike. "Right
now, he's in control. I like the kid because he doesn't ask for
respect. He demands it. I never saw him back down from
anybody. The kid is real."

"Man, fuck him and the goons!" I shout.

"Cash, you have to respect the game. It's a new day and
time. It's their turn."

"Mike, you sound like you have softened up."

"Nah, I ain't softened up!" Mike shouts. "I've
just smartened up. Them teenage niggas, they fresh off the
porch. They fired up. I'm 40 years old. My flame is dying
down. Some of the shit I used to do, I don't have the heart to
do anymore. Think about some of the crazy shit you've done.
Could you do it all over again?" he asks. "You got kids, right?"

"Yeah!"

"How many?"

"Two."

"All right, two kids and a girl?"

"Nah, a wife."

"OK, two kids and a wife who love you and need you at home every night. Them kids don't have anyone at home waiting for them. They don't even care if they make it home or not. Jail or home is the same for them. Think about the heart you had before the kids. Stone cold, right?" he questions.

"Yeah!"

"Well, think about this. They've just developed that heart. What's more dangerous is with that big heart, they don't have any smarts. They're not smart enough to know they have to pay for their actions. They don't realize the seriousness of their acts until ten years into their 30-year sentence. I mean, I know you hold your own and all but it's hard to beef with them and still use your common sense. These young boys will cause you to get 30 years. I know you might say, 'I'll do mines different. I'll do mines smart, I'll do mines in the dark when no one is watching.' But guess what. They're doing theirs broad daylight. If they catch you slipping, you'll have to handle it right then. What if they don't let you make it till later when no one is watching? Picture this: It's 12 in the afternoon, broad daylight, the block crowded as hell. You got your banger on you. You see the young jack reaching for his gun; you beat him to the draw. What are you going to do? A, let him live and take a chance of him killing you later? Or B, kill him in front of everyone and get 30 years? Before you answer, think about your wife and kids. You got too much to lose. They don't have shit to lose. You feel me?" he asks. "I'm not telling you to fear them. I'm telling you to respect what you're up against. Cash, the game has changed."

I sit quietly as I think about what he just said. He's absolutely right, but my stubbornness and my ego won't let me admit it.

"Cash, these young niggas can murder a motherfucker and get sentenced to ten years. They can do their time and still

63

come home in their early 20s. They'll still be young enough to start their lives over. Let us get caught, and we're finished! Ten years will fuck us right on up; coming home in our 50s, what the hell can we do?"

"I feel you, but I ain't going to let these young niggas dictate to me what I can or cannot do," I shout.

"Nah, I ain't telling you to do that, cause I ain't going to let them dictate to me either. I mean, the Mayor can get it just like anyone else. I just want to make sure you know what you're up against. And any way it goes, I'm rolling with you; you know that!"

That's what I want to hear. Now I feel better about him. That's the Mike I know.

Do you see what I told you about the go - go Bar? I just found out everything I need to know. Now it's time to put it together. Slowly but surely, I'll put my team together. I'm the brain; Slim is the past with all the experience. Little Wu will be my soldier. Mike will be my muscle. Now all I need is a trigger nigga and a connect, and everything else will fall in place.

You see, everyone has a position to play. The brains can't be the trigger nigga. If he busts somebody's ass and gets caught, who is going to run the operation? The experience, which is Slim, can't be the muscle. So that means everyone has to play his part.

CHAPTER 6

September 14

Three days pass and it's Saturday again already. I'm up bright and early. Tonight I'm supposed to hook up with the Mexican cat from Connecticut. Last night I could barely sleep, I'm so anxious to get rocking and rolling. I had the runs all last night. Every time I think of making a money move, I get the shits. I've always been like that, ever since back in the day. The closer I get to touching the money, the more it feels like I'm going to shit on myself.

It's 7 am; I'm out walking two dogs that I bought yesterday. I love dogs. One of my dreams is to one day own my own pet store, so I can mate dogs to sell. These two pit bull puppies are so cute, but they're mean as hell. One of them has an all-white body and his head is half black and half white. The other is a red- nosed pit. He's light brown with one hazel eye and one green eye. They're so feisty. They bark and growl at everyone as they pass us.

The block is crowded as usual. As I get close to the short, dirty man who is pitching the dope, he has the nerve to scream out "Block Party" as if I'm coming to purchase dope. I ignore him and continue to walk my puppies.

As I'm standing on the corner in an open field watching my dogs run wild, I'm startled by the loud sound of a car's tires screeching as it turns the corner. The car is speeding down the block. He must be doing at least 85 miles an hour on this narrow street. It's a white Lexus Gs with tinted windows. He's hauling ass. It must be a stolen car.

By the time the Lex gets to the middle of the block, another car comes along behind it. This car is coming even faster than the Lex. It's the blue Intrepid. One of the passengers is hanging out the sunroof with a chrome handgun in his hand, and another passenger is hanging out of the back window, with a small black handgun.

I grab the puppies and run to the back of the lot. Before I can get to safety, I hear rapid gunshots. **Boc, Boc, Boc, Boc, Boc!** *Then I hear,* **Screech!** *Like someone is slamming on the brakes. Finally, I hear a crash.* **Crash!** *When I look up, I see the driver of the Lexus jump out of his car and take off running down the block. He just crashed into a park car; he lost control of the wheel. By now everyone on the block has fled from the corner trying to run for safety. It's crazy watching almost 100 dope heads running in slow motion. The ones, who use canes to walk, just limp away extra fast.*

Boc, Boc, Boc! *The back passenger fires at the young boy as he quickly run offs. The look on his face shows fear. He's running for his life. The guy in the back seat jumps out of the car and chases him on foot.* **Boc, Boc!** *He fires again and again.* **Boc, Boc!** *The kid hanging out the roof fires twice. The boy begins to run faster. Seconds later, the driver of the Intrepid drives onto the sidewalk, recklessly. He's gaining on the kid. I don't want to see this.*

Before I can turn my head, the Intrepid hits the kid full speed. He flips in the air about 12 feet high, then he tumbles onto the ground. The driver then backs up as the kid tries to hurry onto his feet. Before the kid can get onto his feet, the dude who was hanging out the roof is now out of the car and standing directly over the kid. The kid lays there helplessly. He doesn't say a word but his eyes beg for mercy. Before I can blink I hear, **Boc, Boc, Boc, Boc, Boc!** *Then both of Junebug's boys jump in the Intrepid and speed off, leaving the kid squirming on the ground.*

Blood is everywhere. He's not looking good. It doesn't look like he's going to make it. Apparently, no one has called the ambulance; I pull out my cellular phone and call the ambulance. I don't want to see this kid go out like this. I don't know what he did to deserve this, but I sort of feel sorry for him.

I put the leashes on the puppies and run over to the kid. He's laying still with a look of shock on his face. His eyes are wide open. He's staring at me like I'm coming to finish the job. **"The ambulance is on its way,"** *I shout.* **"Breathe, baby breathe!"** *He's looking at me like he doesn't have a clue of what's going on or what I'm talking about. Now he's trying to say something to me.*

"Don't talk. Just breathe," *I instruct.*

My puppies are going crazy. They won't let anyone come near us. They're barking and growling like two guard dogs. Then I see a look of fear in the boy's eyes. He stretches them open wider as he looks over my shoulder. I look up to see what he's looking at. It's Junebug.

He walks over wearing a silver, German helmet and some aviator shades. Through all of the madness, I didn't hear him pull up on his black and silver Harley Davidson. He walks over with a big smile on his face. When he reaches us he kicks the boy directly in his head. The boy's whole body shakes from the impact of the kick. **"Chill man, the boy is about to die,"** *I state.*

"I know. He should have been dead," **Junebug says harshly.**

Junebug then bends down, takes off his shades and points his finger in the kid's face. **"You see, it didn't have to go like this. We could have handled this like men, but you wanted to talk that gangster shit. I told you not to put no dope on that block, but no, you didn't want to listen. Now look at you, you all fucked up!"** *he shouts as he stands up, walks to his cruiser, and hops on it.*

He sits patiently until the ambulance finally arrives and carries the boy away. Then he revs up the bike, **vroom, vroom! Pop, pop, pop!** *He pulls off.*

I leave immediately after. I don't want to be around when the police get here, knowing that I witnessed everything. I'm still on parole; I don't need any problems with the law.

I jump in my car and drive as far away from the scene as I can. As I'm riding I replay the whole incident over and over in my head. Them young boys were very persistent. They were determined to get him. They were not going to let him get away.

But one thing I did learn from this situation is that they were very amateur like. There is no way in the world they should have missed that boy as close as they were on him. It took them almost 20 shots just to hit him. With all that money, Junebug needs to get them some shooting lessons. I swear to God, I can't stand them niggas!

CHAPTER 7

This morning I woke up to the loud sound of a motorcycle zooming up and down the street at 6 am. It was Junebug. His goons blocked the street while he wheelied and did stunts all over the road. He had a female passenger on the back of his bike. All she was wearing was a two-piece bathing suit- a g -string bottom and a spaghetti- strap top. From a distance, she appeared to be naked, the way the tiny string disappears into the crack of her behind. My wife Love couldn't believe her eyes. She said she had never seen anything like that in her life. She thought it was disgusting; I thought it was a pretty sight, watching her big ass bounce as he hit every bump in the street.

After the show, I showered and went to pick up Slim so we could start our trip.

It took us a little longer than I expected to get to Connecticut. The traffic was crazy.

When we arrive at the gas station at the ramp of the exit, I call the Mexican boy just like he instructed me to do.

"Slim listen, when we get with these guys, just sit back and cool out. Don't go in there with all that nodding and shit."

"Bang Man, I got you! I ain't gone be nodding cause I ain't high. I haven't had a bag since this morning."

"Yeah right," I blurt out.

"I'm serious man. I wouldn't lie to you, Big Time."

I believe Slim. I haven't seen him nod out one time since I picked him up. He's really trying to clean up his act. Ever since we had the conversation in the car, he's been doing a lot better.

"I think this is the car right here. He said he would be in a white Toyota Celica." *By this time, the Toyota has pulled up* *on the side of me and the driver gestures for me to follow him.*

    This guy is taking all the back roads. He's speeding. It's hard for me to keep up with him. The big boat bounces up and down as we ride over the dirt roads. I don't even think these are streets. It's like we're in the woods or something.

    Finally, we pull in to a little rundown bar, and the man parks directly in the front. I park, jump out, and we followed him.

    The bar is your typical Mexican bar, just like you see on television; pretty long- haired Mexican women serving drinks while the men throw darts against the wall and shoot pool. The man leads us all the way to the back of the bar. Everyone stares as we follow the short, stocky guy. I must admit that for once in my life, I really feel uncomfortable. We're the only blacks in the entire bar. I can't understand anything the people are saying.

    Finally, he points to a man sitting at a table with a pretty Mexican girl sitting on his lap. She's beautiful. She has long, jet- black hair and big brown eyes. Her white, see- through, silky blouse is plastered to her skin, fully exposing her cantaloupe- sized breasts. The top of the blouse is cut real low. All you can see is cleavage.

    The man looks us up and down with the dirtiest look. He then says something to the girl in Spanish, and she gets up and walks away. I peek at her ass as she walks away from the table. I want to see if she has the whole package. But just like I figured, her ass is flat as a board.

    I look into the eyes of the man. His face shows sign of arrogance. He twirls a toothpick in his mouth, as he looks us over. Finally, he stands up. I almost laugh in his face. He's even shorter than the other man. He can't be no taller than 5 feet 2inches. I tower over him.

    He extends his hand to shake mine. Then he totally disrespects Slim by not even acknowledging him. When Slim extends his hand, the Mexican boy just looks at him, leaving Slim's hand dangling in the air.

"He's cool. This is my father." *I try to reassure him. He just looks at me with a blank look on his face. Then the driver of the Celica speaks.* "He doesn't speak English."

"None at all?"

"No, none."

"So, who did I speak to on the phone?" I ask.

"That was me. I do all his translations." *The Mexican boy finally speaks in Spanish. Judging by the way he's yelling, I can tell he's angry about something.*

"Juan said his brother told him about you, not about the old man. He said he won't talk business until the old man leaves. He doesn't deal with people he don't know. The only reason you're here is because his brother speaks highly of you."

"Tell him this is my father. He's cool."

He translates what I said to him, then Juan speaks and his boy translates his words to me. "He said he understands all that, but he doesn't feel comfortable."

"Yo, tell him this is my man. He won't do him any harm," I explain.

"Bang Man, just give me the key. I'll wait in the car, Big Time."

"Nah, you with me."

"It's OK. I don't want to make anyone feel uncomfortable," Slim explains.

I pass Slim the key and he walks to the exit of the bar.

Juan speaks again. "He said thank you very much and have a seat. He also asks do you want anything to drink?"

"Nothing, thank you. I don't drink."

"He said his brother told him so much about you, and if half of those things are true, you're still a great man." *I smile bashfully.*

"He said ask you, what is it you want to do?"

"Tell him I want to get money, and his brother told me he's just the man I need to talk to."

He laughs, and then he speaks again. "He said no

disrespect, but normally he doesn't do business with the black people."

His honesty catches me off guard. "Ask him why." *I sort of feel disrespected.*

"He said he has dealt with a few in the past. In the beginning everything was good business, until they built up his trust, then he hit them with something big and they never came back."

"Tell him, I'm sorry to hear that, but maybe he's done business with the wrong black people. Every race has good and bad people. I'm sure some Mexicans will do the same thing. Let me tell you something about me. I'm a businessman. I make money, not take money. I've been handling big money my entire career. I'm sure you can't put anything in my hands that I've never dealt with before or that would even tempt me to run off. I promise you, the only way I won't come back is if I can't come back; that's if I'm in a body bag." *I'm getting to him now. He's sitting there nodding his head up and down. How true he is. As a race, it seems like blacks are the worst people to do business with. The majority of us lack loyalty and patience. Some of us will cross our own mothers for a few extra pennies. That's our downfall; some of us will do anything for money.*

"He said, ask you how many bricks can you move in a month?"

"Tell him, that I'm not too sure about. I'm just getting home. I'll have to start slow until I get my clientele up."

"He said there's no need in making this a long meeting. He just wants to get to the point. How many bricks can you buy?"

This catches me off guard. I didn't know we were talking about buying. I thought he was going to front me the work and I pay him later. "Tell him I have a few dollars to move with. Ask him what price he's letting them go for."

"He said $16,000 a kilo. He said they're beautiful, pure, shiny, and white. He said he only deals with Scorpion *(fish*

scale.) **He said ask you, what is it that you want to do?"**
"Tell him I want to start small with a few of them,
maybe two or three."

Juan sits there like he's debating. Then he speaks again.
His boy translates. **"He said that's small. Normally he won't**
make a move unless a guy is buying at least ten. He said he's
willing to start you off with three, then he'll know from there
how many you can handle. When you come back with the
$48,000 then ya'll can take it from there. He said he normally
doesn't work like this, but he's doing a favor for his brother.
He said if you come back, that's good, but if you don't it's
no sweat off his back. He'll just take the $48,000 out of his
brother's account. He said you're his brother's boy, so you're
his brother's risk. He won't lose anything either way."

Finally, the translator leads me to the back of the bar. We
walk into the bathroom where he lifts the toilet from the floor and
starts turning the dial on the safe. When it pops open, he digs in
and pulls out a bag with three kilos in it.

"Normally, I wouldn't open the safe in front of anybody,
but being that you're Jose's boy, I guess you're cool." *Yeah*
right! The next time I come here, the safe won't even be here.
They'll move it somewhere else. How does he think he can run
game on a gamer?

I open one up and examine it. Here goes that queasy feeling
in my stomach that I told you about. Beautiful she is- snow white,
fish scale. This kilo has two layers, one stacked on top of the other.
Each layer is about an inch thick, 9 inches long, and about 6 inches
wide. Each layer weighs 504 grams. The total weight is 1,008
grams. Normally, they come in one solid brick form, but every now
and then you'll see them like this.

Their stamp imprinted on the top is the initials J.S. My man
Jose told me the story behind these initials. They had an uncle
named Julio Sanchez. That's who introduced them to the game.
He was killed by one of his business partners, who got greedy and
wanted the whole business to himself. Ever since they got their

own connection, they've been stamping his initials on their kilos in memory of him.

The man places the bricks in a shopping bag, and I walk out the door behind him. Juan gives me a head nod as I pass him. When I get in my car, I tell the translator to tell Juan I'll call him tomorrow and let him know how I'm doing.

Slim is sleeping. I nudge him to wake him up. I drop the three bricks onto his lap.

"It's on!" I scream, *as I back out of the parking lot.*

"Bang Man, let's get this money! How many did he give you?"

"He just gave me three to see how I handle them. Before you know it I'll be getting 50 at a time!"

We get home in shorter time than it took us to get there. I drop Slim off and go home. I'm exhausted from all the traveling.

As I pull onto my block, I see nothing but yellow tape, all over the corner, where the boy got shot. It 's so quiet out here tonight, you can hear a pin drop. The block is empty.

As I pull up to my house I see a burgundy Crown Victoria approaching. When I get in front of my alleyway, I stop and put my blinker on. I let them pass before turning into the alleyway. As they pass, we lock eyes. It's three suit- and- tie detectives. Two rednecks are in the front, and a black, bald headed one is in the back seat. When I get halfway through the alleyway, I look in my rearview mirror. They're backing up. When I park, I look back; they're still there peeking through the alley way at me.

Please don't let it go down like this! Finally, I get out and hit my alarm. I don't bring the bag with the work in it. I don't want them to ask can they check my bag.

I walk out nonchalantly, as if I don't notice them sitting there. I stick the key in the door and they finally take off. Whoa! I'm shitting bricks.

CHAPTER 8

The next morning

This morning I wake up about 8 am. I'm taking my puppies out for their daily walk.

When I step onto the porch, there's no one on the block. It feels strange to walk out my door and not hear the words, <u>Block Party</u>! I walk the puppies down the block to the corner store to get the newspaper for Love. I'm taking her and the kids to the movies tonight. She needs the paper to find out what time they're showing the movie she wants to see.

Sunday is family day. First I'm going to take them out to eat, and then we're going to a movie. Love only asks for one day out of the week, Sunday. That's the least I can do. The rest of the week I can do me.

When I pick up the newspaper, the headline shocks me. It reads: "MAN BRUTALLY MURDERED ON CITY STREET"

This is the kid from yesterday. As I read further it states, he died in the hospital at 4 am. He struggled for his life all night long. They saved him three times, but the fourth time there was no coming back. The motive stated was a drug deal gone bad, but they also say they don't have a clue who the shooter is. It feels crazy reading this story, knowing I witnessed the whole ordeal, but that's the game.

As I'm walking out of the store, the first thing I see is the burgundy Crown Victoria coming up the block. When they reach me, they pull over. It's the same three from last night.

They all jump out and walk toward me. The closer they get to me, the crazier my dogs go. They're barking loud and hard. I guess they hate cops as much as I do.

The black cop speaks. "Hey Donald, what's up?"

Then the white one speaks. "Welcome home! You did just come home right?"

"Yeah," I answer confidently.

"Seven years of FED prison," says the black cop.

"A man was killed out here yesterday. What do you know about it?" the white cop asks.

"I don't know shit about it!"

"Watch your mouth!" says the black cop. "You don't know anything? You have four years of parole left, right?" he asks sarcastically. "I would hate to see you go back for conspiracy of a murder."

Now I'm getting nervous. "Conspiracy?"

"Yeah, conspiracy! We talked to a few people last night and they told us you had something to do with the murder. They said you ordered the hit. They said something about you wanting your old block back."

"That's bullshit!" I yell.

"And they told us about a confrontation you had the other day, with some guys in front of your house. Something about they can't be out here no more cause you're home and this is your old block," the white cop explains.

Now they're putting shit in the game. Somebody's trying to jam me up. One of these dope heads probably told them about the beef I had with Junebug's boys, about them being on my porch. So now they're trying to play on me to see if I know anything.

"I had a confrontation with them about selling drugs on my stoop. I'm a changed man. I'm totally against drug dealing." *They want to play; I'm going to play right along with them.*

"Yeah, we know all about the change," says the black cop. "By the way, that's a beautiful wife you have. Doesn't she work at the high school around the corner?"

"I don't know. Does she?" I ask, as I look him dead in the eyes.

"Here, take my card just in case you hear anything. I'll give you some time. Just think, four years. Can your pretty young wife stand to be alone for four more long years?"

They jump in their car and pull off slowly. I throw the card onto the ground and proceed to my house. You see, I'm hip to their game. When someone gets murdered and they need information, they dig through the files of the criminals from that area. Then they determine which ones have the most to lose; the fugitives, the three-time losers, or the major felons. Then they come up with a bogus story about how they heard you're wrapped up in it so you can tell who really done it. It might work with these young boys, but they can't run that on me. I'm from the old school.

CHAPTER 9

After the movie, I drop my boys off at home. While Love and me are riding home I decide to ask her to go to the bank in the morning and take $20,000 out of my account. My sister has some dough stashed for me also. I'll get $20,000 from her too. This way, I can pay for the kilos tomorrow night, even if they're not finished. Then the Mexican boy won't think twice about hitting me again. I owe him $48,000. I have some money lying around the house because Love made a withdrawal for me when I first came home.

The $20,000 from my sister will be no problem. I'll just tell her I'm about to start paying for the big wedding me and Love are planning. As for Love, this is going to be a problem. She doesn't want me back on the streets, drug dealing. I told her I was done.

"How much?" she asks.

"Twenty thousand."

"Twenty thousand! For what?"

"I got some things I want to do."

"What kind of things?"

"Come on Love, don't do this."

"No, you don't do this! I thought you said you were done? You made me a promise."

"Love, please. I need to get right!"

"You already right! You got money saved up."

"Love, how long do you think that little bit of money is going to last if I'm not doing anything to put some back in?"

"Well, do something to put some back in! Get a job!" she shouts. "What happened to you opening up the store you wanted?"

"I, I," I stutter.

"It was all a dream. You sold me a dream!"

"Love, I swear I'm not going to make a career out of it. All I need is a 90-day run. After that ain't no looking back. I promise!"

"Oh boy, another promise!" Love shouts.

"Please love."

"What the hell am I going to tell them at the bank?" she asks. "I just took out $25,000 not even a month ago. Now you need another $20,000."

"What the hell do you mean, what are you going to tell them? Tell them you want your money!" I reply.

"Anytime you take out $10,000 you have to tell them what you're using it for," she explains.

"They don't ask you why you're putting $10,000 in!" I shout ignorantly.

"Last time I told them I was doing construction on the house."

"Well, tell them you're still doing construction!"

"All right Donald. It's your money. I'll take it out. But listen to this. If you get into trouble and go to jail again, you're on your own. I'm not doing anymore jail time. I did seven years with you! That was the worst seven years of my life, but I held you down. I was lonely, but never did I get lonely enough to search for companionship. Do you know why?" she asks.

"Why?"

"Because I love you." *The tears are running down her face.* "Donald, I know for a fact I can't do no more time," she cries. "I have goals and dreams, and visiting my husband on the weekend isn't one of them. My mother and my sisters called me a fool when I married you in jail. They said you were never going to be anything but a drug dealer. I don't speak to my older sister today behind that. Please Donald, please don't prove them right."

I hug her tight and whisper, "Love, 90 days. I promise, just 90 days. Whatever I don't get in three months, I won't get. After all that's over, we'll have a big wedding and I'll open my

store and we'll live happily ever after. I promise." *All of her crying must be contagious because I begin crying harder than she is.*

I know I've made a lot of promises to her, but I need just one more run. After that, I'm done.

When I was knocked off it seemed so simple. I thought I was never going to hustle again, but once I got back on the street and started seeing the pretty cars and the glamour, the reality set in. I'm a hustler. I have an addiction for the game.

CHAPTER 10

Today is Tuesday, September 18, the second official day of my 90- day run. Yesterday didn't go too well. I just gave out a few samples and passed my beeper number around. Oh, and I called Little Wu. He told me he'd be ready for me today. He wants to buy 300 grams. That's what I'm talking about.

Love and my sister withdrew the money for me yesterday. I didn't call my man yet. If I don't have to touch my money, I don't want to. But if I don't make any moves by tomorrow, I'll have to. I don't want him to think I can't move the work. Hopefully things will pick up by the end of the week.

After dropping Love off, I immediately go to pick up Slim and my sons. They're on the porch and ready to go. Today, they're looking real slick. They have on matching Polo jean suits and all white Air Force Ones. Desire is really mad at me now. I took the boys school shopping myself. She had the nerve to ask me for $2,000, to get their school clothes. I knew what she wanted to do. She would have spent about $900 on them and kept the other $1,100 for herself. She tries to be so slick. Sometimes she's too slick for herself. When I first went away and she stopped accepting my calls and stopped returning my letters, I was crushed. I almost didn't want to live anymore. But after two years, I got over it. Then I realized that was the best thing she could have done for me. Now she wants to get back in the picture. No way. She's the kind of chick whose love stops when your money stops.

"Dad, we're trying out for the school basketball team today," says Ahmad. **"I hope we make it."**

"Hope, it ain't no hope. Ya'll are going to make it!" I shout.

"Daddy, when I grow up, I'm going to be a pro

basketball player. You're not going to have to do nothing but come to my games."

"Do anything," I correct.

"You're not going to have to do anything," he revises. "I'm going to take care of you."

"Oh yeah?"

"Yeah, I'm going to buy you a big house and everything."

"What about you Ahmir?"

"I don't know," he mumbles.

"What do you mean, you don't know?"

"I know, but I don't want to tell you," he admits.

"Why?"

"I don't know," Ahmir replies.

"Go ahead and tell me."

He pauses for about five seconds. "I want to be a big-time drug dealer like you," he says with a stupid grin on his face as if he has just said the coolest shit in the world.

"What?" I ask, hoping I heard him wrong.

Me and Slim lock eyes. He shakes his head in despair. Hearing this breaks my heart. The last thing I want is to see my kids running the streets. What can I tell him about this lifestyle when all his life he's been hearing the glamorized stories of the things I've done. All these years he's been hearing "that's Cashmere's son." Now I have to explain to him that this is not a good thing.

"Listen Mir. Don't ever let me hear you say that again! Do you hear me?"

"Yes," he whispers. *Right now he has a confused look on his face. I really don't think he realizes he just said something wrong. Drug dealing is so common; maybe he thinks it's all right to be a drug dealer.*

"You will not be a hustler or any other kind of criminal!" I shout. "Hustlers are bad guys."

"But you're not a bad guy," Ahmir interrupts.

"No, but I've done some bad things. Things that have sent me to jail for seven years. Do you want to be away from the people you love for all those years?"

"No," he replies.

"All right then. Mir, I grew up with no daddy. That's why I've made so many mistakes. I didn't have a man around to teach me right from wrong. You have a daddy, and I'm not going to let you make the same mistakes I made. You can learn from my mistakes. Will you ever kill me?" I ask.

"No Daddy!" Ahmir replies.

"How about you Mod?"

"Ah, ah, I love you Daddy!"

"Well that's what ya'll will have to do if ya'll turn to the streets. Ya'll will have to kill me because if I find out that ya'll are hustling or doing anything else that's wrong, I'm going to kill ya'll. And I'm holding both of ya'll responsible for the other one. So ya'll better make sure the other one is doing right. Because if one is doing wrong, I'm going to kill both of ya'll. Ya'll hear me?"

"Yes!" they reply.

"Now give me five and get out of my car!" I shout, *with a playful grin on my face. I'm laughing on the outside but crying on the inside. The shit Mir just said really breaks my heart.* "Ya'll got money?"

"No!" they shout.

"Here, take five apiece!" I say, *as I hand Ahmir a $10 bill.* "Never go anywhere without money!" *I try to make them keep money in their pockets. This way, hopefully they won't be tempted to sell their souls for money being that they've always had. Maybe me having a deprived childhood is the reason I resorted to the streets. Maybe that won't work, but it's worth a try.*

I wait for them to go through the entrance of the building. Ahmir is something. I know I'm going to have problems with him. Ahmad is all right-a little nerdy and quiet but he's all right. But when I look at Ahmir, I see myself. He's the spitting image of me.

He walks like me, talks like me, and thinks like me. I'm just afraid he might be like me!

"Bang Man, I like the way you just handled that!"

"Damn Slim, that's the last thing I expected to hear come out of his mouth."

"Not me!" Slim answers. "He's been saying that for a couple of years now. I checked him about it, but a couple of months later he slipped up again. He has pictures of you standing next to your cars with fur coats on and shit. Pictures with you sitting on a bed with money and guns spread out over the whole bed. That's all he sees is the glamour. He didn't see them seven years of prison."

"You know what Slim? You are absolutely right," I admit.

I have to take Slim to get his morning dose. He is really doing good. Ever since the talk we had, his habit has really decreased. Now he's down to three bags a day. He went from nine bags a day to only three a day.

"Stop right here, Big Time!"

The block is extra crowded today being that the other block is shut down. They haven't been out there since the shooting. Now all the customers from over there come all the way across town. They love that Block Party.

Ring, ring! *My phone is ringing.* "Hello?"

"Yo, Cash!"

"Yeah, who is this?"

"This is Wu!"

"Oh, what's up baby?" I question.

"You!" he replies. "I'm ready when you are."

"All right, give me about a half hour!"

"All right bet. I want 300 grams!"

"Ho, ho, not on my phone baby!"

"Oh my bad man, I apologize."

That's one thing I learned, not to talk business over the phone. We learned that lesson the hard way.

"So where are you going to be?" I ask.

"Come to my house. I live on James Street. In the middle of the block. I'll be on the porch waiting for you. Be careful, it's hot as hell out here!"

"All right, I'll see you in a half," I state.

"All right one!"

"Peace!" I shout.

As I'm sitting double-parked, a black Grand Prix pulls up on the side of me. The window rolls down slowly. It's Junebug.

"What are you doing out here?" he asks.

"I'm waiting for my old head," I reply.

"Oh."

"Yo, it's hot over there," I shout.

"I know, they ride through all day long," Junebug replies. "I'm going to let it cool down for a while. I'm just going to bang from this spot. It'll be all right. You see I had to change cars, right? I didn't want to do it like that, but that kid done some shitty shit he shouldn't have did. You feel me?"

I hate that little Black kid. Every time I see him we get into a staring contest.

"You know that thing me and you were talking about?" I ask.

"What?" he questions.

"The powder," I whisper.

"Oh yeah!"

"I'm in position."

"Oh, all right! What are your numbers looking like?"

"What have you been paying?" I ask. *I have to ask him that. I don't want to underbid myself.*

"Like $20,000 for the whole thing," he admits.

"Well I got em for $18,000."

"Yeah?" he questions. "Yo, bring something through," he instructs. "I'll get it and let my little niggas bang it! I'm going to buy it for them, let them keep the profit off it."

"All right then," I interrupt. *Later for the big-time shit.*

He's going to buy it for his little niggas, whatever. "**What time do you want me to come through?**"

"**Whenever! The cash is always there,**" he brags. "**Shit, I'll support you. Anything to help you get out of that old ass car!**" he shouts sarcastically. *Everyone in the car laughs.*

Slim gets back in the car. "**Pop!**" **Junebug yells out.** "**I see you rolling with Cash, huh?**"

Slim doesn't answer he just smiles.

"**Later ya'll!**" **Junebug hollers,** *as he pulls off. I pull off right behind him.*

"**I can't stand that kid!**" **I shout.**

"**Who, the Mayor?**" **Slim questions.**

"**Nah, the kid you were beefing with,**" **I reply.**

"**Oh, you talking about Spook,**" **says Slim.**

"**Yeah. Whatever his name is, I'm ready to see him,**" **I admit.**

"**You have to watch him. He's sneaky,**" **says Slim.** "**He does most of the shooting. They say that little nigga got like eight or nine bodies.**"

Make that ten. He's the one who killed the kid the other day. I pause for a second.

"**He ain't but 18 years old!**" **Slim shouts.**

"**Well, he's playing a grown man's game. If he crosses my path, I'm going to bring it to him like a grown man!**"

CHAPTER 11

---

*It takes me approximately 15 minutes to get the 300 grams
for Little Wu. Big Wu is my man. He would probably be hurt if he
knew I was serving his son. I feel crazy doing it, but shit, he's going
to get it from somewhere. Anyway, this is only temporary. After
I get right, I'll let him be my lieutenant. Then all he has to do is
make my drop-offs for me. I'll pay him like $2,500 a week. That's
easy money.*

*I'm not sure if the measurements are accurate. I weigh the
blow with an ancient triple-beam scale that Slim has laying around
the house. I put an extra 50 grams in for Wu. He can pay me after
he finishes. This is my way of giving him a little boost. A little extra
always helps.*

*As we turn onto his block, I begin looking on porches to see
if I see him. I'm looking on the driver's side while Slim is looking
on the passenger side.* **"There he is!" Slim shouts.**

"Where?"

"Right there, three houses down," Slim directs. *No soon
as Slim says that, two police cars come speeding down the block.
Then a third follows. Finally, I pull over in front of the porch on
which he's standing. He dashes across the street and jumps in the
car.*

"What up Cash?" he asks. *Here comes another police
car. Only this one isn't speeding. He's slow rolling. He slows
down even more as he approaches us. When he gets to us, he stops.
Ah, shit! He peeks in the car. I nod my head at him, and he nods
his head back at me. Then he gives me a dirty look and rolls his
window down.* **"Is everything all right?" he asks.**

"Yes sir!" Slim shouts, *as he lifts up in the seat and takes
his hat off trying to show off his gray hair.* **"We're just coming to**

pick up my grandson," he lies.

"OK, have a nice day," answers the officer. *The cop zoomes away. Whew, that was a close call!*

"I told you it's hot as hell out here," says Wu.

"Is it always like that?" I ask.

"Yeah!"

"Yo, next time we're going to have to find a better meeting place."

"All right!" he replies. "Yo let me go and put this shit up before they come back through here," Wu suggests.

I pass him the zip lock filled with one solid rock. It's a perfectly shaped corner of the brick.

"This 300 right?" he asks.

"Nah, that's 350," I correct. "You can give me the money for the 50 on the next one."

"All right bet, so how much do I owe you now?" he asks.

"Six thousand."

"How much are you selling your grams for?" he asks.

"Twenty dollars."

"All right, so I owe you how much for the 50?" he questions.

"One thousand," I answer. *Damn, this young boy can't count for shit! School is definitely important.*

"All right, I'll be right back!" he shouts. *He dashes across the street and runs in the house.*

As we're waiting, another cop car cruises through the block. "Bang Man, it's hot as hell around here! You gotta get me from around here. I'm scared to death," Slim admits.

"You and me both."

Two more cars speed across the block directly in front of us. "Damn!" Slim shouts.

"This motherfucker is taking a long ass time!" I holler.

"Shit, he probably has to count the money," says Slim. "That could take forever, dumb ass little nigga!"

We both sit impatiently for about ten more minutes.

"Come the fuck on!" I shout. Beep! Beep! Beep! *I'm beeping the horn while looking over at the house.*

Five more minutes pass. By this time Slim is knocked out. **Beep! Beep! Beep!** *I honk again. Slim jumps up. The horn startles him.*

"He still hasn't come out?" he asks.

"Hell no!" Beep! Beep!

I bust a U turn to the opposite side of the street. **Beep! Beep! Beep!** *Still no Wu.*

"I'm about to go ring the fucking bell!" I shout.

I get out and slam the door behind me. **Slam!** *As I'm walking up the stairs, I'm debating which bell I should ring. I look at the nametags on the bell. The first floor has the name scratched out, so I ring the second-floor bell.* **Tick!** *Nothing but a tick. This bell doesn't even work.* **Ring!** *The bell lights up. This must be the apartment.* **Ring, ring!** *No answer. I ring the bell two more times.* **Ring, ring!** *Still no answer. Finally, I turn the knob. The door opens immediately and I go inside.*

The hallway is a mess. I climb over the junk that's in my path. When I get to the door, I knock lightly. **Tap, tap, tap.** *No answer.*

I put my ear to the door and try to listen for any noise. Total silence. I don't hear a peep. I turn the knob but it's locked. **"Yo!" I yell.** *My voice echoes throughout the entire building. Maybe he's upstairs.*

I jump over the first three steps and skip every other step until I finally reach the top.

There's so much junk at the top of the staircase that it's impossible for me to get to the door. The stinking smell of piss fills the air. This doesn't feel right.

I jump down the flight of seven little stairs. When I get to the porch, Slim is at the bottom of the stairs.

"What's up Big Time?"

I guess he can see the baffled look on my face.

"**What did he say?**" **Slim asks.**

"**Are you sure this is the house?**" **I ask ignorantly.** "**Let's go to the back!**"

We walk around to the left alleyway of the house. There is so much junk we can't possibly go this way. Stoves, dressers, and refrigerators, are blocking the path. I immediately run to the other side.

I sprint through the alleyway. When I get to the back of the house, I look up. To my surprise, there is not a window on the whole house. Everything is stripped. I peek through the first-floor window. The smell of newly burned wood is in the air. I run up the stairs. When I get to the door, I turn the knob. It opens right up.

What do I see? ....Nothing. Nothing at all. The entire apartment is empty... No sign of life. The whole house is abandoned.

Slim creeps up behind me. He doesn't say a word. He just glances around the apartment.

"**Are you sure this is the house?**" **I ask again.**

Slim picks his teeth before he speaks. "**Psstt! Big Time, you've been played!**"

CHAPTER 12

Me and Slim ride around looking for Little Wu for almost three hours. Every 20 minutes I go back through the block where we met him. I'm hoping I'll catch him around there. This kid played me the fuck out! I hope he doesn't think he's going to get away with this. I'm going to kill this motherfucker! Nobody plays me like that! I'll just have to deal with his father when he comes home. Fuck it! I'll kill him too if I have to! Damn, I take that back. I can't kill him. He's my man. But something has to give. His son just beat me for $7,000. I might not kill him, but I am going to bust his ass!

Now we're on our way to see Mike Mittens. I gave him 250 grams the other day. He's out there on some little hole-in-the-wall block. He has like five little niggas out there pumping for him. They're scared to death of him. They were out there doing their own thing, but he slid in and made all of them take work from him.

I turn onto the block. I must admit, I'm impressed. They have a nice little flow of traffic coming through. It's nothing compared to Junebug's flow, but it's pretty decent.

I take notice of Mike sitting on a porch in the middle of the block observing everyone. He's been in prison so much that even when he's on the street, he acts like he's still in prison. He's sitting there looking like he's in the yard, of a penitentiary, somewhere. He has on a wool skull cap, a tight gray sweatsuit with no pockets, and some beige state boots tied extra tight. His boots are choking his feet. I hit the horn to catch his attention.

"Slim, don't say shit about Little Wu," I instruct. "I'm going to handle that myself."

"Come on Big Time. You know me better than that."

Actually, I don't want Mike to know I got played like

that. That might give him some ideas, and then there will be two motherfuckers I have to kill.

Mike runs off the porch and gets in the car.

"**What up ya'll!**" he shouts.

"**What's happening Mike?**"

Slim doesn't respond. He never really talks to people he doesn't know. His saying is "I'm 60 something years old. I don't need new friends. If I don't know him by now, I must not need to know him." I respect that.

"**Yo, I have to make 500 more and I'll be ready for you,**" says Mike.

"**Yeah?**"

"**Yeah, I would have been finished but the cops just left. They were out here for almost two hours.**"

"**Is the block that hot?**" I ask.

"**Nah, some nigga was up there beating on his bitch,**" Mike replies. "**They locked his dumb ass up. Yo, they love this coke!**" *He changes the subject.* "**Them fiends clucking like a motherfucker. I'm about to take this whole shit over. This whole side is going to be mines! Either they're going to sell my shit or they're going to have to buy product from you. It's a lot of paper around here and these niggas soft as hell. Oh, I almost forgot. My little nephew is on his way through. He wants a half a key (kilo). I told him I'd call you when he got back.**"

"**Where is he?**" I ask.

"**He went home to get the money. He was out here kicking it with me, and he saw how them motherfuckers was chasing this coke. He said he had to get some of it. He usually buys the whole thing (kilo), but he just bought one off the kid Ice yesterday. So he only has enough to buy a half.**"

"**How much is Ice charging?**" I ask.

"**He charges $24 a gram. But if you buy the whole thing, he'll let it go for $21,000,**" Mike claims.

"**Yeah?**"

"**Shit, I told my nephew you want $20 a gram. I'm going**

to make $1,000 for myself off that deal."

"Damn Mike, you're charging your nephew?"

"Hey, that nigga already got paper! I'm trying to get me some paper!" Mike replies.

Ring, ring! *Mike's cell phone is ringing.*

"Hello!"

"Damn Mike, look at you. You blowing up. You got you a little cell phone and shit!" I shout sarcastically.

"Nah, I took this from one of my little niggas," he whispers. "Hold on. Hello? Yeah! He right here now! How long? All right, come on. All right, I'm about to tell him right now. Peace!" he shouts, *before hanging up the phone.*

"Yo, that was him," says Mike. He said he'll be here in 20 minutes. Go ahead and get that. I'll wait right here!" *He opens the door and climbs out of the backseat.* "You might as well bring me another 250 grams. I'll be done by the time you come back," he says, *before the car door slams shut.*

"Slim, that's one bird down. Mike already finished 250 grams. I'm about to give him another 250. His nephew wants 500 grams. That's done."

I'm not even going to mention the 350 grams Little Wu played me for. I can't believe this shit. That young jack swindled me. He actually took me for a ride down Beat Street. I hope he doesn't think it's that easy.

It took me exactly 25 minutes to get the work and come back. When I got there, Mike had the money counted and ready. Altogether, there was $14,500. It was only supposed to be $13,500: that's $9,000 from his nephew and the $4,500 he owes me. He gives me the extra grand to go toward the new work I just gave him. Now he only owes $3,500.

Later that day I hooked back up with Junebug. To my surprise he bought the remainder of the work I had left. Total he paid me $29,700. The minute I showed him the work, he immediately jumped in his car and told me to follow him. We went to his stash house. Some young chick lives there. He had $160,000 *neatly stacked in a safe in the back room. He took me all the way to the safe, where he pulled 29 neat $1,000 stacks. The other $700 he pulled from his pocket. He made sure I saw the other money he had in the safe. He bragged on and on about how it only took three days to make that money. I must admit I was impressed. For a minute I thought he was one of those fronting ass niggas.*

Before going in me and Slim took a spin through the projects where Little Wu is from. It was crowded as hell out there. The cook up has them going crazy. There was no sign of Wu, or any other familiar face. None of the older guys I used to know from the projects were out there; just a bunch of new face teen-age niggas. Wu won't be able to run forever.

CHAPTER 13

Next Day

This morning I woke up bright and early. We're going to Connecticut. I know we have to get on the road early so we can beat the traffic.

After I pick up Slim, we pull into the gas station to gas up the car.

"Slim, can you do me a favor?" I ask.

"Anything, Big Time!"

"Go in and get me a cup of coffee, light and sweet."

Slim opens the door.

"Here, you can get whatever you want!" I shout. *I hand him a $20 bill. As Slim is getting out of the car, I notice a beggar standing in front of the convenience store. He's tall and skinny, and his clothes are filthy. His hair is braided in thick, messy cornrows and his beard is long and nappy.*

As I watch him, I see him squinting as if he knows me but he's not sure whether it's me or not. Now I'm trying to see if I recognize him. With all that hair, it's hard to tell.

He waves at me. I don't respond. Then he waves again. I still don't respond. Now he begins to walk toward me. Oh boy, here we go. This guy doesn't know me. He only spoke so he can come over and beg. He walks right up to my window and gestures for me to roll down the window. I crack the window. I'm not about to open the window all the way. I don't trust anybody.

"Cash!" he screams. "What up big daddy?"

"What up?" I ask hesitantly, *while trying to figure out who the hell he is.*

"Long time no see!" he shouts.

"Word up," I reply. *I'm still trying to figure out who he is.*

95

I squint to try to picture him without all the hair. Then it dawns on me. This is Latif, b.k.a. Lie through his teeth. That's what people used to call him behind his back. He's a habitual liar. Damn, what happened to him? He looks terrible.

"Latif, what up?"

"Nothing much!" he replies.

Shit, I can see that. He doesn't even have to tell me.

"You the man!" he shouts. "If I had your hands, I'd turn mines in."

I hate that saying. When someone tells me that, it makes me feel uncomfortable. Those are the words of a jealous man. You have to watch a guy who talks like that. Those are the words his mouth is saying, but his heart is saying something totally different.

I look him over again. He looks completely different compared to how I remember him. The smell of funk is barking at my nose as he stands at my window.

"What's up with you, man?" I ask.

He lowers his head in shame. **"Cash, shit happens. That's the game."**

"No, shit happens if you let it!" I shout. "What the fuck are you doing? Look at you. You look like shit!" *He can't even look me in the eyes. Latif was a terror a few years back. He was a notorious stick-up kid. He used to have the whole town walking on eggshells. He was the only guy that I knew who didn't give a fuck about Jake or Ab. I mean he respected them, but he didn't fear them like everyone else did. But now look at him; he's all washed up now.*

"Damn, you got this Benz looking good as hell!" he shouts.

Cut the shit with the flattery. This is a 1993, for crying out loud.

"I had one just like it. Mine was silver though. I just sold it two months ago."

Here he goes with the lying. All the years I've known, him he never had a car. I don't think he even knows how to drive. Every

96

time I saw him he was in somebody else's passenger seat.

> *Slim gets back in the car while the man is snatching the nozzle away.*
> *As I'm paying the man, Latif's eyes are glued to my stack of bills.*

"Big Bro, you got a few dollars so I can get something to eat?" he asks. "A nigga starving."

"Latif, tell the truth. You're dope sick. You want dope right?"

"You got some?" he asks.

"Nah man," I reply. "Latif, you need to get yourself together, man."

"I know Cash. I'm fucked up right now. Shit crazy, I'm trying to get in a program now. Man, my mother didn't raise me like this. She got a big house and the whole shit; I can't even go there. She told me to come back when I get my shit together. A lot of this shit got to do with the people I'm around. If I was around good people like you, I could get right again."

Never! You'll never let me nurse you back to health, then when you get strong again, set me up for the kill. I ain't no fool.

Now he has so much to say to me. Back in elementary school, he didn't even acknowledge me because I wasn't part of the in crowd. Look now; the tables have turned. Look what all that cool, tough shit got him.... Nothing. "Here man!" *I peel a $100 bill from my knot and pass it to him.* "Go get yourself a haircut!"

"All right! Good looking out, Cash!"

"I ain't bullshitting Latif. The next time I see you, I don't want to see you out here looking like a werewolf."

"All right, I'm going to get a cut right now."

I wasn't going to give him shit, but then again he never crossed me. Oh, except for the time he sent one of his boys through the block and they robbed my little man. I could get him back right now. I could take pure advantage of him but what would that prove? It would be pointless. He's harmless. Right now he's paying for all the dirt he possibly could have done.

"Yo Cash, if you have some old boots and jeans, look out for me," he begs. "I don't have shit."

I look down at his feet. I never saw anyone destroy a pair of boots like that. And his jeans are about six sizes too big. He has rope tied through the belt loops to keep them from falling.

"I'll check and see what I have. How will I find you?"

"I'll be right here," he states. "If I'm not here, I'm in front of McDonalds."

"All right later, Latif!"

"All right Cash!"

"Latif, get your mind right," I shout, *as I begin to pull off.*

"Yo Cash, if you need me just holler! For anything, I'm here at your disposal! Dirty work or whatever. I might be fucked up, but I still can bust a nigga's ass. Give me a hammer (gun) and I'll put in work. Ain't shit change!"

"Later Latif," I interrupt. *I pull off. Off to Connecticut we go.*

We arrive at the bar at 12P.M. The bartender instructs me to go straight to the back. He says Juan is in the back in his office waiting for me.

"He's back there, so just knock on the door. If he doesn't answer, he's probably asleep. Just go in and wake him up," says the bartender.

Slim insists on waiting in the car. He's still upset from the last time.

Only one man is in the bar. He's sitting there sipping on a beer. As I walk past him, he gives me a head nod. I nod back and keep it moving.

When I get to the door, I knock three times. **Knock, knock, knock!** *No answer. Then I knock four more times.* **Knock, knock, knock, knock!** *Still no answer. I put my ear to the door. I can hear music, so I knock two more times.* **Knock, knock!** *Still no response.*

I push the door slightly and peek in. I can see the sofa,

but no one is on it. I walk through the door. When I look to my right, I'm embarrassed to see Juan's little, frail naked ass. He's standing there humped over with his jeans down to his ankles. In front of him is a small Mexican girl, bent over. She has her panties wrapped around her ankles, and her little ruffled skirt is up over her back. Juan is wailing on her doggy style. **"Oooh! Oooh!" she sighs. "Si Poppy, si! Mas rapido!" she screams.**

They hear the door open. They both look me right in the face. My entrance doesn't stop Juan. If anything, he starts pounding harder and faster. The girl is screaming her head off and speaking in Spanish. **"Aghh! Aghh! Suave Poppy, suave!" she cries.** *I can't understand a word of what she's saying. It sounds like she's singing. I don't know if she's screaming for mercy or screaming for more.*

I turn my head and begin walking toward the door. Then I hear Juan grunt like a madman. **"GRRR!"** *He's done.*

"Amigo!" he shouts.

I turn around to look at him. He's pulling his pants up. The girl is bent over with her flat ass in the air, fumbling for her panties. Her ass is bruised and discolored from all the pounding.

When she looks up, she catches me staring at her ass. She quickly turns around and faces me.

Her thick curly bush is fully exposed. Her pussy hair is matted down, covering her entire crotch area. She pulls her skirt down as she wiggles into her panties.

I now realize this is the same waitress that was sitting on his lap the other day. Her pale round face is red from embarrassment.

Juan picks up the phone and starts dialing. He speaks in Spanish, maybe three words, then he hangs up. **"Uno momento, mi amigo!"**

The girl leaves with her head hanging low.

Thirty seconds later, the translator walks in. He sniffs the air and says something to Juan in Spanish. They both laugh as Juan sprays half a can of air freshener.

"What's up amigo?" the translator asks. "How did you

like the work?"

"Good, it was good!" I admit.

Then Juan speaks.

"He said how did you make out?" he translates.

"Tell him everything went fine. He didn't think I was coming back, did he?" I ask.

"No, he didn't think that, amigo! When you left he told me you look trustworthy and he likes your style."

I hand them the cash and they begin counting.

After they finish counting, Juan places the bag on the sofa. Then he speaks.

"He said ask you how you liked it?" he translates.

"Tell him it's good. I can really do some things with it."

"He said do you know exactly what you want to do now?" the translator asks.

"Ask him what's the most he'll put in my hand? Tell him the money is good!"

He begins translating to Juan. Juan sits quietly for a few seconds before finally speaking.

"He said ask you how many you want?"

Damn, I want to say ten but I don't want him to think I'm trying to take advantage of him. "Uumm." *I mumble. Fuck it, what's the worst he can say, no?* "Ten, ask him can he give me ten?"

Juan sits quietly as if he's calculating in his head. Then he speaks.

"He said how long do you think it will take you to finish?"

"Tell him to give me a week. If I'm not finished in a week, I'll pay him out of my own money for whatever I have left. Guarantee."

Juan then speaks. Whatever he's saying is a mouthful. I have never heard him talk this much. Usually he says no more than four words. "What is he saying?" I ask.

"He said, he can give you the ten but he needs to know

your whereabouts, you know, where you live."

"That's no problem!" I respond, *trying to give him a sense of trust in me.*

"He said he'll get someone to deliver them to you for an extra $250 per kilo. Altogether that's $2,500 just for delivery. He doesn't want you to get busted with them."

Yeah right, he wants to know exactly where I live just in case I don't come back with his money. That's why he's getting them delivered.

"When they get them to your house, you give them the $2,500 for delivery and you give them a fourth of the price of the kilos. So total you give them $42,500, when they get there. Then three days later, he'll send someone back for another $40,000. Then you bring the other $80,000 when you come back at the end of the week."

I think about it for a second before finalizing it. "Deal!"

That concludes our meeting. He tells me the package should be there at 10 in the morning. That will be perfect. I can meet them at Desire's house. The kids will be off to school by that time. I hate to jeopardize her home like that, but Homicide comes through my block all day. That's all they need to see is some Mexicans leaving my house. They'd run right up in there. Ten kilos would finish me for life!

CHAPTER 14

Desire left early this morning with the kid Ice. After dropping the kids off at school, me and Slim wait patiently until 1: 30 in the afternoon for the delivery. I give them the $42,500 just like Juan instructed. I use the money that Love and my sister took out of the bank for me. That leaves me with approximately $13,000 left in the house. I'll use that as a head start for the next payment I have to give Juan.

I have a few dollars left in the bank, but I promised myself that I won't touch that. The only way I'll touch that if it's a real emergency. If I keep taking money out of my savings, I'll be hustling backwards.

The Mexican boy told me he'd be coming back in three days for another $40,000. It's not too much pressure because I still have that $13,000 head start. Really all I have to do is move about, a bird and a half and I'll be ready for him. The real pressure is the $80,000 I have to come up with at the end of the week. I really have to get out there and make it happen. The last thing I want to do is get stuck with the work or hold it too long. Time is everything. He may think I'm not worthy, and then he may cut me off. I look at this first batch like a test. I figure after I prove to him my capabilities, then him giving me 25 to 50 birds at a time shouldn't be a problem. It's all a matter of trust. I don't want to do anything to mess up this relationship. With a connect like him, I'm sure to take over. In this game, the man with the most cocaine wins. The more you have, the cheaper you can afford to sell it for. It will be impossible for a man with only two keys (kilos) to compete with me if I have 50-bird capacity.

CHAPTER 15

It's mid October. Two weeks have passed. I still haven't bumped into Little Wu. I try not to think about him too much because it frustrates me. I'm just going to do what I have to do: get this money. When I see him, I'll deal with him. He can't hide forever. Even a bear has to come out of hibernation after a while. This is a small town. I'll bump into him when he least expects it. Right now he's probably hiding somewhere wishing he didn't do that dumb shit. I know what he's going to do; he's probably going to send a middleman to set up a meeting so he can apologize and pay me back the money. But I ain't trying to hear that shit. I'm going to make an example out of his ass. It's been too long now. If he had came back the next day or two, I probably would have let him slide, but not now. He's probably flipped my money a hundred times by now.

Besides that, things are going splendidly. The first week was a rough one. I almost didn't make my quota. Had it not been for Junebug, I would've been stuck. He bought four birds that week. That's $72,000 cash money. His block is on fire! Besides the dope flow, he's killing them with the blow, as well. His other block is still dry. Homicide hasn't let up yet. They park on the block and sit there all day, everyday. The block doesn't even look the same. You wouldn't recognize it. The only trace they left is the raggedy house they used to sell the dope from. Besides that, it once again looks like a quiet residential block.

Last week things picked up. Mike Mittens is holding me down. He's killing them with the $20 pieces. He puts a half a gram in aluminum foil and sells it for $20. He doubles his money and pleases the customers. He goes through a half a joint a week easy.

As for his nephew, not only does he get kilos from me, he also turned his entire crew onto me. The ones who buy kilos, he sells it to them for $19,500. He makes $1,500 off each one. The others who buy ounces or quarters at a time, he sells it to them for $22 a gram. I heard from a reliable source that Ice is starting to notice the difference in his flow. I'm definitely going to steal a lot of his clientele. I have better quality blow at a cheaper price. How can anyone refuse me?

Last week, I sent Mike Mittens to speak with Ice about doing business with us. I was willing to give him the special price of $17,500 a bird. That's cheaper than I sell them to anyone else. He told Mike he would talk to him later, but he never got back at us. I guess he let his pride get in the way. Now my plan is to break him. I'll do whatever I have to do. Even if I have to cut my prices so he can't compete with me. Eventually he will have to buy his work from me.

At this moment, me and Slim are at the kids' school. Today they're playing their third basketball game of the season. They both made the team. Ahmir is the team's captain; he's also the key player. His position is point guard. No matter what kind of pressure they put him under, he still manages to get that ball down the court. If that ball touches his hand, he will definitely score. So far he has an average of 20 points a game. I guess he takes after me. In my early years, I played basketball each and every day. Whenever you saw me, I had a basketball in my hand. My dream was to be a professional basketball player until I was introduced to fast money. That's when I lost all interest in the game.

I worry about Ahmad. He doesn't have the heart he needs to survive in this game. He can dribble his ass off, but he's scared to shoot. Even if he's alone, he'll pass the ball to someone who's being guarded. He barely gets in the game. The coach only puts him in the game after he knows there is no hope of them winning.

Right now, it's the4th quarter with 1 minute and 40 seconds left in the game. We're up 56 to 54. The other team has the ball.

They're passing the ball around trying to kill time.

Twenty seconds have gone by. The forward passes the ball to the point guard. The point guard fakes the shot, and Ahmir leaps in the air. The little boy goes around him. He zooms right past the forward as if he isn't even there. He dribbles straight down the middle of the court. When he gets to the bottom, he encounters the oversized center. He spins around and lays it up on him. The ball bounces off the backboard and goes in, causing the score to be tied.

The team is nervous. Tension fills the air; we're tied up with only 40 seconds left. Ahmir is furious, and he's embarrassed. The crowd oohed and aaghed when the kid blew right past him. I have to admit, I'm embarrassed too.

Phwew! *After the whistle, the ball is passed to Ahmir. I can tell he's mad by the way he's bouncing the ball so hard. It's like he's almost slamming the ball into the floor. He's charging right into his opponents.*

"Mir, you the man!" I shout. "Slow down, Mir! Take your time! You the man!"

"Bang Man, he's pissed off! I hope he don't blow the game," says Slim.

"Nah, he'll be all right. Mir, take your time!" I shout.
The clock is running out. Ahmir dribbles to half court. Everyone swarms him, except the center. He crosses over and runs between two of his opponents, causing them to bump into each other. Then he quickly dribbles right past the other two. Then the big center steps up. He's twice Ahmir's size.

Ahmir dribbles to the left, then to the right. The big boy doesn't budge. Ahmir stops dribbling and fakes. Still he doesn't respond. Finally, Ahmir jumps and releases from damn near half court. The big awkward kid jumps up. As he's coming back down, he falls clumsily on top of Ahmir. **Phew!** *The whistle blows as the ball is gliding in the air.* **"Foul!" screams the referee. Swish!** *All net. Ahmir shockingly scores a three pointer, and he accumulates the foul.*

As he stands at the foul line preparing to shoot the foul shot, the crowd is extremely quiet. Everyone is anxious to see the outcome. Ahmir bounces the ball four hard times. **Boing, boing, boing, boing!** *He slowly lifts the ball into the air and releases.* **Boom!** *Off the backboard, he misses. The score is now 59 to 56, we're up. Only 20 seconds left in the game.* **Phew!** *The referee blows the whistle. The ball is in play. The ball is passed to the point guard.*

As the boy dribbles down the court, Ahmir runs over to him. This is the same kid who just embarrassed him. They're standing face to face. He tries the same move on Ahmir. This time Ahmir doesn't fall for it.

"Watch him Ahmir!" I shout. "Don't let him get the three pointer!"

Ahmir plants his feet firmly. He slides from side to side with the boy. The boy tries to cross over. Ahmir snatches the ball from him and takes off the opposite way. Time is running out, only six seconds left.

"Shoot Mir Mir!" Ahmad screams out.

As soon as he crosses the half-court line, he launches the ball into the air. The ball is gliding. It seems like the ball has been in the air forever. Only two seconds left. **Swish! Urrr!** *The buzzer sounds off. Another three pointer, he just barely made it. The crowd is going wild. His teammates swarm him. The center picks him up and twirls him around like a rag doll. I'm so proud of my boy.*

After the game, I take my sons out to celebrate the victory. We order two whole pizza pies with extra cheese and anchovies. Ahmir is not a big eater, but Ahmad on the other hand can easily down five slices.

"Daddy, we kick their butts, right?" asks Ahmad.

"We?" Ahmir asks sarcastically. "You didn't even get in. You rode the bench the whole game!"

Ahmad lowers his head in embarrassment.

After I finish my mouthful of food, I slowly place the crust down. Ahmir has a dumb smile on his face. Ahmad can't even finish his food. He's fumbling with his hands under the table.

I look Ahmir right in the eyes. He can see the anger in my face. He stops smiling.

"Apologize before I smack the shit out of you," I whisper, *in a low but meaningful tone.*

"Apologize for what?" he asks innocently.

"Apologize for belittling your brother."

He hesitates before speaking. "I'm sorry," he whispers, *while looking out the window.*

"No, you look him in the eyes and apologize like you mean it!"

"I apologize," he says quickly.

"Say, I apologize for belittling you, and I'll never do it again," I instruct.

"I apologize for belittling you, and I'll never do it again," he repeats.

"Don't you ever as long as you live let me hear you do that again! Do you hear me?" I ask. *I can see the tears building up in his eyes as he looks everywhere but in my eyes.* "Do you hear me?"

"Yes," he whispers.

"Look me in the eyes when you talk to me!" I shout. *He slowly lifts up his head.* "Real men look you in the eyes whether they're right or wrong. Now, I'm going to ask you again. Do you hear me?"

He looks me dead in the eyes with a stern face. His eyes are as cold as stone. He's pissed off at me.

"Yes Daddy, I hear you," he says, *with a loud, clear voice.*

"That's your brother right there. That's all you have. Fake friends are going to come and go. They're going to do everything in their power to tear ya'll apart. Never let anyone or anything come between ya'll. Are ya'll listening to me?"

"Yes," they reply simultaneously.

"You two are brothers for the rest of your lives. You don't need friends. You got each other. Never trust anyone but your brother. This is the only person who has your back. You will meet people who say they have your back. They'll be there until you need them, and then you won't be able to find them. But your brother is your brother regardless of what. Do ya'll understand?"

"Yes," they reply.

"Ahmad, do you accept his apology?"

"Apology for what?" he asks.

"For belittling you," I reply.

"Oh, yeah, I accept."

Everyone begins eating again.

"Daddy, what is belittling?" Ahmad asks. *Slim busts out laughing.*

"What?" Ahmad asks, *with a clueless look on his face. Now all of us are laughing.*

That's one thing I'm not standing for. I want them to grow up tight. I wish I had a brother when I was growing up. Then maybe things wouldn't have been so bad. It's hard out here by yourself. You need a partner in this crazy world.

"Daddy, do you still like my mommy?" Ahmad asks.

This question baffles me. Ahmad asks some of the weirdest questions. Every time I'm around him, I have to be on point, because I never know what he'll ask next. He's so up front. Whatever is on his mind, he just let's it out. "Why do you ask that, Mod?"

"I just want to know," he replies. "She still likes you!"

"No she doesn't," I answer.

"Uh huh!" he shouts, *as he nods his head up and down.*

"How do you know?" I ask.

"Ice said it," he replies.

"Who?"

"Ice. He said it last night when him and my mommy was fighting."

"Shh," **Ahmir whispers,** *as he elbows Ahmad under the table.*

"Fighting?" I ask.

"Yeah fighting," he replies.

I look over at Slim. He won't even look in my direction.
"What were they fighting about?"

"He kept asking Mommy do she still like you. And then I heard him smack her," Ahmad replies.

"Where were ya'll?"

"In our room," Ahmad answers.

"Ahmir, what did you do?"

"Nothing," he whispers. *Before I realize it, I've already slapped him across the face.*

"What the fuck do you mean, nothing? You're the oldest. If a motherfucker ever put his hands on your mother, you better pick something up and try to kill him! Do you hear me?" *He doesn't answer me.* "Do you hear me?"

"Yes," he answers.

I look in his eyes. He doesn't have a single tear in his eyes, but he's pissed. If he thought he could beat me, I think he would go for it right now.

"Slim, where were you when this was happening?" I question.

"Bang Man, I was in the other room! When I heard the noise, I ran in." *Slim is talking real fast. I guess he thinks I'm going to slap him too.* "I pulled my razor on him. I tried to cut his throat, but Desire stepped in between us. She talked real bad to me. She called me a dope-shooting-junkie has-been. Big Time, she really hurt my feelings. I told him, if he ever put his hands on my baby, I'd kill him. But she was steady yelling at me."

"Yeah?" I question.

"Bang Man, that nigga got her going crazy. His money is blinding her! Being that he has a little money, she lets him get away with anything. His other bitches are calling our house

109

and everything. Big Time, I even found a prescription for gonorrhea," he whispers.

I'm just listening to him. I can't believe my ears. I know what the problem is. He knows I'm getting money again, and he's afraid Desire will leave him to be with me.

"Mir, I apologize." *I pull him close.* "But don't let nobody hit your mommy. When Slim leaves, you'll be the man of the house. You have to hold it down."

I can see me and Ahmir are going to have a lot of problems. I know I'm a little too hard on him, but I just want him to grow up right. I don't want him to be like me.

As the kids are getting in the car, Slim speaks. "Big Time, don't do nothing stupid. No matter what, she's still going to be with him. She thinks she loves him, but she really loves his money."

"Slim, this nigga ain't gonna be hitting on her in front of my kids! It ain't her I'm worried about. I'm worried about this shit having an effect on my kids. That shit can traumatize them!"

"Bang Man, I feel you but this is a tough situation."

"Ain't nothing tough about it! When I see him, I'm going to tell him about it, and if the shit happens again, I'm going to handle his punk ass."

The situation has me pissed. The punk ass nigga really is mad at me for taking all his customers. He ain't man enough to take it out on me, so he takes it out on Desire. Now I'm really going to make it hard for him, and I hope he steps out of line so I'll have a reason to do him. Then no one can say I'm hating on him cause he's fucking my baby mother. You know how it goes.

While driving them home, I decide to stop in and talk to Desire before I leave. I need to know what's on her mind.

"Slim, when you go in there, tell Desire to come here."

"You got it, Big Time!"

"Later fellas," I shout.

"Bye Daddy," they reply.

"Later ya'll!"
I'm waiting impatiently. I wonder what she's going to say.

Here she comes. She's looking fashionable as usual. She has on a red and white, hooded velour sweat suit. The pants are tight fitting around her thighs, revealing their thickness. The bottoms of the pants legs are bell-bottomed. Her hair is shiny and straight. The only thing messing her up is her dark sunglasses. It's 9:00 at night. Why does she need shades on?
"Huh? You wanted me?" she asks.
"Yeah, get in!"
She gets in slowly. Not one time has she looked at me. She's looking straight ahead. I know she feels crazy with those sunglasses on. It's pitch dark out here.
"What's up?" she asks.
"You," I reply.
"What about me?"
"Desire, what's up with the shades?"
"Nothing."
"Isn't it too dark for shades?"
"No," she replies.
"Take them off!"
"Why?"
"You know I like to look people in the eyes when I'm talking to them. Take them off."
"No!" she shouts.
I reach over to take them off. She grabs my hand. I squeeze her wrist until she lets go. **"Aghh!" she screams.** *I snatch her shades off. Her eye is swollen shut. The corner of her eye, which used to be white, is now cherry red. The entire area underneath her eye is black as can be. She's embarrassed. She lowers her head.*
"What happened?" I ask.
"You already know!" she shouts. "Who told you, Ahmad? I'm going to whip his ass!"
"For what? He didn't give you the black eye," I shout

111

sarcastically. "Anyway, that's not who told me!"

"Well, my dope fiend ass father must have told you."

"Damn Desire, you mad at everybody except the motherfucker who gave you the black eye. I bet you're not mad at him, are you?"

"Mind your business, Cash!" she shouts. "This don't have nothing to do with you!"

"This got everything to do with me. He thinks you still want me."

"They told you that too?"

"It's true, ain't it?" I ask. "Desire, you're too old for that bullshit. Too old to let that little ass boy beat on you. Listen, whatever ya'll do is between ya'll, but I'm not going to let him disrespect you in front of my boys. If they watch him disrespect you, then they'll grow up disrespecting you, and I'm not having that."

"Cash, stay out of this."

"You better tell him before I do, cause I ain't gone talk to his ass," I admit. "Actions speak louder than words. First he disrespected me, telling them I'm broke and played out. Now this. I let him slide the first time, now I have to get at him."

"Cash, please let it go," she begs. "Please stay out of it and let me handle it."

"How are you going to handle it?" I ask.

"I'm going to leave him alone," she replies.

"Yeah right. He knows how much you love that money; that's why he beats on you. He knows he can give you a brand new Gucci pocketbook and you'll forget all about it. Yeah, he might be taking care of you and giving you whatever you want, but look at the price you have to pay. You have to let him punch you in the face and slap you around just to look fly. That's a lot of tax to pay!" I shout. "Desire, get yourself together. You're getting too old for the bullshit."

"Look who's talking!" she defends. "You're older than me and you still on the bullshit too!"

"What bullshit?" I ask.

"That street bullshit!" she replies.

"What you talking about?"

"Cash, stop acting stupid. You know exactly what I'm talking about. That hustling shit!" she states. "You better not come over here giving me a speech while you out here acting like a kid. You damn near 40 years old too. You have two sons, who look up to you like you're a god. You're not 18 anymore; you're a grown ass man. Your sons need you. You can't keep running in and out of their lives. How about you go to jail again, then what? And don't think for one minute, they don't know what you doing. That's all they talk about. Ahmad told his classmates that you rich. He also told them you're a big-time drug dealer. His teacher called the house; luckily she's a friend of mines. I went to school with her; that's the only reason she didn't tell the principal. You need to get yourself together too!"

"I am together!"

"No, you are not!"

"Desire, I ain't hustling!"

"You are a damn lie!" she shouts. "Everybody is talking about it. I took the kids to the barbershop; niggas were in there talking about you. I overheard someone say you got those things for cheap. I ain't no dummy."

"You must be. You keep letting that young ass boy play you the fuck out!"

"Don't change the subject. Cash, get your shit right before you come around here telling me how to live my life!"

She gets out of the car and slams the door. Her ass jiggles like Jell-O as she stomps up the stairs.

This cat Ice is starting to be a problem. I can't believe he told Desire all of my business like that. I definitely have to tighten him up.

CHAPTER 16

A few things have changed in the past two weeks. For one, I'm no longer riding in the prehistoric Benz I had. Me and Slim are sliding down the Ave. in my brand new CL 55 Mercedes Benz coupe. It's beautiful. It has a wine color exterior and a tan interior with shiny chrome rims. I traded my old car in and gave the dealer $65,000 cash. It feels good to ride brand new again. I almost forgot what a new car smells like.

Love is upset with me. She complains about me buying the car. She says I'm supposed to be saving, but instead I'm spending the money up. She's right, but I wanted this car so bad. After test-driving it, I had to have it. Besides, the $65,000 didn't hurt me at all. I've only been hustling one month, and I've already made $100,000 profit. I didn't spend any of my new money. I spent the money I started off with. The way things are going, I'll make that $65,000 back in two weeks.

Things are going terrific. Just last week, I went through 20 kilos. I have the cocaine market on lock. No one buys work from Ice anymore. Everyone is buying from me, Cashmere. The young kids don't call me Cashmere. They call me Old Head. Who would imagine I'm not even 40 years old yet and they consider me an old head.

As for Desire, she claims she hasn't spoken to Ice. She says she's done with him. I haven't seen him either. As a matter of fact, I haven't seen Wu either. I've been looking all over for both of them. Mike told me Ice heard we were looking for him, so he's been laying low down in North Carolina. As far as Wu goes, I go through the projects at least twice a day. I haven't seen a sign of him. He's probably somewhere out of town hiding out.

*Today is Sunday, which is supposed to be family day, but
I have to go to Connecticut to meet Juan. He told me it's very
important. I can't imagine what it could be. I just got my package
of 20 birds two days ago. He can't be calling for the money,
because we don't do business like that anymore. Now he gives me
the package, and I pay him entirely when I'm done, not like the way
I used to pay him in portions. That was security just in case I ran
off; at least he'd have some of his money. But now I guess I've built
up a certain amount of trust.*

*I have to ride past my house to tell Love, we have to cancel
our plans for the day. I know she'll be upset, but I'll make it up to
her with the surprise I have for her.*

*Today marks our five-year anniversary. What is a better
present than a gleaming, six-karat platinum ring, fully loaded with
a princess-cut diamond and baguettes covering the sides. The stone
itself is four karats. I spent so much money for the ring that the
jeweler gave me matching earrings for free. That should shut her
mouth.*

*When I get inside, Love is sitting in the kitchen with her coat
hanging on the back of the chair. She's been waiting for an hour for
me to get here.*

"Finally!"

"Baby, something came up. I have to make a move," I
mumble.

"What?"

"I have to handle something. It's very important."

"Oh, and I'm not?" she asks, *with sarcasm in her voice.*

"I didn't say that Love."

**"You didn't have to; you're showing me. Every since
you've been back on the streets, we haven't spent one Sunday
together."**

*I think for a second. She's right. With all the ripping and
running, I've totally disregarded family day.*

"All I ask you for is one day, and you can't do that!"

"Love, please don't start," I beg.

"No Donald, listen. I told you I'm not going to deal with this bullshit. I'm not going to live this lifestyle! All the secrets! All the lies! I want to live a regular life! The traditional American husband and wife, not a mob-oriented husband and wife. My friends can't even come to the house anymore!" she cries. "My best friend invited us over for dinner the other night. I had to lie. I told her you were sick, all because her husband is a cop. I knew you wouldn't want to be around him! Now, you're telling me that we're selling the house. I don't want to sell the house! I love this house. So I guess when we move, I can't tell my mother and sisters where we live, right?"

She's going on and on. She won't even give me time to get a word in. She's furious. She must have been holding all of this in for a while.

"Love, please." *I finally manage to squeeze two words in.*

"Please, my ass! I'm not about to live this drug-dealing life you want me to live. You're the drug dealer! Not me!"

Now she's starting to piss me off, yelling shit like that.

"I'm a schoolteacher! Oh by the way, you need to conduct your business a little better. One of my students saw you drop me off the other day. He knows everything about you! I mean everything! He whispered to me how you have the town on lock. I was so ashamed I had to tell him you were my husband's brother. Here it is, I'm telling my students to say no to drugs and you're the biggest drug dealer around!" she screams. "Are you selling drugs to any of my students?"

"Huh?" I question, *as if I didn't hear her.*

"You heard me!"

"Love, don't come at me like that!"

"If you are and they find out, I'm sure to lose my job. And if I lose my job, I'm going to be working with you!"

I laugh right in her face.

"You laugh, but I'm serious," she claims. "I've worked too hard to let you mess up my life. The only reason I married you was because you promised me you were done. Everyone else looked at you and saw a drug dealer. I saw a loving, compassionate man who made a mistake and was paying for it. That's why I never left your side. But if it happens again, I'm going to be forced to look at you like a foolish drug dealer. Donald, I need stability. I need to know when I come home that you'll be there. Right now, I can't be sure of that. With the lifestyle you live, anything can happen. I don't know if you're going to make it home."

She's venting. I didn't have a clue I had her under so much pressure. I always thought I was doing this for us, when in all reality, I've been doing this for me. Damn, I didn't realize I was being this selfish.

"I want to go on vacation to Jamaica next year." *She interrupts my thoughts.* "I can't plan it yet, because I don't know if my husband will be around next year."

"I'll be around!" I shout stupidly.

"I hope so!" she replies. "You know, sometimes I wonder how my life would have been if I had married a regular Joe Blow."

That crushes me. What is she telling me? Is she unhappy with her life? Is she living with regrets? I step closer to her. My lips are touching her forehead. I put my finger damn near in her eye. Now she's piping down. She knows I'm pissed off. She's scared to death. I can feel her heart thumping through my body. "What the fuck do you mean, had you married Joe Blow?" I ask, *while slightly poking her eyebrow after each syllable.* "If you had married Joe Blow, you would be stressed out of your mind, living from paycheck to paycheck! Your credit cards would be up to the max! You would be renting an apartment, not owning your own home! You and your 9 to 5 ass husband would be broke! That would be your last name, Joe and Love Broke."

"No, but instead of stressing over money, I'm worried about my husband getting killed on the streets or slipping up and having to spend the rest of his life in prison. Either way, I lose. Wow, that's so much easier to live with," she shouts

117

sarcastically.

"Love, don't come at me with that dumb shit! You knew who I was when you met me. I was Cashmere, not Joe Blow!"

"No, you were never Cashmere to me! To me you were Donald, and you'll always be Donald to me!"

I totally ignore her last statement.

"I'll never be Joe Blow, and if you want Joe Blow, you're welcome to walk out that door whenever you get ready! I'll get over it!"

"Walk out?" she asks, *with a high-pitched voice. I think that might have done it.* "It's that simple to you, huh? All the years I stood by your side, and you tell me to walk out the door? You know what, maybe that's what I'll do!" *She grabs her coat and storms out of the kitchen. I trail close behind her.*

"Here, take this with you!" *I reach into my inside pocket for the two boxes. I toss them at her.* "Happy anniversary," I shout, *as I'm walking to the door.* "Joe Blow wouldn't be able to afford that," I brag. "It would take him a lifetime to save up enough money for that ring!" *I slam the door behind me.*

"Donald! Come here, Donald. Wait!" she screams from the porch. *I get into the car and pull off, leaving her on the porch.*

She has truly hurt my feelings, but I understand where she's coming from. She deserves more, and that's what I want her to have. That's why I'm selling the house. I'm going to buy a condo in the suburbs. We're supposed to close the deal in a week or two. She doesn't understand. All the secrets are for security purposes. I'm Cashmere. I'm getting too much money to live in the hood. It won't be long before the wolves try to get at me. I'll fuck around and come home and niggas will be sitting in my living room waiting for me. Then what?

"Bang Man, slow down. You're speeding! Are you all right? You look stressed."

"Yeah, I'm all right!" I shout. "It's my wife. Bitches ain't never satisfied!" *I know I'm pissed off now; I have never called Love a bitch.* "When you broke, they want a rich motherfucker. When a motherfucker got a little dough, they want stability. They need to make up their minds! They're not happy no matter what you try to do! They're ungrateful!"

"Listen, Big Time! They want the best of both worlds. You can't be mad at them. They want lots of money and a good, stable relationship. Is anything wrong with that?" He asks. *I don't answer.* "Huh, is it?" he asks again, *in a demanding type voice.*

"Nah, I guess not," I mumble.

"You're just mad because she's right. You want to be the husband she's always dreamed of, doing all the husbandly things, but you can't because you're a drug dealer. You can't have a houseful of friends over. You can't let everyone know where you live. It's hazardous to your health." *I just sit back listening. He's hitting the nail on the head with his little speech.*

"Slim, how do you know that?"

"Bang Man, I used to be the same kind of nigga, just like you! Did you forget? Don't look at me in the present! Look at who I was in the past, then compare me to now. If you're not careful, you'll end up just like me! A has-been. When I was your age, no one could tell me I would end up like this. I was the richest nigga in this town, but look now. It's over! Listen Big Time; you have a wife who loves you. Don't lose that. Get this money and get out. Remember when you first came home and you said all you want is one more run?"

"Yeah."

"You have to be careful with that, because the funny thing about a run is that while you're having one, you don't realize it. Being that shit is moving so fast, you don't have time to sit back and think. You don't realize it until the run is over and you're sitting in someone's prison somewhere, telling stories about how you were running things. Listen to me!" he demands. "You might don't see it, but I do, so let me tell you. Right now you're having a run. So play the game; don't let the game play you. I scored my last point already. I'm retired!

You still have a couple of good games left in you. Remember, I told you this. Ten years from now, I don't want you to be sitting somewhere saying, "I wish someone would have told me" cause I told you!"

"Big Time, get what you can and get out. You're a good guy. You got a good heart, but guess what? It ain't no room for good guys in this game. The streets swallow up dudes like you. Think of all the successful guys you know in the game. Name one who isn't sheisty or who isn't a back-stabbing motherfucker. Just name one!"

I think for a second. Before I can answer, Slim interrupts. "You can't name one because there isn't one. In order for you to be successful in this game, you have to be willing to step on motherfuckers or wipe out anyone in your path."

"Big Time, you ain't built like that. I'm not built like that. That's why I wasn't successful, because I wasn't willing to do anything for money. I had a good heart. In order to win in this game, you have to be heartless. You can't give two fucks about a nigga. Don't get me wrong, I made a lot of money, but I couldn't get to the next level because I wasn't willing to cross niggas. Niggas who I knew would cross me in a heartbeat, but I still remained loyal. Look at me now. It might look like I don't have shit, but I do. I still got my morals, and I still got my dignity. A lot of niggas lose that in the game, but I still got mines. When it's all over, will you be able to say the same?"

"Big Time, remember this; it's not if you win or lose, it's how you play the game. I played fair. I can go to the grave today with no remorse about the game. Sure, I'm not rich like I should be, but I played fair. I never snitched on no one. I never robbed anyone, I never set anybody up, and I never hurt anybody who didn't deserve it. I played by the rules. That rule book is played out now. The jitterbugs got a new rule book. Their book teaches them to do anything and everything to make a come up."

I look over at Slim in admiration. He made a lot of sense.

He really has lived it. He is definitely proof of the end results of the game if things don't work out in your favor. Everything he talks about, he really has lived it; this is why I love him and keep him with me. He keeps me on point.

"Big Time," he calls out.

"Huh?" I reply, *as I look him in the eyes.*

"I love you," he shouts.

"I love you too Slim."

When I pull to the traffic light, who do I see? Junebug is directly across from me. He's in his Benz, and his goons are behind him in the black Pontiac Grand Prix. I can see him squinting, trying to see who's driving this car. He hasn't seen me in it yet.

Yes, finally, I will get him back for all his smart remarks about my car. I just want to see the look on his face.

Before the light changes to green, he speeds through the intersection. As he gets close, it's all eyes on me. He blows right past me. He's going so fast, he doesn't even realize it's me in here. **Beep, beep, beep!** *I hit the horn. I won't miss the chance to get even, for anything in this world. I can see his brake lights in my rearview mirror. He stops and puts his car in reverse. When he finally realizes it's me, his mouth drops open. He didn't expect to see me riding like this. He thinks he's the only guy who can ride in a brand new Mercedes. Not only does my car cost $20,000 more than his, mine is much faster. Mine's the sport, coupe version of his.*

In his passenger's seat sits a beautiful girl, not the Chinese girl he's usually with. This one is a long, blond-haired, white girl. She's really beautiful. He must have snatched her right out of a magazine. One thing about him, he has taste. Every time I see him, he has a better-looking chick than the one before, unlike his brother Dre. Dre could have had any chick he wanted, but he always chose the ugliest ones.

"Damn Cash, you riding, huh?" he asks.

"Yeah, a little something," I answer modestly.

"She looking good," he admits. **"What size are those rims, 18s?"**

121

"Na, 20s," I reply. "I couldn't play myself and put 18s on here." *His mouth drops even lower.* "What size are yours?"

"Eighteens," he whispers.

Got him.

"Shit must be picking up for you, huh?"

"Yeah, shit all right, but I bought this with old money. I'm still spending money from the late 1980s. If you think this is something, wait till you see what I do with that money from '92. 1992 was a good year!" I shout. "This is that back-in-the-day, 15-year-old money. You don't know anything about that. You were nothing but a little baby back then. You couldn't even buy yourself a soda at that time. I said to myself, "self, you better spend that money before the numbers fade off and you can't tell if it's a $100 bill or a $5 bill." *He gives me a half ass smirk. All my bragging is getting to him. He doesn't find it funny, but his white chick is laughing hysterically. He looks over at her and gives her a dirty look until she stops laughing. She's been watching me the whole time we've been talking. I can't help but notice her big blue eyes. I know she would play if I gave her the opportunity.*

Junebug is speechless. I take a quick glance at the car behind him. Me and the kid Spook lock eyes. We begin our staring contest, the same way we do every time we see each other. I turn back to Junebug. "I'll holler at you later!" *Before he can respond, I speed off.* Screech!

"Bang Man, I don't like the way he was looking at you! He had a lot of hate in his eyes. You better be careful."

"Fuck him! Now, he finally got a taste of his own medicine." *It feels so good to finally get even with Junebug.*

Ring, ring! *My phone is ringing.* "Hello?"

"Yo!"

"Hello?"

"Yo, Cash!" *This is Mike.* "Where are you? I need to holler at you."

This is something serious. I can tell by the sound of his

122

voice. "I'm tied up right now," I reply. "Why, what's up?"
"When will you be free?"
"Mike, what's going on?"
"Cash, I don't really want to talk on the phone."
"Is everything all right?" I ask. *Mike has me worried.*
I'm anxious to find out what it is.
"No, everything ain't all right!"
"What is it, Mike?"
"Cash, I just heard some crazy shit!"
"Some crazy shit, like what?" I ask. *What the hell is he*
talking about?
"About Little Wu!" he replies.
Oh shit. I wonder who told him.
"Is it true?" he asks.
"Is what true?" I ask, *as if I don't know what he's talking*
about.
"I heard Wu played you the fuck out! I know that ain't
true, is it?"
"Yeah, he got that off," I mumble.
"Why the fuck didn't you tell me?" he asks. "How can
you keep something like that a secret from me? Cash, I feel
disrespected! I thought I was your man."
"You are my man," I shout. "I just didn't want that shit
spreaded all over the street. That can ruin my reputation."
"Too late. It's already all over the street."
"Who told you?" I ask.
"My nephew told me. Someone pulled his coat to it.
I heard that kid is bragging to everyone. He said you were
begging for your life."
"Begging for my life?"
"Yeah, you and the old man. He said the only reason he
didn't pop you was because the old man was there. That's why
he just pistol-whipped you."
"Pistol-whipped me? That punk motherfucker ain't
pistol-whip me! It didn't even happen like that! Yeah, he

123

played me, but he did it like a coward. I would have respected him if he pistol-whipped me and all that other shit. But instead he pulled a dope fiend move. He didn't do it like a man!" *Now I'm pissed!* "I'll tell you all about it in person! I'll hit you as soon as I get back in the area."

"All right Cash!"

"All right, later!" Click! "Slim, did you hear that bullshit? Wu is running around telling motherfuckers he pistol-whipped me and we were begging for our lives!"

"Nah man, he ain't say no shit like that!" Slim responds.

"Yes the fuck he did! Slim, I swear, when I catch him I'm going to deal with him just like he did all the shit he said he did. He should have killed us!" *Slim sits quietly. I can't believe this shit. This young motherfucker is fucking up my reputation. He's trying to gain fame off of my name. I'm going to kill him! Fuck his father! This shit is personal, now! I'm thinking he's somewhere regretting what he done, and he's out here bragging about the shit; straight disrespecting me. Now niggas might think shit is sweet. Soon everyone will be asking for consignment thinking I'm soft and they don't have to pay me back. I know what I'm going to do. I'm going to bust his ass, broad daylight, in front of the world. These motherfuckers are going to know not to play with Cash!*

CHAPTER 17

It's a long aggravating ride to Connecticut. Besides the ride, the shit with Wu makes it even worse. I can't wait to catch him.

When we arrive at the bar, Slim is knocked out. He's snoring as loud as he possibly can. I have to turn up the volume on the radio just to drown him out.

As I'm turning into the parking lot, I see Juan and his translator standing in the doorway. I get out and walk over to them. Juan looks upset. He immediately starts speaking. Now the translator starts to speak.

"Juan said he's disappointed in you."

"Ask him why."

"He says take a good look at the parking lot and tell him what doesn't belong."

I look around once, then twice, then three times. I don't have a clue what he's talking about. **"I don't know."**

Juan starts to speak again.

"He said take a look at the cars in the lot," *says the* **translator.**

I look around. I see the old Celica the translator drives, and I see Juan's old blue Camaro. Across the parking lot are a couple of Firebirds, an old Chevy Blazer, and two raggedy pickup trucks. **"Yeah and?" I ask.**

Juan speaks again. This time he speaks with a sharp tone.

"Juan said don't ever bring that car to this bar again," **he translates. "He said you'll make him hot."**

Juan speaks again.

"He said he has never had trouble with the law in all his years of business. He keeps a low profile, and he's not going to

125

let you get him busted by driving around here with that hot ass car."

Juan speaks again.

"He said if the cops ride by here, they would want to know who the black man with the Mercedes is and what his business is here. Whenever they see the black people and the Spanish people together, they already know what is going on."

Juan speaks again.

"He said that is the problem with the black people. They love to show off," he translates.

Juan speaks again.

"He said in this game, you have to keep a low profile. You will last longer. Then after you're done, you go legal, then you can do all the showing off you want. They won't be able to touch you because you are clean."

Juan speaks again.

"He said you were in federal prison all those years, you should know better. Did you learn anything from that?"

I'm getting pissed. Who the hell does he think he is? Matter of fact, who does he think I am? I don't care how much money he has, he's not going to be talking down to me. He ain't nobody. He just happens to know somebody that I don't. If I had his connect, I would be in charge. "Tell him to lower his voice when talking to me! I don't talk to him like that, and I'm not going to allow him to talk to me like that," I shout, *as I look Juan right in the eyes. He mellows right out. He turns his head the other way. He can't look me in the eyes. He's used to everyone jumping when he says 'jump.' That's how it is when you got money. But guess what? I been had money.*

I'm hot under the collar, but I'm not going to argue because he's totally right. I just don't like the way he said it.

Juan speaks again. This time he's speaking civilized, like he's talking to another adult.

"Juan said, please park your car in the back and come through the back door of his office," says the translator.

I jump in the car and pull to the back. It's secluded back here. It almost looks like a forest.

When I walk through the door, Juan starts speaking immediately. Then the translator speaks right over him. **"He said he would appreciate it if you don't ever bring that car up here again."**

The translator then walks over to a closet, pulls out a small box, and hands it to Juan. Juan speaks as he fumbles inside the box. After he finishes talking, the translator begins to speak. **"Juan called you up here because he wants you to see something."**

Juan reaches over and drops something into my hand. Then he speaks.

"Juan said, do you know anything about this?" he **translates.**

I open my hand to see what it is. I don't have the slightest clue. It's a tiny, off-white, egg-shaped rock.

"It's raw dope," says the translator. "Heroin."

"I know that," I lie. *I never knew dope came in this form. Actually, I never cared. I never sold dope. I've been selling blow all my life.*

Juan speaks.

"He said can you do anything with this?" the translator **asks. "He has a lot of it, and he needs it moved."**

I pause for a moment. I don't know shit about heroin. I should take it. But what if I can't move it? Then I'll be stuck owing this man money. But damn, Slim did say this is where the money is.

"Tell him yeah!" I shout. "I can move it. I'm a hustler. **I can move anything."**

Juan speaks again.

"He said are you sure?" the translator asks.

"Of course, I'm sure," I lie again.

"He said if you can move it, he has a half a kilo for you."

My eyes stretch open. A half a kilo? What the fuck am I getting

127

myself into? **"He said he wants $45,000, for it."**

Damn, $45,000 for a half a kilo? I start calculating. That's $90 a gram. Hell no! How much can I make off of it at that price? They're both staring at me, waiting for my response. I don't want to look dumbfounded, so I'm just going to roll with the punches.

Juan speaks again.

"He said that comes out to $90 a gram. It's pure, untouched. You won't have any problems moving it," he claims.

That's what you think. I don't know about this. I should just back down while I have the chance, instead of getting it, knowing I don't know the first thing about it; $45,000 is too much paper to be playing with.

"Do you know how to cut it?" the translator asks.

"Nah, but I know somebody who does," I reply.

"Good," says the translator.

Juan speaks again.

"He said he'll get the package to you in the morning. He said he doesn't want you to drive it home in that car of yours. You won't make it to the highway before they pull you over. What time will you be ready?"

"Tell him to come first thing in the morning," I reply.

"All right, 9 o' clock," he affirms.

"All right then. Adios, hasta manana," I shout.

"Manana," Juan shouts back.

I proceed out the back door. What the fuck did I get myself into? I don't know shit about dope, and my greedy ass gone take a half a joint. I hope Slim knows what to do with it.

Slim is still knocked out. I knock on the window, to wake him up. **Tap, tap!** *He wakes up and looks around. He has a confused look on his face. He doesn't know where he is. He reaches over and opens the door.* **"Bang Man, where the hell are we?"** he asks, *as I sit down.*

"At the bar in Connecticut. I parked in the back. Slim, do you know what to do with raw dope?" *Please say yes.*

"Do I know what to do with it?" he asks, *as if I just spoke*

French to him. He starts picking in his teeth. **Psstt, psstt.**

Oh boy, he doesn't know. He's taking too long to answer. If he has to think about it this long, he's as clueless as me.

After a few seconds, he finally answers. **"Yeah, if you a junkie, you shoot it, and if you a hustler, you sell it," he answers sarcastically.**

"Slim, cut the shit. I know that much!" *Now isn't the time to play. I just made a big ass commitment.*

"Nah, I'm just kidding," he laughs. "What do you mean? Do I know how to cut it?"

"Yeah, do you?"

"Of course! I'm the best when it comes to cutting dope," he claims. "In my day, everyone wanted me to go to the table for them!"

"So, how much can you make off of a half a kilo?"

"A half a kilo? That's a lot of bread," he answers.

"About how much?" I ask.

"Bang Man, let me see! A half a kilo is 500 grams, right? Each gram makes about one brick of dope."

I begin calculating. A brick of dope is $500, if you take it to the ground (meaning sell it on the street) so that's $500 x 500 grams, which equals $250,000. Damn! That's a big difference compared to a half a kilo of cocaine. All I have to give Juan back is $45,000; that leaves me with $205,000.

"A gram can do a little over a brick, but if you want it strong, you don't want to put too much cut on it," Slim explains.

"Nah, one brick is good. Are you sure you know how to do it?" I ask.

"Bang Man, I'm positive!"

"Slim we're about to blow! This nigga just hit me with a half a joint, and he has a lot more!"

"Yeah?"

For some strange reason, Slim doesn't look excited at all.

"Psst, psst!" *He starts picking his teeth.* **"Big Time, are you sure you want to fuck with the dope?"**

"Why wouldn't I be sure?" I ask sarcastically.

"I mean, with the Mayor running around here like that," he whispers. "He thinks the dope game is his."

"Slim, fuck Junebug! Fuck his goons! And fuck everybody else who ain't with us! I just had a seven-year layoff. I'm starving. I'm not going to let these young niggas stop me from eating! Besides, I'll be moving it out of town. I don't want to work too close to home."

"Big Time, the dope game is a lot different from cocaine. A different kind of heat and everything."

"Slim, make up your mind. When I first checked out *(came home),* you told me dope is where the money is. Now you're trying to talk me out of it! But it's too late now; the package will be there first thing in the morning."

On the way home, we don't talk much. I try to figure out how I'm going to move all that dope. By the end of the ride, I come to the conclusion that I'm only going to wholesale the bricks. Once I find out how much other cats are wholesaling for, then I can determine the price I'll be selling mines for. I know a couple of cats out of town who only sell dope. I'll make a few phone calls and it will be on.

As soon as we get back into town, my phone starts ringing. Ring, ring! "Hello?" I answer. "Yeah? Right now? All right bet!" Click.

"That was Mike's nephew. He said he just dropped his chick off at the projects, and he saw Wu out there balling *(hustling).*"

Slim doesn't respond. I begin to speed through the streets recklessly. As I approach the traffic light, it turns yellow. I speed right through. I speed through the light at the next corner and the next corner, too. The last light I couldn't catch. It turned red while I was halfway through the block.

While sitting at the light, I'm startled by a tapping on the window. Tap, tap. *I look over. There stands a bum. He's old; he appears to be a crack head. I'm already pissed about Wu. I'm so anxious to get there, and on top of that, this motherfucker is tapping on my window. I roll the window down slowly.* "What?" I snap. "Excuse me, do you have a little change for the homeless?"

"No! I don't have shit, and don't be banging on my window like that!" *I roll my window up right in his face.*

"Hold up, Big Time!" Slim screams. *Then he gestures for the man to come over to his side. He digs into his pants pockets. The man runs to the passenger side as the light turns green.* Beep, beep, beep! *Slim pulls from his pocket three wrinkled dollars and a handful of lint.* "Here!"

"Thank you, sir!" the man shouts, as I speed off.

I watch Slim out of the corner of my eye.

"Psst, psst!" *He begins to pick his teeth, just like he always does when he's in a thinking process.*

"Why did you give that motherfucker your money? All he's going to do is buy drugs with it!"

Slim stops picking his teeth. He keeps his eyes straight ahead. Never once does he look my way. "It doesn't matter to me what he does with the money. When I look at guys like that, I see myself. Big Time, if it wasn't for you and Desire, I would probably be in that same position. Yeah, I gave him my last three dollars, but do you know why?"

"Why?"

"Because I know how it feels to be sick and can't get off E," he replies. "I don't wish that feeling on nobody. Big Time, never shit on anybody. You never know when you'll need a hand. I'm a prime example of that. At one time I was on top of the world. Now look at me. Who would have known shit would have turned out like this? But throughout all the bullshit, I'm still blessed. I think God takes care of me from all those old blessings. Sure I done did some terrible shit, but I done did some righteous shit, too! Big Time, you gotta keep your shit balanced. You never know when you'll need some of those old blessings. Every time you do a good deed, look at it like another blessing in the blessing bank. When you get my age, you can

live off of the blessings you have accumulated. Hopefully, you've saved enough to carry you through your entire life. Me, I might not have no money, but my blessing account is flooded."

I'm speechless. All I can do is snicker. You have to admire Slim. Through all the bullshit, he still looks at life from the bright side. Not only does this guy keep me on point, he never lets me forget what life is really about. I really don't know what I'd do without him.

I'm approaching the projects, finally! I slowly pull in the parking lot. I see small huddles of people in front of every entrance of each of the six buildings. There's a hot dog truck in the middle of the parking lot. Everyone is focused on that. At least 20 children are lined up at the truck. Besides that, there is a black, convertible Porsche with a temporary plate parked right behind the truck. A small crowd has also formed around the car. Everyone stares at the car in admiration as the driver shows off the interior of his car. No one even notices us pull in.

"Do you see him?" I ask.

"Nope," Slim answers slowly.

I cruise around the entire complex, looking in everyone's face trying to see if I spot Wu. I don't see him anywhere.

I then take a second spin around. Now everyone is staring at us as I slowly circle the lot.

"I don't think he's in here, Big Time."

"He must have left. Damn!" *As I get to the exit, I step on the brakes. I take one more look over the entire complex. I happen to lock eyes with two kids to the right of me. They're looking at me and smiling from ear to ear.*

"What the fuck are they looking at?" I ask.

"Who?" Slim questions.

"Them two over there!" *Now I put all my focus on them. They begin to ease away, but they're still smiling.*

I turn to my left just in the nick of time. To my surprise, standing not even ten feet away is Wu with a long-nose revolver aimed at us.

"Duck!" I yell.

Scuuurrrr! *The car peels off sluggishly.* **Boom!** *He fires again. I tuck my head down by the steering wheel. Slim has his head between his legs.* "Go Big Time, go!" **Boom!** *He fires again.* **Boom!** *And again. I finally make it through the exit.*

As I turn onto the street, he fires again. **Boom! Thump!** *This one hits the back window. The entire glass shatters. The whole window is out. I can feel a draft of wind blowing through the car.* "Slim, you all right?"

"Yeah, just go!" **Scuurrrr!** *I lose control of the car. I lift my head up slightly to regain control. I quickly glance back to make sure he's gone. The coast is clear. Exhale! I slow down.*

"He's gone!" *I shout. Slim lifts his head slowly and looks back. In the rearview mirror, I can see the kid who was smiling at us. He's at the entrance, celebrating and jumping for joy.*

"Bang Man, that motherfucker tried to take us out!"

"I'm going to kill that motherfucker!" *I shout.* "I don't believe this shit! This nigga must don't know who the fuck I am! He done fucked up now! This motherfucker just played me out!"

Slim is in shock. His hands are shaking uncontrollably. Beads of sweat are dripping down his face.

Sniff! Sniff! *The tears are rolling down my face.* **Sniff!** *I can't believe this shit. I've never been disrespected like this.* **Sniff!** *Wu is going to pay for this shit.* **Sniff!** *That stunt will cost him his life. If I don't do anything else in life, I'm going to finish his ass!* **Sniff!**

CHAPTER 18

Today Love didn't go to work. Late last night we got a call from the realtor telling us to come in today and sign all the papers to finalize everything for the condo. We're out of here, finally! Now I can really do my thing. This is the best news I've heard in a long time, especially since that shit Wu pulled last night. He's going to pay dearly. The good thing is that no one will know where to find me. They'll be expecting to find me at the old house, but I'll be long gone.

Deep down inside, I really hate the fact of selling the house. This is the only concrete memory I have of Big Ma. Hopefully, Big Ma understands that this is for security purposes. Big Ma hated me being on the streets. But she always told me, if you're going to get into trouble, it better be worth it. That's why no matter what, I always think big. I always said if I'm going to do this, I'm going to do it big. What's the sense in risking your freedom for a couple of pennies? If you get caught, you're going to do the same time as a cat who's doing major things. Besides, if you only want a little money, you might as well get a job. That's always been my motto.

Big Ma, I hope you're resting in peace. I know I'm living wrong, but God knows I want to change. And I will change. Just bear with me and continue to pray for me.

Love complained about selling the house, but she didn't sleep all night, thinking about our new condo. She even had me looking in furniture books at four in the morning. Oh, and the ring, she loves it. All last night, I kept catching her posing in the mirror, trying to see how it looks on her. She asked when we're getting married. I told her to set the date for two months exactly. By that time, I should have all the dough I need, and I'll be done with the streets. Especially if this dope thing goes the way I plan. With the coke and the dope, I should be rich in no time.

The incident with Wu last night is a wake up call for me. I was supposed to spend the day with my family, but instead I chose the streets. Look what that almost got me.... murdered. I wanted to go right back to the projects and do me, but I couldn't stop thinking about what Mike Mittens told me, about having too much to lose. That's so true. I can't be stupid like these young niggas. They do everything for the people. I'm not doing it for the people. Fuck what the people think. Worrying about what people will think will get me 100 years. In my earlier years, I was just like them, trying to impress the people. But now I'm almost ten years older and twenty years wiser. Fuck the people; I want self-satisfaction.

Right now, I'm waiting for the delivery. Desire went on a job interview this morning. Thank God! I gave her $1,000 to get three business suits. She didn't have one presentable outfit in her entire wardrobe. The only job she could've gotten wearing the clothes in her wardrobe would be a job on the hoe stroll.

I guess her not dealing with the kid Ice is starting to take a toll on her. She needs money. She's so broke, not only did I have to feed her baby, I also had to pay for the babysitter to mind her son while she went on the interview.

Me and Slim have been together since early this morning. We even went to the smoke shop to get all the ingredients he needs to cut the dope. Some of the ingredients I've never heard of. The only two things I was familiar with were quinine and bonita. The rest I was totally in the dark about.

After about an hour and a half of waiting, the bell rings. I peek out the window. When I spot the green Toyota Land Cruiser, I quickly run to the porch and grab the package. I step back in and immediately open the package. Slim starts to examine the contents.

"Bang Man, this is definitely the right shit!"

"Yeah? Are you sure?"

"Hell yeah!"

"How you know?" I ask.

"Besides me being a junkie, this was my game right

here," he admits.

Slim rolls up his sleeves. Damn, I see why he keeps long-sleeved shirts on. He doesn't have a clean spot on his arm. Needle marks cover his entire arm. As long as I've known him, I've never seen his arms. I sort of wish I hadn't seen them now.

Slim sees me staring at them. He shamefully pulls his sleeves back down.

"Slim, are you sure you know what you doing?" *I have to ask; $45,000 is too much money to play with.*

"Big Time, have I ever steered you wrong?"

Before I can answer, Slim is already going to work. He puts on his mask. Then he starts mixing and doing his thing.

I tried to watch him, so I could see the entire process, but I fell asleep. I'm so tired from Love keeping me up all night. The last thing I remember is Slim saying, he's only going to cut a little bit just to see if it's strong enough. The next thing I know, he's waking me up. He's done. He has a big mound of beige powder on the table in front of him.

"You all done?" I ask.

"Yeah, I'm done."

I want him to check it out, but I know he won't do it in front of me. He has too much respect for me.

So what we did is fill a couple of the tiny envelopes with powder. I tell Slim to call a few of his buddies up and we take the samples to them. This way we'll know what we're working with.

Altogether we give out six samples, three to mainliners or Old School as they call it, (Shooters). The other three, we give to some sniffers.

Our last stop is Slim's main man, 'the Doctor' as everyone calls him. He earned the nickname because he's the guy who shoots everyone's dose for them. All the junkies trust him to poke them. They won't let anyone else do it. He's supposed to be the best. Slim says he's gentle and takes his time. Supposedly, he can find veins that no one else can find. Slim purposely saved him for last.

So far everyone else says it's good, Slim knows The Doctor will keep it real whether he hurts your feelings or not. Slim says, he'll tell you to your face whether or not it's garbage, unlike the other guys, who tell you it's good just because it's free. This is the guy that Junebug lets test his work before he puts it on the street. He knows that if it's good, the Doctor will spread the word; if it's bad, he'll tell that, too. He claims that he's the consultant in the ghetto. Everyone comes to him to find out who has it good, and he refuses to mess up his reputation by putting his clients on some bullshit.

As the Doctor comes walking out of the backroom, unrolling his sleeves, Slim sits there with a long face waiting for the results. The Doctor walks out just as straight as he walked in. I look him in the eyes.

"Well, what's up Doc?" I ask. *He stands there face to face with me. He's not even blinking.*

He pauses. The anticipation is killing me.

**"Youngblood, you got yourself a nice batch of garbage,"
he admits.**

"Huh?"

**"Yeah, pure garbage," he repeats. "The shit so bad, you
won't be able to sell it for $7 bags. This won't even get a nigga
off E! Whatever you do youngblood, don't buy it. Give it back
to whoever you got it from."**

"It's too late. I already got it," I admit shamefully.

"Do you have a lot of it?" he asks.

"Yeah, almost a half a kilo," I reply.

"Oh, you have it raw?"

"Yeah!"

"Who cut it for you?" he asks.

"Slim."

"Slim?" *He busts out laughing.* **"He ain't no chemist! I
used to do all his chemistry!"**

"Yeah? Slim told me he was the best."

"No, he had the best. He had me!" the Doctor boasts.

"Don't fuck with Slim; you'll fuck up the whole batch."

"Motherfucker, I know how to cut dope. I just haven't been in the lab in a long time!" Slim shouts.

"Yeah right," the Doctor replies.

"Listen youngblood; bring the rest of that smack to me. I'll take care of it for you. I guarantee you, nobody will be able to beat you out. I bet you I have every dope fiend around leaning, bent over, sucking his own dick. When I put the chemistry on some smack, ain't a motherfucker around can stand up straight after he gets hold of my work," the Doctor brags.

Me and Slim go to retrieve the rest of the dope, or smack as the Doctor calls it. I'm pissed off at Slim when I realize he has fucked up over 60 grams. That's 60 bricks down the drain.

After dropping the smack off to the Doctor I leave. Slim stays with him to watch him and make sure he doesn't dip. Normally, I wouldn't leave two junkies alone like that, but I have some major business to handle. Besides, I have trust in Slim. Plus, he knows he's already in the doghouse for fucking the dope up.

My man is up from Virginia; he's buying six kilos. He always comes like that. He's my heavy hitter. He comes up once a week for six pies. Him and his boys put their money together and he comes to get it. They have Virginia on lock. This was another one of Ice's plugs, but I stole him too. Mike's nephew put us together. Ice was robbing them. He was charging them $25,000 a kilo. He figured being that they are from down south, they're slow. Them guys are coming with over 200 grand; you don't treat them like that. That's bad business. When I gave them the price of $20,000, they almost lost their minds. I give Mike's nephew $1,000 off of every pie they buy. That leaves me with a profit of $18,000 every time I serve them.

I know if Ice isn't missing anyone else, I know he's missing the hell out of them. It's no way you can get used to making $18,000 profit off one guy, then all of a sudden, out of the blue, he doesn't come anymore. There's no way. He's taking it better than *me. Had it been the other way around, I would have killed the competitor and them country boys. Shit!*

CHAPTER 19

The deal with the kid from Va. went smooth. Immediately after that, I had to meet with another kid. He bought one bird. Altogether, I sold seven pies in that little time frame. I made $20,000 profit before the Doctor even finished. Today is a good day.

I call Slim to check up on him. He tells me to come over and to bring more envelope packets for the dope. So before going to the Doctor's house, I stop at the smoke shop.

By the time I arrive, five other guys are in the house. All of them including the Doctor and Slim, are walking around like zombies. They're bent over and scratching like flea-infested dogs. They say when it makes them itch, that's a sign of good dope.

"What we look like Doc?" I ask.

"Ask your boy," he replies.

"What's up Slim?"

"Bang Man!" he drags, *on with a dry, aggravating voice.* **"We got a smoker!"**

I laugh.

"Come on youngblood; let's get this shit bagged up," **says the Doctor.**

We begin dumping the powder into the tiny envelopes.

It took us forever to bag up, and we still didn't finish. We ran out of envelopes before we ran out of smack. I was uneasy about letting the dope fiends help bag up, but The Dr. insisted. He said it would take three of us a lifetime to finish. I know they probably robbed me blind. I watched them as close as I could, but after a few hours, I was so busy trying to finish that I didn't pay much attention to them. My fingers are cramped up from handling the little packets. We must have used a whole box of masks. The Dr. said the masks are a must when bagging up pure dope.

In total, we packaged 460 bricks, which equals 23,000 bags of dope. That's a little more than what Slim said it would make. The Doctor stretched it a little bit, but it's still strong. He called a friend of his to check it out. He said on a scale of one to ten, he'd give it the whole ten. They're begging me to put it on the street. Really they just want to have access to it. They say it's much better than Junebug's Block Party. They say the reading on his is only an eight, but he's consistent. No matter what, he always has something good. Other spots will have a nine, and then next week they have a five. Not Junebug; when you go to him, there's no gamble.

"Where's this going to be so I'll know where to go?" asks the dope fiend.

"I'm not sure yet," I reply.

"Well, at least tell me the name so I can listen out for it," he says.

"I don't have a name for it yet. What do ya'll think I should name it?" I ask them.

"Uh, name it High Power!" screams the Doctor.

"High Power?" I repeat. "What do you think about that Slim?" *I look at Slim; he's standing there bent all the way over, sucking his own dick as the Doctor calls it. He's in one of the biggest nods I've ever seen.* "Slim!" I repeat.

He quickly snaps out of it. "Bang Man!" he shouts, *while lifting up his head for a fraction of a second before fading back into his nod.*

Everyone waits for him to finish his statement, but he doesn't. He just nods out again. "You heard the man. I'm going to call it Bang Man! I'm naming it after Slim." *They all laugh.*

"Listen youngblood, go to any office supply store and get a rubber stamp made with Bang Man. Get it in red letters so it will be easy to read, all right?"

"Alright Doc," I affirm. "How much do I owe you?"

"Just give me a little something, but you have to promise me a job if you get some more. Is that a deal?" he asks.

"That's a deal," I answer. "Here!" *I toss him two bricks. The rest I pack into cardboard boxes. I don't give the other guys anything. As high as they are, I'm pretty sure they have stole enough. Besides, the Doctor has 100 bags; he'll take care of them.*

The Doctor helps me and Slim carry the big boxes to the car and we leave. Before dropping Slim off I give him a brick for his self.

Now I'm on my way to one of the houses my sister owns. This is where I'm going to stash the dope for now. I'll stash it in her basement. Her or no one else will ever know. Ever since I've been home, I've been maintaining the house for her. It's a three-family house. She has tenants on all floors, but no one has access to the basement. I have the one and only key.

Now that I'm thinking about it, I'm a little worried about the Doctor and Slim. Maybe that was a bad idea giving them all that dope. I hope they don't overdose, especially the Doctor. I gave him 100 bags. He better not overdose. I need him.

Before pulling into the garage of my sister's house, I begin calculating. In, total I have 460 bricks. I gave three away. That leaves me with 457. If I wholesale them at $300 a brick, I can make $137,100 total. After subtracting the $45,000 for Juan, that leaves me with $92,100 profit. Damn! I love it when a plan comes together.

CHAPTER 20

The next morning

The first thing me and Slim did, was go to the car lot. Not to buy another Benz, oh no. Today I picked up a black Ford Taurus (SHO). It's a five speed. It's in mint condition, and it's superfast. She'll definitely serve the purpose. As soon as I drove her off the lot, I took her directly to the tint shop. I got the darkest tint I could get.

This car won't be used for flossing. Tonight I'm going to take her for a nice test drive. She's perfect; she's jet black, no one will see her coming. Her windows are so dark that no one can see in, and she's fast. Just in case shit gets hectic and the police jump on us, we'll be able to get out of the hole with no problem.

Tonight is Judgement Day for Wu. He will wish he never fucked with me.

After dropping the car off, me and Slim start our day.

"Bang Man, I'm hungrier than a hostage! Can we go over to Mickey Dees to get a bite to eat?"

I make the quick left into the parking lot, only to be greeted by lying ass Latif. **"Damn! I'm not in the mood for this bullshit today!"** *I pull into the space closest to the entrance. Latif dashes over to me. He has on the exact same clothes he had on the last time I saw him. When he gets over to the car, he puts on a big kool-aid smile. He then snatches his skullcap off his head.*

"I told you!" *he shouts. I smile. He has a haircut. The nappy cornrows are gone. His hair is cut down to a Caesar.* **"I told you!"** *he repeats, with a big smile on his face.*

"Latif, what up?"

"You, Cash!" *he replies.*

Slim goes inside the store.

"Cash, what happened to the boots I asked you for? Did you find anything for me?"

"Nah, Latif, I haven't had the time to look. I've been running so hard."

"Yo Cash, let me hold a few dollars."

"Come on Latif, damn!"

Slim returns with the food. When I see Slim's face, I automatically think about what he told me the other day about the blessing account. I then hand Latif a $20 bill.

"Good looking out, Cash! I owe you a million, baby!"

"Shit, if you don't, you will," I reply. "All the money you've borrowed over the years."

"Don't worry; one day when I get back right, I'm going to repay you every penny I owe you," he claims.

"Yeah right."

"Nah, I'm for real Cash. You a good nigga. I told you before; I'm here at your disposal. Anything you need, I mean anything!"

My mind begins to run wild. Should I? Na! Fuck it, it's worth a shot.

"Yo, I might have some work for you," I whisper.

"What up, what is it?" he asks anxiously.

"We'll kick it later," I whisper. *I don't want to tell him what it is just yet. He might run around telling the whole world.* "Check, if you're serious, meet me right here tonight," I whisper.

"What time?" he asks, *with a look of starvation in his eyes.*

"Meet me right here as soon as it gets dark."

"Bet!" he shouts. *His eyes light up.* "I'll be right here! Don't bullshit me, Cash. I need some work."

"All right then, later La!"

"Later Cash!"

We pull off. I wait for Slim to respond. I don't want to ask him for his opinion. I hope he offers it. I need to know if using Latif is a good idea.

I wait and wait; Slim doesn't say a word. I take it that he thinks it's OK. If he didn't he sure would have put me in my place.

We're on our way to make a drop-off to Mike's nephew. He has a sale for a bird and a half. This young cat keeps me so busy. What would I do without him?

CHAPTER 21

I'm late. It's been dark for over two hours now. Me and Slim have been working all day. Today has been the busiest day yet. Juggling the coke and dope is mind-boggling. Two different hustles, two different methods. You can't deal with them the same. They both need their own special attention. It's almost like juggling two full-time jobs.

After the last drop-off, we picked up the other car from the stash spot. Slim hasn't said a word since we changed cars. He's been constantly picking his teeth. That tells me he's in deep concentration.

Tonight is the perfect night. We couldn't have picked a better night. Tonight seems darker than normal. It could be from the thick fog that's in the air. **Click, click! Click, click!** *That's the sound of two nine millimeters. Slim is loading them up and making sure they're in working order.* **Click! Click, click!** *He's a gun expert. He can take a gun apart, and put it back together in a matter of minutes.*

"Pssst, pssst!" *Slim picks his teeth.*

"What's the matter Slim?"

"Nothing," he replies. **"Why do you ask that?"** *Pssst, pssst!"* *He picks his teeth again. I'm not going to respond. I'll just let him concentrate.*

This tint is so dark I can barely see where I'm going. I can't even read the traffic signs. No one will be able to see in here, especially with this thick fog. They probably won't even see the car coming.

I make the left turn into McDonalds parking lot. **"Watch it!"** **Slim shouts. "You almost hit the curb!"** *See, I told you these windows are dark. I glance over the lot. There's no sign of*

Latif. I stop and look harder; still no sign of Latif. **"I knew his lying ass wasn't gone be here! I'm out! I'll have to do this myself!"**

Slim doesn't respond. I'm waiting for him to respond, but he doesn't. He's looking as if I haven't said a word. **Click, click!** *He's fumbling with the guns.* **"Yeah, Big Time, they ready now! They're fully loaded and ready to go! Sixteen in the clip and one in the pipe! Thirty-four shots altogether. A blind man can't miss with thirty-four shots!"** *He laughs.*

Fuck it, I have to ask him. **"Yo, you haven't said a word about any of this!"** *I shout.* **"What do you think? Should I handle it myself or what?"**

"Pssst, psst!" *He picks his teeth before speaking.* **"Bang Man, this something that gotta be dealt with, right?"**

"Yeah," *I reply.*

"Well, let's deal with it."

That's what I was waiting to hear. I just wanted him to give me the green light.

"Anyway, you ain't by yourself I got your back! What do you think I'm here for, my looks?" *he asks, smiling from ear to ear, exposing his raggedy mouth. We both laugh.*

I turn out of the parking lot. As I cruise down the block, I decide to let Slim take the wheel now, while no one is around to see our faces. After switching seats, Slim pulls off slowly. **"Let's go,"** *he shouts.*

"When you get to the projects, go through the back entrance," *I instruct.* **"Don't go through the front!"**

"OK, you the man," *says Slim.*

We cruise past the gas station. **"Hold up! There's Latif,"** *I point out.*

"Man, later for Latif!" *Slim shouts.* **"If his punk ass wanted to go, he would have been there. You can't force a man to do something if he don't want to do it. His heart won't be in it. He'll be doing it for you, not cause he wants to. Fuck around and get us all an asshole full of time,"** *Slim explains.*

"Just pull over there and let me hear his punk ass excuse."

Slim pulls directly in front of him. He's startled. He doesn't know who's in here. He tries to see through the tint. He's bending over and squinting. Finally, we come to a complete stop. Now he's really scared. We pull up on the side of him. He begins walking a little faster. We go faster. Now he's taking full strides. Slim steps it up. Finally, he sprints off. **"Bang Man, he gone! Look at this motherfucker go!"** *Slim laughs.* **"And this is the punk ass nigga you want to do some dirt with? You gotta be out of your mind."**

"Go Slim, catch up with him." *Slim gasses up. We catch up with him immediately. I roll down the window.* **"Latif!"** *I yell. He's still running full speed.* **"Latif, this Cashmere!"** *He slows down. Finally, I roll the window down all the way. He sees me and stops. He has the dumbest look on his face. I bust out laughing.*

"Nigga, what up?" *I ask.*

"What up, Cash?" *He's embarrassed.* **"I waited over two hours for you,"** *Latif shouts.* **"I thought you were bullshitting, so I left."**

"Have you ever known me to bullshit?" *I ask.* **"Get your scary ass in!"**

"I ain't scary! I didn't know who the fuck you were," *he says.* **"Boy, I have done so much dirt; I thought my past had caught up with me!"** *he hollers, as he grabs the door handle, and gets in.*

"Latif, let me know now if you don't want to roll."

"What, don't want to roll? Nigga, you sound stupid. I wouldn't miss this for the world. This is what I live for! Put this tape in," *he hollers, as he digs into the inside pocket of his raggedy, flannel, lumberjack coat. As he reaches over to hand me the tape, the stench of old socks out of a wet, dirty clothes hamper fills the air. I stick the tape into the radio. The music that's coming out of the speakers is foreign to me. I don't know who the artist is, but the hook goes like this: I play rough!*

I sit and listen to the entire song before I ask.... **"Who is this?"**

"Oh, you ain't up on this shit? This is 'I Play Rough' by Mob Style," he states. **"This is riding music! This is how I prep myself to put in work."**

After that Latif doesn't say another word. He sits there in a zone. He has his eyes closed, and he's bopping his head real hard to the beat.

"Rewind that!" he shouts, *as the song fades out. I press the rewind button. The song replays.* **"Turn it up, Cash!"** he instructs, *with his eyes closed.*

"Hand me the bangers," I whisper to Slim. *Slim passes me the two twin, rubber gripped p89s. I sat one in my lap, and I hand the other one over my shoulder to Latif.* **Click, click.** *He checks to see if the gun has one in the chamber. He doesn't say a word. He just continues bouncing to the beat.*

"Rewind that again," he shouts.

I look back at him. Now he's in a full zone. He has his hand gripped tightly around the handle of the gun, and he's bopping his head crazily like a maniac.

Five minutes later, we pull to the back of the projects. Latif is still zoning. As we near the entrance, my heart starts pounding. My mind is running wild. Wu standing at my window is playing over and over in my head. **Inhale! Exhale!** *I take a deep breath.* **"Pssst, pssst!"** *There goes Slim.* **"I play rough!"** **Latif sings.** *I turn the music down. Latif doesn't even notice. He's singing loud.* **"I play rough!"** he shouts.

"Latif!" I call. *He doesn't answer.* **"Latif!"** I shout again. *He still doesn't answer; he just opens his eyes.* **"We're here,"** I inform. *He looks around. His face shows no sign of emotion.*

We've been together for 20 minutes, and not one time has he asked who or what the beef is about.

I grip my gun tightly. **"Pssst, pssst!"** *Slim picks his teeth. He pulls up so we can view the parking lot. I look around. The* *parking lot is emptier than usual.* **"Turn the lights out, Slim. Pull up a little closer."**

Two dudes are standing next to a black Cadillac Escalade. **"Slim, do you see him?"**

"Nah."

"Sit tight for one minute; maybe he's in the truck," I **instruct.** *The truck has out-of-state plates. The two dudes are laughing and playing around the truck. One of them is opening the passenger's door, back and forth.*

We sit and watch for about five minutes.

"Slim, pull a little closer. The tall one looks like it could be him." *The taller one is wearing the same kind of army camouflage jacket, Wu was wearing.* **"Is that him?" I ask.**

"Nah, Big Time, that kid has braids."

"Are you sure?" I ask. "Wu might be in the truck."

Latif hasn't said a word since we pulled up. I wonder if he's scared. Maybe he's ready to back out. **"Latif, what's up? You're kind of quiet back there. Are you all right?" I ask.**

"Yeah, I'm good! I'm just waiting for you to give me the word. I know one thing. We have to hurry up. We can't sit here all night. It's hot as hell down here. Five-0, stay coming through this motherfucker."

The interior light of the Caddy truck comes on. The driver's door opens up. A girl with skintight jeans jumps from the truck. She has the tightest little body. She's short and stacked. She runs around to the passenger side. Her and the boy start play-fighting. He lifts her by her ass and begins pumping on her like a maniac. Then the passenger door opens up and a second girl jumps out. She is even thicker than the first girl. Together they jump on the boy.

"Damn, a truck full of bitches!" shouts Latif.

The back door then opens up. A foot dangles in the air. It's the boot of a man. **"Hold up," I shout. "This might be him, right here."** *Seconds later, he sticks his other leg out. Now both of his legs are dangling in the air.*

"**Bang Man, here come the police!**"

"**Where?**" I ask.

"**Coming down the block!**" *Just like Slim said, a police car is cruising up the block.*

"**Turn the car off!**" Latif shouts.

The police car has a bright spotlight on top. The light is shining as they cruise through the block. "**Slim, lay your seat back so they can't see our shadows.**"

"**They won't be able to see in here,**" says Latif. "**I couldn't see shit when ya'll pulled up on me.**"

The cop car is easing up on us. Their light shines directly through our windshield, brightening the entire car. I can see their faces clearly. Now the light is on the side window. Now the back window. Darkness again as they pass us. They turn into the parking lot and pull parallel to the truck.

"**Bang Man, I think we need to get out of here before they come back!**"

"**Nah, we can't move, they'll notice us,**" I explain. *The man finally jumps from the backseat, but it isn't Wu.* "**Damn, that ain't even him!**"

"**Big Time, that's the other kid that was out there with him,**" says Slim.

"**Oh, his little cheerleader?**" I ask.

"**Yeah!**" Slim confirms.

"**Man, we sat out here all this time for nothing!**" I shout.

"**What should I do?**" Slim asks. "**Should I pull off when the cops leave?**" *Just as the words leave his lips, the cop's siren starts to echo and the lights begin flashing. They speed out of the parking lot recklessly. The group immediately starts wrestling again.*

"**Big Time, we might as well leave. He ain't nowhere around.**"

"**That's his man right there, right?**" Latif asks.

"**Yeah,**" I reply hesitantly.

"**Fuck it, let me do him then!**" Latif shouts aggressively.

"**Pssst, pssst!**" *Slim starts his shit.* "**Bang Man, them little girls out there. They ain't got shit to do with it.**"

"**They shouldn't be out here!**" **Latif shouts.** "**I didn't sit out here all this time for nothing! Cash, give me the word!**"

I pause before speaking. "**Hold up La; let's wait for the chicks to leave.**"

"**Come on man, we can't sit out here all night,**" **Latif replies anxiously.** "**Give me the word. I'll jump out and do him, and we're outta here.**"

The girl jumps back into the passenger's seat. One of the kids chases the driver around the truck. She jumps in and slams the door. He tugs on the door handle, trying to get in. The brake lights come on, then the reverse lights. The passenger leans her head out of the window and kisses Wu's man. "**Bingo,**" **Latif hollers.** "**Better make it a long kiss; this will be the last one,**" **he shouts sarcastically.**

The kid slowly backs away from the truck.

"**When they pull off, let me out,**" **says Latif.**

"**Nah, if they see you, they might take off,**" **I explain.** "**We're going to ride up in the lot. Slim, as soon as they pull off, pull up in the lot.**"

The brake lights finally disappear.

"**Start the car up,**" **I instruct. Vroom!**

The girl slowly circles the lot. I grasp my gun tighter. The tighter I grip it, the slippier the handle gets. My palms are leaking sweat.

The girls approach us. The bright headlights almost blind me. The kids back up against the building. You can barely see them, it's so dark out here. All the lights in the court are knocked out. They purposely do that so no one can see them back here.

"**Bang Man, be careful! Them boys might have guns on them.**" *I didn't even think about that, but I doubt it though. If they have guns on them they wouldn't have let the cops get that close up on them.*

"**Slim, roll my window down,**" **says Latif.**

The window slides down automatically. The girls zoom right past us. Slim turns the lights on. **"Now!" I shout.** *Slim steps on the gas.* **"La, how do you want to do it?" I ask.**

"Just follow my lead!" he shouts. "Watch my back Cash!"

As we come through the entrance, they all step away from the wall. They're trying to get a look at the car, but Slim has the high beams on. The bright lights are making it difficult for them to see. We slide directly up on them. They stand there trying to see in the car. Only Latif's window is halfway down.

"What up fellas?" Latif greets. "Ya'll seen Wu?"

"Nah," Wu's boy answers aggressively, *with a cold look in his eyes.*

"Nah? Yo, if you see him, give him this," Latif shouts. *Latif extends his hand from the window. The chrome reflection dangles from his white latex glove.* **Boc! Boc! Boc!** *The shots echo.*

"Agghh!" the kid screams, *as he grabs hold of his chest. All three shots hit him. The impact knocks him about ten feet backwards. His body slams into the brick wall.* **Thump!** *His head bangs into the brick. His body ricochets, and he splatters face first onto the asphalt. Latif jumps out. I follow behind him. The other two kids dash off into flight. I chase behind them. I aim. I squeeze.* **Boc! Boc! Boc! Boc!** *I stop in the middle of the parking lot. They're almost out of sight. I squeeze.* **Boc! Boc!** *I know it's impossible to hit them with the distance between us. I just fired again so they wouldn't look back. I don't want them to be able to ID the car.*

I turn around and see Latif bending over the boy. He grabs him by his shoulders and turns him over. He digs into the kid's coat pockets and then he digs into his pants pockets. From his pants pockets, he pulls out a big sloppy knot of money. He then stands up straight and aims. **Boc! Boc! Boc!** *The boy's lifeless body absorbs the shots. His body jolts after each bullet penetrates. Latif is still aiming at him. I run over to him.* **"Let's go!" I shout.** *Latif*

153

doesn't respond. He's still standing there as if he's ready to squeeze again. "Let's go," I repeat. Boc! Boc! *He fires again. The kid is laying there stiff. Blood is pouring from his mouth, and his eyes are wide open. His body shows no sign of life.*

   I grab Latif by the arm, push him in the car, and slam the door. I jump in the front seat. Slim speeds out of the parking lot. Latif finally snaps out of his zone.
   "Motherfucker," Latif shouts. "Did you see his body bounce off that wall?" he asks cold-heartedly. "Yeah! Stupid young motherfucker! That's how Latif get down! I'm an asset! You need a motherfucker like me on the team! Wait till those bitches hear about this in the morning! I told you that was his last kiss! That bitch gave him the kiss of death! Put my motherfucking tape back in," he demands.
   "I play rough!" *He sings along with the verse that bursts through the speakers.*
   Within the last ten minutes no one has said a word. All I heard was the now-irritating noise of Slim picking his teeth during the interludes of Latif's tape. I must have played it over at least ten times.
   Twenty minutes later, we pull into the garage where my car is stashed. We change cars and exit the garage.
   Slim still hasn't said a word. "Good looking out, La."
   "No problem Cash. I told you before, I'm here at your disposal."
   Latif still hasn't asked what the beef is about. He doesn't even care. "How much do I owe you, La?"
   "Come on man, don't insult me like that," he replies. "I done that from the heart."
   "I feel you La, but you gotta charge me something. Business never personal."
   "I'm good Cash, for real."
   "Charge me something," I demand.
   "Go ahead, Cash!"

I have to pay him something. I won't have it any other way. If I don't pay him something, he'll throw this in my face for the rest of our lives. He'll think I owe him forever. **"How much, La?"**

He pauses. **"Get me a brick of dope,"** he mumbles.

Damn, one brick? Fifty bags of dope is all he wants? He just slaughtered a man, and all he wants is one lousy ass brick! **"One brick?"**

"Yeah," he replies. **"That way I can get on my feet. I'm going to turn it up from there."**

Yeah right, you're going to turn it up all right... right up your nose.

CHAPTER 22

Two weeks has flown by. Damn, it's December already. Everything is going terrific. Love and I have officially moved into our new condominium. It's already fully decorated and everything. As for the old house, the realtors are trying to get a sale for it now. The wedding plans are starting to come together. We're getting married in Central Park.

Our entire wedding party will be entering by horse and carriage. After the ceremony, me and Love will take off for a balloon ride over New York City. And finally, for the honeymoon, we're taking 20 guests with us to Jamaica. You know, that's Love's dream vacation. We're staying for two weeks. I don't want to be away for two whole weeks, but I know how bad she wants to go there. The date is set for April 1, 2001. You're all invited. Come January, I'm supposed to be done with the streets. Love is giving me two more months to get a little extra money to pay for this expensive ass wedding. Plus, she says she wants to give me ample time to get the streets out of my system.

Oh, I bought another little hooptie to move around in. It's a 1996 Lincoln Town Car with limo-tinted windows. I still park the Benz at the old house so people won't know we moved. What Juan said to me about my car really makes a lot of sense now that I've thought about it. I mean, I already knew it's best to keep a low profile, but I let my ego get in the way. That kid Junebug was really getting to me. You know, the way he continuously tried to belittle me. Something inside me just wanted to prove to him that he isn't the only one who has money.

By the way, Junebug hasn't bought one bird from me ever since he saw my new car. I guess he feels that him buying kilos from me helped me get the car. I had a feeling that was going to happen. When I looked into his eyes that day, I saw nothing but jealousy. Him not buying from me doesn't stop anything. I picked up two new plugs, and believe me they buy heavy! Anyway, that dope has taken off! I finished the first package, and now I'm working on another one. I didn't receive all the money from the work yet, because I put everything out on consignment. I gave it to a couple of guys I know from other towns; 50 bricks here, 100 bricks there. The response was incredible. Everyone is trying to get their hands on "BANG MAN". The stamp is in red letters with an exclamation mark at the end of it. "BANG MAN!" Slim is famous. I took another half a joint from Juan yesterday. I took it over to the Doctor so he could do his chemistry.

I only have one problem. Last week, me and Mike had a slight falling out. He's mad because I won't give him any dope to move on his block. I told him I don't want to move it around here. But he got real mad at me. I don't know why he wants the dope anyway. He doesn't need it. He's killing them with the twenties of powder in aluminum foil. He goes through two pies a week out there. Overall, he grosses about $75,000 a week. After he pays his workers, he steps off with about $18,000 profit. That's damn good for a motherfucker who has never made any money on his own. All his life, he's been taking money from hustlers. He was an extortionist.

After a week of not speaking, I called him and told him I would hit him when I get the new package. Although I don't want to do it, I will have to. I'm going to do it because we're a team. That means if I'm eating, the whole team has to eat. If one teammate isn't eating, that's a problem in the making. Eventually, jealousy will set in. Then all kinds of problems will arise: setups, stealing, snitching, and so on. Not to say Mike will do any of those things, but I really can't afford to find out.

Oh, I almost forgot; the other day Ice slid into town. He went to Desire's house. Slim told me Desire didn't let him in. He was on the porch, begging and pleading for her forgiveness. Slim said he was out there crying like a baby, telling her how much he really loves her and how he wants them to spend the rest of their lives together. Slim said she didn't give in. She told him to leave her porch before she calls the police. My oldest son called me so I could come over and catch him, but I missed him. I'm glad I did. I don't think I'm going to do anything to him; he's already going through enough. I've been there before. Trust me, I know how a broken heart feels.

Right now, I'm walking down the block to my kids' house, me and my two pit bulls. You should see how much they've grown. They're only a couple of months old, and they already look full-grown. They're so strong and so mean.

I'm taking the kids to the park around the corner from their house to shoot some hoop. They begged me to bring the dogs. They love them. I have to bring their muzzles. I don't think they'll turn on the kids, but I can't take a chance. I wouldn't be able to live with myself if these dogs were to hurt my boys.

Beep! Beep! "Cash!"

Before I even look over, I already know who it is that's calling me. It's Junebug; I can tell by the horn. I know how Mercedes horns sound.

"Cash, what's up?"

"You!" I reply.

"Nah, you the man," he shouts sarcastically.

Seconds later, the Grand Prix rolls up behind Junebug as usual. Immediately, me and the driver, Spook, start our staring contest. He isn't blinking, and I'm not blinking.

"I'm hearing big things about you," says Junebug. *I don't respond; me and the kid Spook are still at it.*

I laugh. **"Your little man back there, he real funny!"**

"What did you say?" Spook asks. "You talking about me Old Head?"

"Yeah, I said you're a real clown!" I reply. *By this time, my dogs are going wild, barking and growling. They sense a threatening situation. Spook slams the car into park and starts to get out.*

I got something for his ass today; 17 shots. If he thinks for one minute he's about to play me out again, he has another thing coming.

He gets out, leaving the door wide open. The rest of the goons follow. I switch the dogs' leash to my left hand. With my right hand, I sneakily reach for my nine inside my coat pocket. By the time they're all out of the car and approaching me, I have my gun out. They halt. **"Nah, don't stop! Keep coming so I can let this motherfucker go!"**

"Spook, ya'll get the fuck back in the car!" *shouts* **Junebug.** *Spook is really mad now, but he isn't coming any closer. The rest of them are already getting back in the car.* **"Spook, did you hear me?"** *asks Junebug.* **"Get the fuck in the car!"** *Spook walks to the car slowly. I put my gun back in my pocket, but my finger is still on the trigger. I'm not a fool. I'm not sleeping on these motherfuckers. One false move and I'm going to tear that car up. They might kill me only because I'm outnumbered, but I tell you one thing; my family won't be the only family in mourning.*

"Cash, don't mind him," says Junebug.

"You need to teach him some manners!" I reply.

"You teach me some manners!" Spook shouts.

"Get out the car, I'll leave your little ass right here in the middle of the street!"

"Yeah, right," he challenges. **"You ain't nothing but a punk ass old head! I know your kind!"**

"You little punk ass nigga, you ain't never met a motherfucker like me; my guns bust," I shout. **"This some new shit to you. I was doing this when you was a baby."**

"You ain't never done nothing," Spook shouts. **"What have you done?"** he asks sarcastically.

"I'm not about to sit here and run down my resume to your little punk ass. I let the streets tell my story," I reply.

"What story? Ain't nothing for the streets to tell," Spook claims. **"I already did my homework on you. You ain't**

never did shit but call them punk ass niggas Jake and Ab when you had a problem."

"Who?" I ask. "You got me fucked up! I put in my own work! I'm good with mines."

"I'm good with mines too," he shouts.

"Yeah, I saw your little work over there on the block," I admit. "I wasn't impressed. It took you almost twenty shots. Not me. I'm guaranteed to finish the job with no more than two."

"Your punk ass ain't gonna finish shit. Stop lying to yourself! You ain't gonna kill nothing, and you ain't gonna let nothing die," he replies. "You ain't fooling me. I already did my homework on you."

"Yo Spook, shut the fuck up," Junebug interrupts.

"Get out again," I shout. "I bet you I finish your ass right here." *He has me pissed now, talking that Jake and Ab shit. This young cat don't know me. I'll bust his motherfucking head!* "Listen, you little young motherfucker, we can do it however you want to do it. We can go toe to toe on the yellow line in the middle of the street, or we can go from corner to corner with the hammers. It's up to you; my gun bust and I can fight."

"Cash, cool out," Junebug mumbles.

"Fight?" Spook asks. "I ain't about to wrestle around with your ass out here. Nobody ain't fighting no more. That shit played out! I'll put some hot shit up in you," he shouts, *as he digs up under his shirt and grabs his gun from his waist. I raise my gun slightly just in case he decides to start firing.* "I'll hit you with this forty-five, have ya old ass walking around here like 115 pounds," he says sarcastically, *as waves his gun in the air.*

"Spook, shut the fuck up," shouts Junebug. *Spook doesn't respond. He's just sitting there nodding his head up and down with a devilish smirk on his face.*

"Yeah, back to what I was saying. I've been hearing big things about you," Junebug repeats.

"Like what?" I question.

"I heard you got it good," Junebug replies.

"I can't tell. I haven't heard from you in two weeks."

"Oh na, I chilled with the blow. I'm just concentrating on that BLOCK PARTY, but I heard you got your hands on a smoker," he shouts.

How does he know about that? I wonder who could have told him. "Where did you hear that?" I ask.

"Listen, I'm the Mayor! I might only run this town, but I politic with other Mayors and politicians all over the world. You feel me?" he asks. "I heard you're making a lot of noise other places. The big dogs from other towns are calling me up questioning me about you," he informs. "They say you're making it hard for them to eat ever since you put out that BANG MAN."

Damn, he really does know. He even knows the name.

"Listen, Cash. I don't have nothing to do with that out-of-town shit. I don't care what you do out there. I'm only concerned with right here. Please Cash, I'm begging you to keep that shit out there wherever you have it at. Not even on no tough shit," he claims. "This is man to man, from the heart. This is how I feed my family. This is how I been feeding my family. You watched me grow up. I spoke to my brother Dre the other day; he's real big on you. That first day you came home and you were telling my people where they can stand, niggas wanted to off you then," he admits.

"You being the powder connect, I didn't mind. Shit, I don't like Ice anyway. I'm glad his punk ass is outta here. But this new shit, with this dope, that can be a problem. On the real, if it were anybody else, I would have got at you."

That's it. I can't take no more. "Yo, it ain't that easy," I interrupt.

"Nah Cash, I ain't coming at you like that. Let me rephrase that; maybe my niggas would have got at you, or maybe your niggas would have got at me. Who knows? But what I'm saying is, if it were anyone else, I would've nipped it in

**the bud," he says calmly. "I can't have nobody running around
here with better smack than me. I'm the Mayor!"** *He raises
his voice.* **"Listen, I got a lot of respect for you and the things
you've done. Please keep that shit out of this town," he begs.**

*He pauses for a second or two. Neither of us says a word. I
still have my finger on the trigger. My dogs are still going bananas.
I look at Spook; he still has his gun out. We go at the staring bout
again. He starts bopping his head up and down.* **"Cash, I'll
holler at you later," Junebug shouts.** *He pulls off quickly. Spook
follows. As he passes me, he winks at me and blows a kiss. I grab
a handful of my dick and shake it at him, gesturing for him to
blow me. Then I smile. He mumbles something to me as the other
passengers smile. I read his lips; he said, 'I got you, I got you.'
Now I realize it is officially on with me and him. I'm not worried; I
don't go nowhere without mine.*

*I picked the boys up. Now we're on our way to the park.
I want them to practice, because by the looks of it, they might be
going to the championships. Right now their record is 14 and 1.
The team they may have to go against is 15 and 0. They're tough.
It's going to take a lot of hard work to beat them. But with a lot of
practice, I'm sure we can pull it off. We have a few more games
before the finals, so I'm going to stay on them.*

*On the way to the park, I let them walk the dogs. Ahmir
loves the red-nosed one, and Ahmad loves the other one. I guess
they love them because they share the same characteristics. The
red-nosed one is aggressive and moody just like Ahmir. Wherein
the other one follows the first one's lead. He doesn't get ruffled up
unless the other one does. Just like Ahmad, he doesn't get hyped up
or upset unless he sees Ahmir get angry.*

*The dogs drag them all the way to the park. The dogs are
entirely too strong for them, but they refuse to let me walk them. I
laugh as the dogs run, causing the boys to fall on their faces. One
time Ahmir must have gotten dragged for a half a block when the
dog tried to get hold of this lady's poodle. I didn't stop him. He
couldn't hurt it. He had his muzzle on. I wish I had a video camera*

to tape that. That was the funniest shit I ever saw. It feels good to laugh! That's the only thing that is keeping my mind off of Junebug and his little goon squad. I hope I don't have to get into this with them, but it seems like I'm not going to be able to avoid it.

CHAPTER 23

Later that evening

Someone gave us a tip on where Wu and his baby's mother live. Twenty minutes ago, Mike received a call. Someone informed him that Wu's girlfriend just came through and picked him up. They're on their way home. But guess what? We're already here. At this moment, we're sitting three houses down from his house. When he comes through the block, he won't even notice us. We're in Mike's van. The windows are so dark, it's impossible to see inside. He just got the van about a week ago. He keeps it stashed, so no one has seen it.

Slim is at the steering wheel. I'm in the seat directly behind him, and Mike is sitting in the passenger's seat. Mike has a nine millimeter, and I have a sawed-off shotgun. When Wu comes through, he's going to get the surprise of a lifetime.

"Listen. Let's go over this one more time," I suggest. **"Slim, when they come through, what are you going to do?"**

"I'm going to cut them off," he replies.

"Mike, what are you going to do?" I ask.

"I'm going to jump out, snatch the girl out the car, and lay her face down," he replies.

"OK, then I'm going to do him, right there," I state. **"Mike, make sure you get her far away from the car. I don't want any mistakes. She's innocent."**

My heart is racing. I have never wanted anything this bad. You can't imagine how bad I want this.

Minutes later, Slim spots the Mitsubishi Eclipse, slow rolling up the block. **"Bang Man, here he comes!"**

As the car creeps up, I notice their windows are slightly tinted. You can only see shadows. The car pulls up and stops in the middle of the street. Slim steps on the gas. They begin to turn into their garage. **Scuuuurrrr!** *Slim takes off in the nick of time.* **Crash!** *Their car smacks into the back of our van. Mike jumps out with no hesitation. He aims at the driver's side window. Then with his left hand, he reaches for the door handle. I jump out. I'm already at the passenger's side. I have the shotgun aimed at the window. Mike yanks the door open, as planned.*

"**OWW!**" *The girl screams at the top of her lungs.*

"**Get the fuck out**," **Mike shouts.** *The girl freezes. She's in total shock.*

"**I said get the fuck out**," **he repeats.** *He drags her out of the car and pushes her to the back of the van.* "**Lay the fuck down!**" **he demands.** *She's crying hysterically.* "**Now!**" *Mike gives me the OK. I snatch the door open with my left hand, while aiming the shotgun with my right. My finger is on the trigger ready to squeeze. It's over. The moment I've been waiting for; sweet revenge. The interior light comes on.* "**Aghhh!**" *Surprise- no Wu! The barrel of the shotgun is resting on the forehead of a small boy.* "**Aghh!**" **he screams.** *The kid looks into my eyes with fear and helplessness. I look back at Mike. He has a confused look on his face. He's waiting to hear the sound of the shotgun ringing off, but instead he hears the sound of an innocent kid screaming for his life.*

"**He ain't in here!**" **I shout.**

"**What?**" **he asks.**

"**He ain't in here!**" **I repeat.** *The boy is about five years old. He's scared to death. His eyes are stretched wide open.*

"**Aghh!**" **he cries.**

"**Don't worry little man; we're not going to hurt you,**" **I mumble,** *as I hide the gun behind my leg.* "**Pull up**," **I instruct Slim.** *I then run to the back and pull the girl to her feet.* "**I'm sorry**," **I plead.** "**This wasn't meant for you.**" *She's screaming bloody murder.* "**Go ahead and get in your car**," **I shout.** "**I'm not going to hurt you.**" *Mike is already in the van. He has the door stretched wide open for me. I jump in the van and slam the door.* **Scuuurrr!** *Slim peels off.*

"**Damn! A fucking baby!**" **I shout. "I was two seconds away from killing a baby! She must have dropped him off and picked up the kid.**"

I sit quietly. Right now I feel like shit. I've never seen anyone as scared as them. That girl thought we were going to kill her and her son. Wu doesn't realize the jeopardy he has put his family in. He doesn't know. That dumb shit could have cost him dearly. He doesn't realize the seriousness of the game he's playing. These young boys just don't get it!

CHAPTER 24

It's been two days since I've seem Slim. I haven't seen him since the night we almost killed Wu's girl and son. This isn't like him. He usually calls me before he goes anywhere. I've checked all his hangouts; everyone claims they haven't seen him. Desire said he came in late last night and left early this morning. I'm confused. I don't understand why he hasn't called me. It's not like we had a falling out. Everything was fine, at least I think everything was fine the last time I dropped him off.

Ring! Ring! *My phone is ringing.* **"Hello? Yeah! Oh, what up baby? Alright! How long? Bet, I'll meet you there."**

That was my man, AJ. He's one of my out-of-town plugs. He wants 50 bricks. I have 70 stashed at Desire's house, so there's no use in me going all the way to my sister's house.

I pull up to Desire's house. While parking, I notice Ahmir in the backyard bouncing a basketball. I back up; I don't want them to see me. They'll want to talk, and that'll slow me down. I slam the car into park, snatch the keys out, and jump out of the car. I run up the stairs and ring the bell. Desire comes out almost instantly. I blow right past her.

"Damn Cash! You could at least say hi," she screams sarcastically.

"What up Dee," I shout. *I run into Slim's room and slam the door. I go to his closet and reach all the way to the back. I fumble around for a few seconds until I feel the strongbox. I grab it and pull it off the shelf.*

This is Slim's strongbox. Only two keys fit this box. I have one and he has the other; just in case something happens to me, he can get in it. Slim is the only person I trust like that.

The first thing I see after I get the strongbox open is two packs of unused syringes. This makes me feel uncomfortable. Even though I know he shoots dope, I still hate to picture him all slumped over, poking himself like a junkie. I mean, I know he's a junkie, but I sort of hate to admit it.

I know the entire world looks at him like a filthy junkie, but I see past that. When I look at Slim, his outer shell is invisible to me. It's like I'm looking and talking to his inner self. It's like reading a good book that has its cover snatched off. At first you say to yourself, I'm not reading that raggedy old book, but once you get into it, you realize it's the best book you've ever read. Once you start reading and enjoying the contents of the book or appreciating the knowledge the book has to offer, you forget about the fact that the book doesn't have a cover.

I grab a sleeve. Each sleeve consists of five bricks taped together in a line. Each brick is individually wrapped in newspaper. There are fifty packets of dope to each square brick . The total size of a brick is about, two inches long, and two inches wide.

Two, three, four, five, six, seven, eight. What the? The eighth sleeve has been tampered with. The seal is broken. Instead of five bricks, this one only has four bricks. I examine the other thirteen sleeves. One, two, three, four, five, six, etc. The rest are all in place. I don't understand this. Each sleeve had five bricks in it. I wrapped them up myself. I brought these here a few days ago. My man was supposed to pick them up, but he never showed up.

I dig further into the strongbox. Maybe this one came loose. Maybe there's a single brick, somewhere, in the bottom. I dig further. I feel something deep in the corner. I grasp it and pull it out. It's a piece of torn newspaper that matches the tear on the sleeve. Someone tore this one open and took a brick out. **"Hmphh!"** *Not someone, Slim did it. I can't believe him. This is why I haven't seen or heard from him. He's ducking me. Right now he's probably somewhere high as a kite. I don't believe he'd steal from me. He's never done this before. I have left up to fifteen* *kilos in his possession. Sometimes he has held all of the buy money overnight before going to see Juan. Never has it been a penny short. Why would he only take one brick when he could have taken all seventy of them? Damn, Slim! I can't believe him! I can't fully blame him. I should have never put him under that kind of pressure. After all, he is a junkie.*

CHAPTER 25

One day later

I still haven't heard from Slim. I'm fucked up behind this. I didn't think he would ever betray my trust. It's not even the fact of the $300. It's the principle. I've been taking care of him ever since I came home. I bought him all new clothes. I make sure he has money in his pocket every day. Why would he steal from me?

Last night before going in, I stopped by Desire's house to drop off some money. She needed pamper money for her baby. She was ashamed to ask me. When I got to the house, little man was so wet, his soggy pamper was leaking all over his legs. That was one time I sincerely felt sorry for Desire. In fact, I felt so sorry for her that I ended up giving her $250, instead of $20 like she asked me for.

When I handed her the money, she was almost in tears. Desire has really put herself in a terrible situation. She's 36 years old, no job, no degree, and a 16 month-old baby with a crack addict for a father. And to top it all off, she has a teenager for a boyfriend. She's really screwed up. Her greed and passion for the fast life knocked her off course. When she was younger, all she wanted to do was live like the rap stars. Whatever she saw M.C. Lyte or Queen Latifah wear when their videos played on Hott Trax, she just had to have it. I always told her that would be her downfall. If she had listened to me, she wouldn't be suffering like this. But she didn't; now she has to pay the price.

Before leaving the house, I told her to call me as soon as Slim comes in, no matter what the time is. He must not have come home last night, because she never called. I didn't tell her what he did. Our business is our business. I would never cross him like that.

Ring! Ring! *My car phone is ringing. I press the intercom button, which sits on my steering wheel.* **"Hello,"** **I answer.**

"Cash, this Mike! Where are you?" he asks.

"I'm around. Why?"

"Come through!" he shouts. **"I have something important to tell you!"**

"All right, I'll be there in ten minutes." Click! *Now what?*

It didn't even take me ten minutes. I was right around the corner when he called. I got there in four minutes.

As I turn the corner, I can barely drive through the block, they have so much traffic coming through. Mike has turned a dead-end street into a main avenue. As soon as he sees me, he jogs over to the car. He grabs the door handle anxiously.

"Did you hear what happened?" he asks, *before he sits down.*

"Huh?"

"Did you hear what happened?" he repeats.

"With who?" I ask.

"Your boy," he replies.

"My boy, who?"

"Your boy Wu."

My heart beats a little faster. With a confused look on my face, I ask, **"Na, what happened?"**

"He got mirked last night."

"Get the fuck out of here," I shout.

"No bullshit," Mike replies.

"Yeah?'

"Word up!" Mike replies.

"Where at?" I ask.

"In the PJ's."

"What happened?" I ask.

"The word on the street is he ran up in some Jamaican boy's house, tied him up in front of his family, robbed him, and killed him."

"Yeah?"

"I heard he came off!" Mike shouts. "They say he got like 10 pounds of boogie (marijuana), 2 kilos, and $40,000."

"Damn, he came up!" I shout. *That sting made the little swindle he caught on me look like chump change.*

"No, he didn't. He didn't even get the chance to spend a dime of that shit," Mike replies. "He went in the Jamaican boy's spot at 1 in the morning. By 9 the next night, the boy's family had the projects sealed off. I heard they had all kinds of machine guns. Them dreads were like 40 deep!"

"Yeah?" I ask.

"Peep this," he adds. "This is the fucked-up part, right here."

"What?"

"They ran up in Wu's house and got all the drugs and money back."

"Get the fuck out of here," I shout.

"That ain't the worst part though," Mike claims. "Check this. After they got everything back, they raped and killed his bitch. They shot her in the face twice. When the police found her, she was gagged with her own bloody panties."

A lump forms in my throat. Damn. I instantly picture the pretty little young girl we dragged out of the car that night. She was so beautiful. Damn, she was innocent. She didn't have anything to do with Wu's bullshit. The only thing she was guilty of was being in love with the wrong dude. "That's fucked up," I reply. "She was innocent."

"Hey man, Wu should have thought about that when he did that fuck shit," Mike shouts.

"I know man, but damn, she didn't have shit to do with it," I shout back.

"Yes she did. She was his bitch."

Whoa! I didn't know Mike was this cold. I feel sorry for the young girl. I feel sorry for her mother and father. I feel sorry for her baby. Her baby? "Where was the little boy?"

"I don't know. No one mentioned him. He must not have been there."

"That's a good thing." *Damn, now he's going to grow up with no mother or father.* **"How did they find out who did it?"**

"They say his stupid ass was bragging around town all day. Somebody must have gave him up," Mike replies. **"They went to his girlfriend's house first, and then they went to the projects."**

Well, that's one problem out of the way, even though I would have loved to have the satisfaction of doing it myself. This feels just as good. It also saves me the risk of me doing 30 years if I would have got caught. No need in feeling sorry for Wu; you do dirt, you get dirt.

"Ride with me real quick," I suggest.

"Where to?" Mike asks.

"Through the projects. I want to see their faces."

"Hold up, let me tell my little man to hold it down while I'm gone." *Mike rolls down the window.* **"Yo Rah Rah, I'll be right back! Hold it down!"** he yells, *from the window.*

We pull off. I just want to see the looks on their faces. Two fallen soldiers in less than three weeks. I still think about the other kid. I didn't really want Latif to kill him I just wanted him to pop him a few times to teach him a lesson. I wanted him to realize that shit is real out here.

Before I know it, we're at the projects. The parking lot is rather empty. I don't know if it's because it's early in the morning or the fact that Wu got murdered last night.

As soon as I pull into the parking lot, my attention is drawn to the first building. That's the building where Latif murdered the kid. Right against the very wall he flew into is a makeshift memorial. It has a big stand with flowers on it. On top of the cross sits a white t -shirt with a picture of the boy on the front. It reads: R.I.P. 1986 - 2001. Damn, he was only 15 years old.

As we pass the memorial, I notice a small crowd in a huddle about 25 feet away. One kid is bent over. As we pull up a little

173

closer, all five of the kids look up at us. The kid who was bending down begins to stand up. He shakes a match. I now realize he was lighting a candle. There are about five glass candles blocking the passageway. There is also a bloody army jacket with an old white, filthy teddy bear sitting on top of it. Right next to the bear sits a big baby picture of Wu in a golden frame.

All the kids are sad. At least they're acting like they're sad. They probably don't give a fuck. When someone dies in the hood, everyone crowds around the memorial crying, knowing they hated the motherfucker, just fronting for the people. Deep down inside, they're just as happy that he's dead as I am.

As I slowly pass, someone points at me and all the other kids start to stare. The one who's pointing has a big, cheesy smile on his face. He must have been out here when Wu shot at me. I get pissed all over again. I put the car in park and jump out. **"Cash, where are you going?" Mike asks.** *I don't respond. I get out and walk in the direction of the kid who's smiling.* **"Cash!" Mike shouts.** *I ignore him again. As I get closer, they all rise up and stand attentively.*

"Is something funny?" I ask. *No one answers.* **"I said, is something funny?"** *Still no one responds.* **"Do I look like a fucking clown?"**

"Cash!" Mike shouts. "Cool out Cash!" *Before I realize what I'm doing, I've knocked down all five of the candles. I did it with one sweeping motion of my foot.* **"Cash!" Mike shouts.** *Everyone's eyes are stretched wide open. They're surprised that I disrespected them like that.* **"Sniff!"** *I suck up a mouthful of snot.* **"Spit!"** *I hog spit at the memorial. It lands on the glass eye of the teddy bear. The flim stretches from the teddy bear's eyes to the sleeve of the bloody army jacket. It's so cold out here; the dripping snot freezes before it falls, causing the iced flim to dangle from the teddy bear's eyes to the jacket.*

"Fuck Wu!" I shout. "Spit!" *I spit again.*

"You disrespecting my man," says the kid, *who was laughing at me. I look at him. Now shit isn't funny. He's enraged.*

174

He quickly spits a razor from his mouth into the palm of his hand and runs in my direction. Mike jumps out of the car. The kid gets about three feet away from me. He raises his arm in the air as if he's about to slice me. I snatch my gun off my waist. He freezes. The other kids back away. He's motionless. I reach over and grab him by the neck.

"Go ahead, cut me!" I shout. **"Cut me, you little punk motherfucker!"** *I jam my gun into his mouth.* **"Ucckkk!"** *He chokes as the barrel touches the back of his throat.*

"Cash, cool out," Mike begs, *as he grabs me by the shoulder.*

"Mike, get the fuck off me," I shout. **"You were about to cut me, huh? Drop the razor,"** I demand. *He quickly drops the razor.* **"Are you ready to meet Wu? Do you love him that much that you ready to die with him?"** I ask. **"Huh?"** *The kid doesn't answer.* **"Answer me!"** I yell. **"You'll only be one day behind him. Answer me, you bitch ass nigga!"** *The kid isn't responding. He has a slight smirk on his face. He's not even worried. Fuck it, I'm about to do him right here, right now. He must think I'm soft. He thinks I won't do it. I quickly glance around. I take the gun out of his mouth. I cock the hammer back. I'm biting my bottom lip so hard, I can taste the blood from my teeth breaking the skin.*

Now the kid is showing a sign of fear, but it's too late. I glance around again to make sure no one is watching. I back the kid into the alleyway.

"Cash," Mike whispers. *I look over at him. He's shaking his head no. The minute I see his face, I think about the conversation we had in the bar. The words "You have too much to lose," echo in my head. Love's face appears, then my two boys' faces.*

I push the kid with all my might. He stumbles backwards. I backpedal to the car and Mike follows. We both get in the car. All the kids are watching as we pull out of the lot.

The car is completely quiet; no radio or conversation for five minutes before I finally speak. **"Thanks,"** I mumble.

"For what?"

"For not letting me go through with it," I reply.

"I told you, these little dumb ass niggas will get you 30 years!"

Ring! Ring! *It's my car phone. I press the intercom button without looking.* "Hello!" *I shout. No one answers.* "Hello," *I* repeat.

"Big Time," Slim mumbles.

"What?" I ask sharply.

"Come by, I need to talk to you," he whispers.

After dropping Mike off, I go over to Desire's house. I'm still furious. When I pull up, Slim is sitting on the porch waiting for me. When he spots my car, he limps over to the car. He gets in. Never do I look in his direction. I have my eyes fixed on the car directly in front of me. He extends his hand in my direction.

"Here, take this $250, and I owe you $250 more," he whispers.

I totally ignore him. "What happened to the other brick?" *I can't even look him in the eyes, maybe because he betrayed my trust. I'm so mad at him right now, I could smack the shit out of him.*

"Big Time, I gotta keep it real with you. It's Desire's momma," he explains. "I got to thinking about her, and one thing led to another."

"Slim, I don't want to hear that shit! What the fuck happened to the other brick?" *I finally look him in the eyes. He has dark rings under his eyes. He looks like he hasn't been to sleep in days.* "All I've done for you, you gone steal from me?" I ask. "From me?"

"Big Time, at the time that was the only thing that could ease my pain."

"So you just said fuck it, I'm going to steal this brick from Cash. He won't notice it, huh?"

"It wasn't like that. Please don't look at it like I stole

from you," he begs. "Here, here's half of the money. I'll get the other half to you in a day or two."

"Fuck that money!" I shout. "How the fuck are you going to steal from me?"

"Here Big Time, take the money, please!" he begs, *as he extends his hand again.*

I snatch the money from his hand, roll the window down, and throw the money out. "Slim, get the fuck out my car."

"Huh, Big Time?" he asks, *as if he didn't hear me right.*

"You heard me, get the fuck out my car. When you crossed me, you lost me!"

"Come on, Big Time," he begs.

"Get the fuck out my car, you fucking junkie!" *He backs away from me with a baffled look on his face. He reaches for the door handle. He opens the door and gets out.*

As he stands in the doorway, he speaks. "Bang Man, you gotta make me a promise." *I'm looking straight ahead as if he isn't standing there talking to me.* "Big Time please promise me one thing, OK?" *I look over at him. The tears are pouring down his face.* "Big Time, please don't have me killed." *I step on the gas.* Scuurrrr! *I burn out with my door wide open.*

The tears that dripped down Slim's face are nothing compared to the tears that are dripping down my heart. I wish I hadn't used the word junkie. Have him killed? What the fuck is he talking about?

CHAPTER 26

Early this morning, I received a shocking call from Desire. She told me they just admitted Slim into the hospital. As if me tossing and turning all night thinking about what Slim asked me wasn't enough. Desire said this morning the ambulance had to come pick him up. She said he was in real bad shape.

I just step off the elevator. Slim's room is directly across from the elevator. I knock on the door. **Knock! Knock!** *He doesn't answer, so I walk right in. My heart is pounding. I don't want to see him like this. I feel terrible about the way I talked to him yesterday. Then, for him to beg me not to get him killed, that took the cake. Does he really think I would do something to harm him? I would never do anything to hurt him no matter what he did. Slim means so much to me. He's like the father I never had.*

Right now, he's sleeping. He looks a mess. He has a tube running through his nose and IV running through his swollen, tracked-up arms. The creaking of the door awakens him. He cracks one eye at me.

"Slim, get up from there. Stop faking. You're all right!" I yell, *trying to cheer him up, hoping he forgot the last words I said to him last night.*

"Bang Man," he whispers. **"I ain't faking. I wish I was. I'm fucked up, Big Time. My whole body hurts."**

"What is it?" I ask.

"It's pneumonia. The doctor said due to my condition, a basic cold will break me down like this."

"Yeah?"

"Yeah man," he replies.

Slim is talking about the AIDS virus. I feel guilty. I feel like it's all my fault that he's laying here. He was fine until I said what I said.

"The doctor said I should be all right, but from time to time, I'm going to feel very sick. You know, some days I'll be up and others I'll be down. That's the effect this disease has on you," Slim explains. "Big Time, I couldn't even get out the bed last night. I tried to get up in the middle of the night to take a piss, I couldn't move. I felt like I was going to die."

"You'll be all right." *I try to comfort him.* "Just remember you're the man. You're not going anywhere unless you want to."

"Did Desire say anything to you?" Slim asks.

"Anything like what?" I ask.

"I told her everything," says Slim. "I told her about me having AIDS, I told her about her Momma, everything. Bang Man, I thought I was about to die! I wanted to leave with a clean slate."

"What did she say?"

"She didn't say anything; she just screamed the word junkie, and ran out the room."

Junkie, twice in one day. I know he feels terrible. "She didn't tell me anything about that."

"I had to tell her. I couldn't go out like that." *He starts to cry.* "I didn't want to hurt her, but I had to tell her. The word junkie didn't hurt me half as bad as the tears that rolled down her face. They cut like a knife."

I sit with Slim for an hour or so before I have to leave. I have to meet with my man A.J. He wants another fifty bricks. I have to stop by Desire's house to get the ones that are there, and then I have to go to my sister's to get the rest to complete the order.

When I get to Desire's house, I ring the bell twice. **Buzz! Buzz!** *I hear the peephole.* **Click!** *Then I hear the top lock opening. When the door opens, I don't see anyone at the door. She opens the door slightly. I slide in the little opening. After getting in, I'm greeted by Desire's naked body. The first thing that catches* *my attention is her erect nipples. They're standing attentively. Her nipples are too big for her titties. They look mix and match, like someone glued them on. Her titties are not small; they're just too small for her oversized nipples. That's one thing I used to admire about her, her hooters. Even now after three kids they still don't sag a bit. As she turns around to walk back in the house, her big ass just bounces up and down, one cheek at a time.*

She has no shame. Back in the day, Desire never wore clothes while she was home. Maybe now she does, being that she lives with her father and the two boys. But before, whenever I came home, I was welcomed by her nudity. It feels crazy seeing her like this on the count of us not being together anymore. Actually, I feel uncomfortable. I don't think it bothers her. She's walking all over the house like she's fully dressed. She's not even looking my way. She even has the nerve to stand up on the countertop and stack some dishes away. Through the big gap in between her legs, I can see every dish that's stacked in the cupboard. I'm just kidding, but whoa! This is too much temptation for a married man.

She continuously bends over to pick up each dish one by one, poking her ass in the air as she slowly stands up. I'm starting to get the impression that she's trying to turn me on. Every time I look at her, the thought crosses my mind, but Love comes into my mind and wipes the thought out. Love is such a good wife. I would hate to lose her for ten minutes of meaningless fucking. It's not worth it.

I hurry to Slim's room, grab the work, and come right back out. On my way through the doorway, there stands Desire. We're standing face-to-face. **"Cash, I have something I want to tell you."**

"Desire, go ahead."

"Nah, I'm serious," she claims. "This ain't about sex! For so long I wanted to apologize to you for leaving you when you needed me the most. I know I turned my back on you, and I know you probably will never forgive me for that. But I apologize. It wasn't all my fault. You're part the blame. You

spoiled me. **You wouldn't even let me work. All you wanted me to do was stay home and fuck your brains out,"** she says sarcastically.

I laugh. That she did. What she's saying is true. I was so scared that someone would take her from me that I didn't want her to leave the house.

"Cash, you didn't even let me cook. We ate out every night. To this day, I still can't cook. Then when you went away, my world stopped. I didn't know what to do. I didn't have any skills. I didn't even have a high school diploma. What could I do, work at McDonalds? I had two kids to take care of. True indeed, your sister helped, but I had my own needs. You showed me the finer things in life. You helped me develop bad habits. I have a shoe fetish you won't believe. If a shoe costs less than $300, I can't wear them. My feet will hurt me all day." *I laugh again.* **"You laugh, but I'm serious. What was I supposed to do? I had to keep it moving. I had to find someone just like you."**

"Did you find him?"

"No, I didn't, but I came to the conclusion that it takes four of these half ass niggas to make one of you." *My face heats up. I'm blushing like crazy.*

"I hate the fact that you're married, but I can't change it; as much as I wish I could, I can't. I just wish you all the happiness in the world. I know I fucked up, but I'm a big girl." *I look her up and down. Yes you are!* **"I made my bed, now I have to lay in it."** *She falls into me and embraces me. At first, I pull away from her until I hear her crying like a baby. I pat her back, trying to comfort her. The tears are soaking through my shirt. It feels awkward holding her soft, naked body. Love would kill me if she could see this. But it's totally innocent, except for the bulge that's growing in my jeans. I know Desire feels it.*

Just as I'm letting her loose, I notice a shadow on the front porch. Someone is peeking in the window. I push her away and run to the living room. When I look out the window, no one is there. They must have jumped off the side of the porch. I run out of the house to the front porch. To my surprise, I see a black Denali speeding down the street. He runs the first two red lights. He didn't expect me to be here. He doesn't know about my Lincoln; all he knows about is the Benz. He was probably scared to death when he saw me. He thinks I'm still after him for beating on Desire.

I jump in my car and dial Desire's number. She answers.

"Desire, that was your little boyfriend."

"Who?" she asks.

"Ice."

"Later for him," she shouts. "I don't know why he still comes here. I told him we're done."

"Later Dee!"

"All right Cash!" Click! *We hang up.*

On my way to the meeting spot, I can't help but think about what Desire said to me. I never, in all the years I've known her, heard her say anything that made that much sense. I truly feel sorry for her. Yeah, she left a nigga when he was down, but it's over now. I'm back up. Even though she crossed me, I still hope she gets herself together. I really do for my kids' sake.

CHAPTER 27

One week later

Today they released Slim from the hospital. It's freezing out here today. It's so cold they didn't want to release Slim. They say it could be a hazard with his condition.

These past days have been hectic. It feels strange making moves without my road dog. Slim is like my other set of eyes. He sees whatever I don't see, or should I say, what I don't want to see.

I brought him home from the hospital earlier. He didn't look too good. The doctor said he would be all right as long as he takes his medicine as prescribed. I almost cried, watching my main man barely able to walk. He has to use a cane until he gets his strength back. It took him so long to get from the car to the porch that I finally had to pick him up over my shoulder.

I think that made him feel worse. That must have made him realize how helpless he really is. I know that had to hurt his ego. He grunted as I lifted him. He said his entire body was hurting. He told me what hurt the most was Desire and the boys seeing him like that.

The doctor says some days he'll be up and others he won't be able to get out of the bed. He'll have a nurse to take care of him. She's supposed to come by every day until he gets better. She has to change him, feed him, and bathe him. The reality of it all has really set in now. I never thought of Slim not being here, but seeing him all fucked up like this makes me realize that he really has the deadly disease, and one day I could wake up and he won't be here. Damn!

Before I dropped him off, I had to apologize to him for the way I talked to him that day. I wouldn't be able to live with myself if he died without me apologizing. I asked him, did he really think I would have him killed. He told me ever since I've been back getting money, a lot of things have changed.

He said sometimes I don't act like the Cash he used to know. I don't act like the good kid he raised. I act like a greedy hustler who doesn't care about anything but making more money. He said lately I've been acting more like the back-stabbing, shiesty individuals he warned me about. The guys whose main objective is to win no matter what they have to do. I've been moving so fast that I haven't noticed the change in my personality. Have I really turned into that kind of person?

As of right now, I've been without cocaine for four days now. I don't know what's going on with Juan. He told me something about a drought. Actually no one anywhere has cocaine. I was the last one in town with it, but that's only because my last package was 25 birds. Juan tells me he has something coming through tomorrow. The only thing is, the price is going to be a little more expensive. Instead of $16,000 a pie, the price will be $21,000 a pie. I'll be selling them for $23,000 or $24,000. That's still good because the average guy will be paying $25,000, and trying to sell them anywhere from $28,000 to $30,000 a kilo. That means I'm still ahead of the game, thanks to my man Juan. That's the advantage of having a strong connect. Where would I be without Juan, I don't know.

There's a drought every year traditionally. I learned that many years ago. Supposedly the Coast Guards catch x amount of pounds. But why do they catch these kilos at the same time every year? Is it coincidence, or is it bullshit? If you ask me, I think the people up top throw a bunch of bullshit work out and purposely let them get caught just so it looks like they're doing their job. Then the big-time cats can hold the real work and sell it for whatever price they want. They know after a couple of days with no work, you'll be desperate enough to pay whatever price they ask. I think it's all politics. But it's cool with me. I'll just concentrate on this dope money until I get my hands on some work. Shit, the day isn't over yet, and I've already sold 175 bricks of Bang Man.

Ring! Ring! "Hello?"

"Cash!"

"Yo, who is this?" I ask.

"Cash," the caller shouts again. *His phone is full of static.* "Cash?"

"Yo!"

"Cash, can you hear me?"

"Now I can, barely," I shout. "Your phone is full of static. Who is this?"

"This Sal," the caller replies.

"Oh, Sal, what's up?" *This is Sal, one of the cats who buys blow off of me. He's not a heavy hitter, but he is consistent. He only buys a half a bird at a time and it takes him about two weeks to move it. That's slow money, but it's sure money. He must be finished. He should have called me last week. The last time I served him was almost three weeks ago. He must not know about the drought. It just came in effect about a week ago.*

"Cash, what's up?" *The phone is still not clear. His voice has an echo on it, making him sound like a robot.*

"Sal?"

"Yeah!" he replies. "Cash, I'm ready. Meet me at the spot. I'll be there waiting for you." *Then the dial tone. His phone cuts off. I try to call him back, but I get his answering machine. I'm going to go over to the spot. Besides, I can't tell him over the phone that I don't have any work. He would ask me a million questions. When will you have something? Will the price go up? All those questions on the phone could get me back to the fed pen. I learned my lesson. I don't trust cell phones.*

It takes me approximately 20 minutes to get to the spot. The grocery store parking lot is extra crowded today. We always meet here because it's so busy that no one pays attention to us. I quickly glance over the parking lot looking for a silver, convertible BMW. I don't see it. I decide to walk over to the Jamaican store to get me some oxtails and rice while I'm waiting for him. If he comes, he won't leave because he'll see my car parked in the spot.

185

I walk over to the store. A few people are sitting there eating. "Yes, may I help you?" asks the dread-headed woman.

Her dreads are salt and peppered. I have never seen anyone with dread locks this long. Not only are they long, but they're thick, too. They hang to the back of her thighs. She's an older woman in her fifties.

"Yes, I'll have a small order of oxtails and rice, please."

"OK, that'll be ten minutes." *Her accent is so strong, I can barely understand what she's saying.*

"No problem." *I walk back to the doorway to see if Sal has pulled in.*

As I approach the doorway, I notice a short, cocky man coming in. I slide over so he can pass, but he comes right at me. He bumps me with his shoulder. He knocks me off balance. He's a solid little, wide-framed motherfucker. "Watch where you're going, motherfucker!" *he shouts. All the customers stop eating to see what the ruckus is about.*

"You watch it! You bumped into me," I shout.

"So what, you saw me coming. You should have moved," he yells back.

"I should have moved?" I question. *The nerve of this guy! I step closer to him, and he steps closer to me.*

"What!" he barks.

"Sir, your order is ready," hollers, *the lady at the counter.* "Sir!" *I look over at the counter.* "Small oxtails and rice, you're ready to go." *She shakes her head, gesturing for me to stop.*

"Boy, oh boy," I whisper, *as I walk away.* "Can I have a Guinness Stout with that?"

"You sure can," she replies. "That'll be $6 even."

"Here you go, ma'am."

"Son, let that go. It's not worth it," she whispers. "You're too handsome to be out here fighting. Look at him, he's ugly. That's why he's jealous of you." *I crack a smile as she hands me my food. No matter how old a woman gets, she never loses her touch. They know just what to say to have you eating out of their hands.*

"Have a nice day," I shout.

"You too, son."

I walk to the door where the man is still standing. Only now he's not by himself. He's with another man. This man is much taller than him, but not as wide. I lock eyes with both of them as I walk out the door. Neither of them says anything.

Before getting in my car, I look around once more for Sal. He's still nowhere in sight. I sit in the car and start opening my container. I'm starving.

After putting a hefty forkfull in my mouth, I look up. I see a black car with pitch-black windows coming at me, full speed, head-on. **Beep! Beep! Beep!** *I hit my horn to catch his attention. Maybe he's not looking.* **Beep! Beep!** *My heart is racing. The car stops right before he rams me.* **Sccuuurrrr!!**

I sit up with my hands raised in the air, like what's up. Then comes another car to the right of me, and then another to the left of me. They have me blocked in. Then the two men come running out of the Jamaican store, full speed. As they get closer, all the passengers of the three cars charge me. I'm baffled. I don't have a clue what's going on until I see badges dangling from all of their necks. It's the police. **"Put your hands in the air," the white cop yells.** *What the fuck is going on? I quickly throw my hands in the air. The man who bumped me in the store runs over to my side, while the man who was with him runs to the passenger's side.*

"Don't move punk!" barks the man on my side. *He opens my door and snatches me by the collar, while the other cop has his gun aimed at my head.*

"Go ahead, tough guy. Say something. Give me a reason to bust your motherfucking head open." *He drags me out of the car like I'm a rag doll. He's strong as hell.* **"Lay down!"** *Before I can lay down, he punches me right on my chin. My legs buckle immediately, and I fall right on my face. I'm dizzy as hell. Everything is blurry. I try to shake it off, but he kicks me in the ribs.*

187

"You think you tough, huh?" he asks.

"What's up?" I ask. "What the fuck did I do?" *He kicks me again.* "Aghh!" I grunt. *That kick was harder than the first one. That one really hurt. I'm furious, but I can't do anything. By now all the police are searching my vehicle. I don't understand what's going on. Do they know me? I never saw any of them before.*

"Cashmere!" the white cop shouts. "Where is the shit?"

Cashmere? This cracker knows my name. What the fuck is going on? "What shit, sir?" *The cop kicks me again.* "Ugghh!" I grunt.

"Don't act stupid, motherfucker. Where is the shit?"

"I don't have shit."

"Don't make this hard for yourself!" he threatens. "Tell us where it is."

The cocky officer drags me onto my feet and bitch slaps me. "Turn around!" *As I turn around, through the corner of my eye, I see the silver BMW pulling out of a parking space. Right next to his space sits a white Chevy Lumina with two white men in it. Sal is now pulling out of the parking lot.* "Give me your hands," the cop shouts. *He twists my arms and puts them behind my back. He then handcuffs me and drags me to the car that's parked directly in front of mine. He throws me in the backseat of the car and slams the door, catching my foot in the door.* "Aghh!" *After sliding my foot over, he slams it again. The other cops are tearing my car up. They're searching everywhere. They're looking in places I didn't even know existed.*

I don't believe this shit! I wonder did Sal set me up? I don't think he would do that. He's a real nigga. He's done three bids. I've never known him to be a snitch. Maybe they didn't know he was with me and he snuck off. I don't know. This shit doesn't look right!

The cocky cop comes over to the car and gets in the driver's seat, leaving the other officers searching my car. "Cashmere, where is the shit?" he asks calmly.

"Listen man, I don't know what you're talking about. I came here to get something to eat. You saw me in the restaurant!" I answer. "I ordered oxtails and rice." *I look down; the whole order is all over my leather coat.*

"Yeah, all right!" he shouts.

By this time, another officer jumps in the passenger's seat. "They can't find it," he whispers. "Yo man, where is the shit?" he asks calmly. "You might as well tell us. We're going to find it. If you cooperate, it'll make it easier for you. The longer you make us look for it, the harder the sergeant will make it for you. The quicker you turn the shit over to us, the quicker you can get processed and get bailed out. If you tell us now, you'll probably be out by tonight."

He's furious. His entire face is cherry red. He wants to bust me so bad. "I don't know what you're talking about. I came here to eat."

"All right Cashmere!" he shouts sarcastically. *He then looks over to the other officer.* "What is it he's supposed to have?" *the cop in the passenger's seat asks the cocky one in a low, whispering tone.*

"A half a kilo," he whispers. "He was supposed to meet him here with it," he mumbles. *Oh shit! Sal did set me up! I'm going to kill that motherfucker! That bitch ass nigga put my freedom on the line. He thought I was going to bring the work with me. It's a good thing I don't have anything, because I surely would have brought it.*

That bitch ass nigga was setting me up all the time. Acting like his phone wasn't working. That was all a front. I swear to God, I'm going to kill him! He fucked up now, cause I ain't got shit. They have to let me go.

Seconds later, a tow truck pulls up. The driver of the car I'm in backs the vehicle up, allowing them to pull in front of my car. The tow truck backs up close to my bumper.

"Yo, what the fuck ya'll doing?" I ask.

"Shut the fuck up!"

189

"Man, ya'll can't take my car! I don't have shit in there!"

The sergeant walks over to the back door where I am at and yanks the door open. He slides in. We're face-to-face. The smell of garlic bites my nose. "Cashmere, I'm going to ask you a question," *he whispers. His breath is atrocious. Each word stuns me.* "Before you answer, think about it. Think about your freedom, and then think about having no freedom. You shouldn't have a problem visualizing that. You just did seven years. If you tell me the truth it will be a lot easier for you. Do you have a stash spot? Think before you answer," *he whispers.*

"No, I don't sir," I reply.

"Listen, we're taking you down. They already issued us a search warrant. If you have a stash spot, they'll find out when we get the car there. Don't make this difficult. If you have one, let me know so we don't have to go through with this. The tow truck and all this shit costs money. No one likes to spend money. Save us the money and the bullshit, and I'll do my best to save you." *Yeah right! Who the fuck does he think he's talking to? Like if I had something I would tell him where it is. Shit, I'm not going to make his job easier; find it. That's what he gets paid $30,000 a year for.*

"You just did almost eight years. I know you don't want to do more time than you have to. Save yourself, Cashmere."

"Sir, I don't have a stash spot," I reply calmly.

"All right!" he yells. "I tried. Don't say I didn't try to help you. Take him in." *He gets out and slams the door.*

As we pull off, the driver speaks. "You should have told him where it's at."

"Listen, I don't have shit."

"I mean, it don't make me any difference either way," the cop admits. "I'm going home in two hours regardless. I don't give a fuck about you. But you should have told the truth for your sake." *I don't even respond. Do they think I'm stupid? If*

I had something, it wouldn't make a difference whether I told them or they found it on their own. Shit will still be the same. They're trying to play me like a young boy.

Before I know it, they're dragging me from the car. I don't know where we are. I've never seen this building in my life. They drag me through the back door and we get on the elevator. When we get off, I see nothing but little cells. The cop at the desk doesn't have a uniform on. He has on a football jersey and some tight ass jeans. They open the cell and push me in. **"Can I make a phone call?"** *I ask.*

"No!" *he replies.* **"You should have cooperated. I would have let you get that."**

"Whatever," *I mumble.*

Two hours later

It feels like I've been sitting in this tiny cell for about eight hours. Maybe it hasn't been that long. It just feels like it. I fell asleep, then I woke up, and then I fell asleep again.

I hate being in a cell. The day I was released, I promised myself I would never be in anybody's cell again. And here it is, not even six months later. All because of this snitch ass nigga. I'm going to kill him. I hope them cops don't plant anything on me. You know how dirty they can be.

I'm going crazy in this cell. I just want to punch the wall. I can't believe this shit! I swear, I hope they don't put nothing on me. Please God; don't let them plant nothing on me, please!

After pacing the floor for an hour, I lay back on the cold, hard floor. I put my coat under my head and fall asleep again.

"Yo, get up!" *the cop yells. I open one eye, hoping all this is a nightmare.* **"Get up!"** *he repeats. I stand up. I look at the clock on the wall behind the cop's head. It reads 10 o'clock. I've* *been here for almost eight hours. I know Love is worried to death. I haven't spoken to her since this morning.*

The officer opens the cell. **"Get out of here,"** he shouts.
"I can go home?"

"Not unless you want to stay," he replies sarcastically.
I hurry out of the cell. **"Where's my car?"**

"Go to that door. An officer will escort you to your car."

One second later, the short, cocky officer comes out of the back room. **"Come on, Cashmere!"** he shouts. **"The world-famous Cashmere, big-time drug kingpin!"** he screams sarcastically. **"I don't know how you did it, but you did it. They checked your car thoroughly. They couldn't find it. Tell me where it is. I won't tell,"** he says, *in a joking manner.*

"They didn't find shit, because it wasn't shit in there."

"Cut the shit," he replies. **"You're over for now, but watch yourself. We're on you. We're going to be up your ass with a microscope from now on until we get you."**

The elevator comes up. We get on. **"You better count your blessings,"** he shouts.

When we get outside, the car is parked right in front of the building. **"Later, Cashmere!"** he shouts. *I don't say shit.*

I get in my car. It's a mess. All my papers are thrown around, and all the shit from my trunk is in the backseat. They even ripped my passenger's seat. Jealous ass motherfuckers!

I look in the glove compartment to check and see if my owner's manual and insurance card are there. Everything is in place except for a stack of photos that were in there. I had pictures of everybody in there; my wife, in front of our house, my kids in front of their house. I also had a picture of my dogs standing on the roof of my Lincoln. Damn, they got everything. I could kick myself up the ass. Now I really have to be careful. Sometimes it seems like the older I get, the dumber I get.

I'm heading home. What a day!

CHAPTER 28

Me and Love argued all night. She insists that the reason I didn't answer my phone yesterday was because I was with a girl. If I tell her the cops had me, she'll really be on my back. I don't want her to worry too much. Being that I'm on her bad side, I decide to spend the day with her. I have to do a little ass kissing.

She has the whole day planned. First, we're going to the bakery to pick out a wedding cake. Then we have to sample some food at the caterer. From there she has to meet with the decorator.

My whole day will be spent on this wedding planning. At first, I was pissed at the thought, but being held by those police yesterday made me appreciate my freedom more. Besides that snitch ass Sal, who I'm going to murder when I catch up with him, I couldn't keep Love off my mind. The whole time they had me, I kept thinking about the long speech she gave me about me going to jail again. I'm lucky I didn't have anything. With my criminal jacket, I would have been gone forever. The thought of Love leaving me drives me crazy. I don't think she'd actually do it, but who knows? How much can one woman take?

Those few hours made me realize that I have to get myself in order. I have to start thinking more like a husband and a father and less like the typical drug dealer.

Later that day

We finished up earlier than planned, so we spent the rest of the day shopping for Christmas gifts. I blew so much cash on my boys. I bought them everything I wanted as a kid but couldn't

afford. I bought them a mobile basketball court for the backyard.
I bought them a new video game, a racing track, and a gigantic
fish tank about the size of the entire wall. And last but not least, I
bought them two racing dirt bikes. No, they can't ride, but I'll teach
them. OK, those might be more for me than them. I'll probably
have more fun with them than they will.

When I was a kid, I wanted one of those bikes so bad, but
we couldn't afford it. I wanted one so bad that me and a couple of
my friends went up to the suburbs and tried to steal one out of these
white people's backyard. The man caught us and held us until the
police got there. Boy, Big Ma tore all our asses up. She didn't care
if their parents liked it or not. Shit, she would have torn their asses
up as well. Big Ma was tough!

I made a promise to myself that all the things I didn't have,
I'm going to make sure they get. Not having is the reason I turned
to the streets. I grew up without, but Big Ma did the best she could
do. I remember days when I had to put cardboard in my sneakers
just so my socks wouldn't show through the big hole in the sole. It
was then that I told myself that one day, all this would be just a
memory. I'm going to make sure Ahmir and Ahmad never have to
see those kinds of days. One way or the other, by hook or by crook,
I'm going to make sure they have.

For my wife, I had to get her out of that raggedy Honda
Accord. I promised myself once I started rolling, I would get her
a new car. Well, I'm picking it up on Christmas Eve. I bought her
a brand new, candy apple red, Mercedes Benz with black leather
interior. It's beautiful. It's a two-door convertible CLK 430. The
top is jet black to match the interior. She's going to be so surprised.
Red is her favorite color.

CHAPTER 29

Christmas morning

My boys spent the night with me last night. I had Slim set up the basketball court in their backyard. By the way, Slim is finally doing better. He hasn't been getting high at all. The doctor told him that in order to survive, he has to leave the dope alone. The dope will conflict with his medication. I bought him a case of methadone, so he can kick his habit for good. We haven't been around each other much. Ever since I've been without cocaine, I've been concentrating solely on the dope; I don't want to put him under that type of temptation.

Love and the boys are still asleep. I can't wait until they get up. I'm more anxious than they are. I couldn't sleep a wink last night. I enjoy making my loved ones happy. I get my satisfaction when I see their faces light up.

I've been up since 6 A.M. It's now 8:30. I walked the dogs already. I parked Love's car in front, and I have the bikes in the garage. They're gassed up and ready to ride.

Love just woke up. I hear the water running. She's in the shower.

I sit in the living room waiting impatiently for her to come out. Finally, she walks in. She has a big box in her hands. She passes it to me. **"Merry Christmas, honey!" she shouts. "Here's one of your gifts."**

I open it quickly. Inside is an NBA leather team jacket. It has patches of every team in the NBA all over it. Damn, she must have read my mind. I wanted one of these jackets so bad, but I just couldn't make myself spend $2,000 for it. **"Thank you! You must have known how bad I wanted this jacket."**

She smiles. **"Your other gift is in the back room. Come**

on; let's go back there," she suggests.
"No, hold up. Take your gift first," I shout.
"No, wait until you see your other one," she demands.
We walk to the back room. To my surprise, in the middle of the floor sits a 60-inch screen. The play station is already hooked up to it. It has surround sound and everything. On the floor right next to it is a stack of about 20 discs. She knows how much I love to play video games. I guess I'm still a big kid at heart. **"Damn Love, you're the best!"** *I give her a big kiss.* **"Smooch!"** *And a tight hug.* **"Here, take this!"** *I shout anxiously. I hand her a huge box. She tears it open. Her mouth drops to the floor when she sees the contents. It's a beautiful, black, full-length mink with a hood.*

"Oh my God!" she screams.
"Put it on!"
She puts the coat on top of her fitted baby phat T-shirt and her spandex shorts. She looks crazy standing there with a full-length mink and big bunny slippers on.

After prancing around in the coat for about five minutes, she finally takes it off and gives me a big hug. **"Honey, I love you!"**
"You are about to love me more," I state. *I open the curtain of the front window.* **"Look out here."**

Her eyes almost pop out of her head. **"Ooh!" she screams.** *I shake the keys in the air. She reaches for them. I extend my hand to give them to her. As she tries to grasp them, I snatch them away from her. She grabs my hand with a tight grip and squeezes it, until I finally let them go. She snatches the keys and takes off out the door. I'm right behind her.*

When she gets to the car, she walks around it, viewing it from every angle. I know she's happy, because it's freezing out here, only 20 degrees and she's out here almost naked.

She gets in the driver's seat; I jump in the passenger's seat. She anxiously starts it up. She mashes her feet on the gas pedal. The car jerks and takes off. **"Whoa, slow down baby," I shout.** *She ignores me.*

She's speeding down the narrow street. I've never saw her drive this fast before.

We ride with no destination. Before I know it, a half hour has passed. I totally forgot about my kids. They're in the house asleep, and we left the door wide open. **"Baby, go back to the house. I forgot we left the door wide open."** *She laughs.*

As we pull back to the house, to my surprise I see Ahmir hauling ass out the back on his dirt bike. I guess I don't have to teach him to ride. He's already riding like a pro. Ahmir is like that; he picks up fast. Anything he tries to do, he turns out to be good at it.

Seconds later, here comes Ahmad. He isn't riding; he's more like walking the bike.

"Damn Ahmir, you ride that thing pretty good," I admit. **"How did you learn to ride that fast?"**

He shrugs his shoulders nonchalantly. **"I don't know. I just got on and tried."**

"Mir Mir, ride me on the back," Ahmad begs. **"Please!"**

"No, you ride your own," Ahmir replies.

"I can't," says Ahmad.

"Never say you can't!" I shout. **"You're the man. You can do whatever you want! Don't ever let me hear you say the word can't! Do you hear me?"**

"Yes Daddy," he replies.

"Now, get on the bike and ride," I instruct. *Ahmad climbs on the bike.* **"Remember, you're the man!"** *He rides for about two feet and falls off.* **"Get up and try it again!"**

He hesitantly climbs on. **"Remember, you're the man!"** Vroom! Vroom! *As soon as he revs it up, he falls. I can see the discouragement in his face as he watches Ahmir ride like a pro.* **"Later for Ahmir. Worry about what Ahmad is doing. If you worry about him, you'll never learn how to ride."** *Damn, I learned that from Ab. He taught me that many years ago. Never worry about the next motherfucker. The time you take to figure out*

197

what the next man is doing is time you could have been using to perfect your thing.

I daze off, thinking about Jake and Ab. I wonder what they're doing. They would be so proud of me, the way I'm holding things down out here. I wonder if they've heard about me? **"Daddy, Daddy!"** *Ahmad interrupts my thoughts. He's riding now. He's gone down the block.*

"That's right," I yell. **"You're the man! You're the man!"** *He's gone. He's not stopping. He crosses the light and goes to the next corner and the next. He's still not stopping.* **"Ahmir, go get your brother. Tell him to come back."** Vroom, vroom! *Ahmir speeds off. It doesn't take him long to catch up with his brother.*

I look over at Love. She's still sitting in the car. She's now reading the owner's manual and playing with the features; you know, turning the volume up from the steering wheel, turning on the fog lights, and dropping the top of her convertible. She's having more fun than the kids. It feels good to make my family happy. This is the reason I do what I do. Their happiness is worth all the risks I take.

Ahmir and Ahmad are approaching quickly. Ahmir is in the lead, but Ahmad isn't far behind. Ahmir hook slides as he gets to me. I can see it in Ahmad's eyes; he wants to try it. He slams on the brakes. I close my eyes. I don't want to see this. I don't hear a crash, so I slowly open my eyes. He slid successfully. **"Yes! I'm the man,"** he shouts.

"That's right, you're the man," I agree. **"Give me a high five!"** **Clap!** *That's what it's about, motivation. I'm going to do my best to be the best father I can be for these boys. I'm going to motivate them to be whatever it is they want to be, except for drug dealers.*

CHAPTER 30

Today is a special day. Not only is it New Year's Day, it's also my born day. Today, I turn 37 years old. That's something in the ghetto, because the average dude doesn't make it past 25. I feel blessed to be on the streets for this birthday. I spent all the other ones behind the wall. Today, I'm going to spend this one with my loved ones. But first I have to go see Mike Mittens. He called and said he needs to speak with me A.S.A.P.

Out of nowhere, Big Ma comes to my mind. I miss her so much. She would always bake me a three-layer cake on my birthday. She never missed one. Even when I was locked up, she would send a card with a drawing of a chocolate three-layer cake with a golden middle. Big Ma was such a sweetheart. This is my first birthday on the street without her. Sniff! Pardon me. The tears are rolling down. Sniff! I look up to the heavens. I love you, Big Ma!

I pass through my old block. The new owners have already moved in. I forgot to tell you, the realtor sold the house two weeks ago. I walked away with $195,000. That's not bad, being that I only paid $160,000 for it.

There's a raggedy caravan parked in the back. The van looks out of place. I'm so used to seeing my car parked back there. Well, that's over. Now it's only a memory, another closed chapter of my life.

The block is still empty. Junebug never opened it back up. I haven't seen him in two weeks. I wonder what he's up to.

Ain't this a motherfucker? Before I can even get the words out of my mouth, I see his Benz coming down the block at full speed. Speaking of the damn devil!

As the car gets closer to me, it slows down.

Finally, it comes to a complete stop. I look over, but there's no Junebug. Spook is driving, and the rest of the little punks are riding with him. They have all the windows rolled down. They're all jumping around, real hyperactive. The music is blasting. They're pumping Juvenile. The hook is going like this "Acting like a nigga that ain't never had shit." I almost laugh out loud. They aren't acting. They never had shit, and they're never going to have shit if they keep running around here up Junebug's ass.

Me and Spook start one of our famous stare-offs. After a few seconds, he smiles a devilish smile and speeds off. One of these days, I'm going to give him what he's been asking for; one of these days.

As I ride a little further, you wouldn't believe what I see coming straight at me. I see an emerald-green, convertible Bentley Azure with a mahogany brown interior. You can barely see the top because it's down. That's right, the top is down. Today is one of the coldest days we've had this year. It's only 17 degrees and some fool has the top down.

The car stops at the red light. I'm trying to see the driver, but I can't because he has both visors down. I guess he's trying to block the sun. The license plates catch my attention. There are two plates in the front. The top one is a regular plate, but the bottom is strange. It's a European-type plate; it reads Ghetto Diplomat. No, don't tell me. I know he didn't do this. He must have lost his mind.

As the car gets closer to me, the high beams start flashing. Yes, he did. It's Junebug. He's going to prison. He has really outdone himself, and he's rubbing it in their faces at that. A Ghetto Diplomat plate? He really thinks he can do whatever he wants. He also has personalized plates on his Benz that read Mayor; his Harley has the letters BLK PARTY. But he has really outdone himself this time.

There he is sitting in the driver's seat with a snow-white mink on and dark shades. As the sun bounces off his diamonds, you see big, pretty rainbows. In the backseat, he has the Chinese girl that I saw him with, and he even has the blond-haired white girl in the back, too. This guy is crazy.

They're both sitting in the backseat with matching two-tone chinchillas on. They're looking straight ahead as he chauffeurs them through the block.

The white one is a flirt. I can see her watching me from under her shades. She wants me; I can sense it

"Cash, what's the deal baby?" he asks.

"Nothing much man," I reply. "This you?"

"Yeah," he answers modestly. *I wonder if he can see the hate in my face? I'm trying to play it off, but this is too much. Until now, I've never envied anyone in my life.*

"Have you lost your mind?" I ask.

"Why do you say that?"

"I got three letters for you!" I shout. "FBI," I then whisper.

He smiles, showing all 32s. "Fuck em! I ain't worried about them. I got the best lawyer money can buy. When they get me, I got a few million dollars for my defense." *This motherfucker is so cocky.* "Do you like it?"

"Yeah, she hot," I reply. "I thought you were one of them rap niggas when I saw you at the light." *He laughs.* "You outdone yourself!"

"I know, but it's a new year!" he replies. "I'm going to be doing new things. I'm going to make a change. No more playing around." *He points to the backseat.* "You see I have both of my ladies back there together," he boasts. "Look at them riding in harmony, Chinese and White, together. I was tired of living a double life, so I decided to tell them about each other. Either they share me or be cut off. What do you think they came up with?"

I don't believe this guy. This money has driven him crazy. "You crazy!" I shout. *I don't believe these women are letting him talk like this. They must be more foolish than he is.*

"I ain't crazy! Every baller has a strong woman behind

him. I just happen to have two. As long as I provide for them equally, they shouldn't have any complaints."

"Look, my Chinese mommy wanted a chinchilla, so I had to get Blondie one too. If I do for one, I have to do for the other." *He chuckles.*

I look at him like he's crazy. They're both sitting in the backseat as nonchalantly as they can, without saying a word as he plays them. Money sure makes the world go around. If Junebug were broke, there's no way they would accept this nonsense from him.

The Benz is coming back. He's coming around the corner full speed. Spook is flooring it.

When he gets close to Junebug's car, he slams on the brakes. **Scccuuuurrr!** *He almost runs into the back of the Bentley.*

"You see, I gave my right hand man the Benz," Junebug states.

"Oh yeah?"

"Yeah, he's coming up in the ranks. He's almost 19 years old. Maybe he can appreciate the little Benz," he says sarcastically. "I outgrew it! When I was a child, I did childish things, but now I'm grown."

"I hear you player!"

"I'm out, Cash!" *He takes off slowly. The white girl sneakily blows me a soft kiss from her pretty lips as they pass me. I told you she wants to play! He thinks she loves him; she only loves his money, young dumb ass nigga!*

About fifteen minutes later, I arrive at Mike's block. It's empty. His entire crew is sitting along the curb with long faces. When I pull up, he jumps right in. "Mike, what's up?"

"Cash, please tell me you have some good news."

"Nope, not yet," I reply. "My connect still hasn't come through yet. I'm waiting for him.

"Damn!" Mike screams. *Mike is hungry. We haven't had any cocaine for over two weeks now. This is a real drought. No one has product.*

"Yo man, I'm starving," Mike says aggressively. "I need some work."

"Mike, be patient baby."

"That's easy for you to say. You killing them with the dope. I'm bleeding!"

Uh oh, there he goes counting my money. That can be a problem. "Don't you have money saved?" I ask. *I know he should have some money, all the coke he's been selling out here.*

"Yeah, I saved some dough. I got about $60,000 saved up, but I can't touch that. If I start chipping off that, I won't have shit," he explains.

"Mike, you ain't about to spend 60 grand before we get some blow and you know that."

"I don't know shit! I didn't know we would go two weeks without work, but we have," he says sarcastically.

"Mike, what can I do? I don't have the shit growing in my backyard. I wish I did, but I don't."

"I gotta eat!" he shouts. *He's not listening to a word that I'm saying.* "Let me get some of that Bang Man!"

"Mike, just hold up for a minute," I beg.

"I can't! Let me get a few bricks so my team can eat. They starving, look at them. How can I keep them motivated, if I can't feed them? I'm not really worried about myself. You're right; I can't go through 60 grand like that. But them guys they ain't got no dough saved.

"I thank you. You gave me a way to make some dough. Look at me, I ain't never seen 60 at one time. Now I got paper. I got my own apartment and a nice little hooptie. I'm all right. You brought a nigga back to life! But right now it ain't about me. It's about my team. Them kids were already doing their thing when I came out here. But they had enough faith in me to get with me. They didn't need me; I needed them. Now they don't have shit, it feels like it's all my fault."

"Mike, I feel you!"

"You ain't really feeling me! You didn't give me the dope yet!"

I debate with myself before responding. I finally give in. "All right Mike!" *His face lights up.* "I'm only going to give you ten bricks. Just give me $3,000 back."

"No problem!" he shouts excitedly.

"This way your soldiers can make a few dollars today."

"All right, good looking!" Mike shouts.

"Listen Mike; we're not turning this into a dope set. As soon as we get the blow, that's it," I explain.

"I know, I know."

We ride to the stash house. I give Mike the ten bricks of Bang Man, and drop him off. From there I go to pick up my family.

CHAPTER 31

The next morning

Ring! Ring! *The phone wakes me. Who the fuck can this be?* **Ring! Ring!** **"Hello?"** **I answer,** *trying to pick up before waking Love.*

"Cash! I hate to call you this early, but shit banging!" *This is Mike.*

"What?" I ask.

"I came out here 4:30 this morning. I had four bricks left from yesterday, and I finished them shits in a half hour."

"Yeah?" *He has my attention. Now I'm fully awake.*

"Word up Cash! Get up and bring me some more," he demands.

"Give me about two hours," I reply.

"Two hours? You can't get here no faster than that? I only got one brick left."

"Nah Mike, I can't get there no faster than that!" I shout sarcastically.

I get up and put on the same clothes I had on yesterday and jet. I didn't even brush my teeth. Halfway through the ride, he calls me again.

"Hello?"

"Cash, where are you?"

"Mike, I'm almost there! Calm down!"

"I sold that last brick in ten minutes!"

"Mike, I'm coming! I'm coming!" *He's starting to aggravate me now.*

"Hurry up!"

Click! *I hang up on him.*

Finally, I get to the stash house and I take out 25 bricks.

*As soon as I turn the corner, I notice dope fiends swarming over
the entire block. When I pull over, one of Mike's soldiers runs to
the car, grabs the bag, and takes off. As soon as he gets to the
alleyway, the fiends crowd him. Another one of Mike's soldiers
starts to scream.* **"Bang Man! Bang Man! Single line, don't
crowd him! Keep it moving!"**

*The crowd quickly clears out after he serves them. But
just as fast as they clear out, another crowd swarms in. Mike runs
over to the alleyway, and then he runs over to my car.* **"See, I told
you. My little man just moved two bricks in ten minutes,"** he
informs. **"That's 100 bags, $1,000 in ten minutes. Man, fuck
that cocaine! I got a new hustle!"**

*This is what I was afraid of. I knew once he saw the dope
flow, he wouldn't want to bother with the blow anymore.*

*Damn, these motherfuckers really are going crazy for the
Bang Man! They're coming for it. I know the dope is good, but I
didn't know it was this good. A.J. told me it's the best shit out. But
this is the first time witnessing it for myself. No wonder A.J. moves
so much of this shit. I sell it to him for $275 a brick. He sells them
for $325. This guy moves about 600 bricks a week. I make so much
profit off of him alone, I really don't have to deal with anyone else.*

**"Cash, they love this shit! They say Bang Man is shitting
on Block Party!"**

"Yeah?"

**"Hell yeah! Cash, we about to blow! The Mayor is
going to be mad as hell."** *You can say that again!* **"Fuck him!"**
Mike shouts. **"They got guns, and we got guns. See my little
man sitting in the cut over there on the porch,"** he asks, *as he
points to an abandoned porch two houses down. The house has a
sun porch. The kid is sitting so far back you can hardly see him. I
never would have seen him if Mike wouldn't have pointed him out to
me.*

"Yeah, I see him."

"He got two big ass 45s on him. Let them goons come

through here with that bullshit if they want to!" *I smile at him.*

The crowd doesn't stop. They're coming in huddles. All you can hear in the air is, "**BANG MAN!**"

I finally leave. I have to go see my boys.

Before I could get there, Slim calls me. **Ring! Ring!**
"Hello?" **I answer.**

"Bang Man, what the hell you then done?" he asks.
"Huh?"

"Don't huh me! You know what the hell I'm talking about! Ever since yesterday, all I been hearing about is Bang Man!"

"Slim, I'm on my way!" Click!

When I get there Slim, is on the porch. "Big Time, what have you done?" he asks. "I thought we agreed on you not bringing it around here."

"I didn't do shit. Mike did it. How did you know?"
"The Doctor told me. He thinks he's famous."
"Yeah?" *I laugh.*

"I thought you weren't going to put it around here," says Slim.

"Hey, shit happens," I reply.

"Bang Man, you need to tell the Doctor to stop running his mouth. He's telling everyone that's his work; he's the chemist behind it." *I can sense a little jealousy in Slim's voice. I don't think he wants the Doctor to get the credit for it.* "I told him to stop telling everyone, but he said I'm jealous because I fucked up the other batch," Slim states. "So is Mike killing them?"

"Slim, I watched them sell four bricks in 20 minutes."

"Bang Man, they killing them!" Slim shouts. "Boy, the Mayor is going to be upset."

"Hey, Mike said fuck the Mayor, I'm with Mike!"
"And I'm with you, Big Time!"

CHAPTER 32

The next morning

I dropped off 50 more bricks to Mike this morning. Shortly after I left him, I got the call of a lifetime. It was Juan's man. He has some blow for me.

I just received it 30 minutes ago. Not only did the price go up, but the product is terrible. Juan charged me $30,000 a bird for some ugly beige shit. Normally everyone hates beige coke. They say it's full of speed. Speed causes the crack head to be jumpy and nervous. Being that they haven't had any cocaine for three weeks, they'll buy anything right now. The bad thing is, I only have eight kilos. I really could sell those with two phone calls if I wanted to.

Juan only got his hands on 16 joints. He gave me eight, and he gave the other eight to another one of his heavy hitters; a Dominican boy from the Washington Heights area in Manhattan. I literally begged him for all 16, but he wouldn't give them to me. He said the Dominican boy is as loyal as me, and he can't do that to him. I respect that. This game is built on loyalty and trust. That's how the survivors survive.

Being that no one else has blow, I can sell it for whatever price I want to. I'm in demand. I'm not going to take advantage of my loyal customers, but all those cats who are just jumping on the bandwagon, I'm going hard on them. I'll sell it to my people for $35 a gram, but anyone else will pay $40 to $42 a gram. That sounds crazy, right? But it isn't because the dealers will break their bottle size down. What they used to sell for $5 they will now sell for $20 dollars. That's the good thing about the drought. If you have work, you can do whatever you want with it.

I'm not going to sell anyone a whole kilo. The most I will sell to one person is 250 grams. This way all my customers will get *some. Plus if I sell someone the whole thing, they may hold onto it until I run out and then try to sell it for $50 a gram and make more off it than I did.*

None of my customers will sell weight. They'll break it down on the street and quadruple their money. If they pay $10,000 for a quarter, they'll make $40,000 off of it. And they'll move it faster than ever because no one else has work.

I make my rounds. Me and Slim drop off work to all my people. It feels good to have my road dog back. I was lonely without him.

I call Mike to inform him. He gives me the brush-off. He doesn't even care about the cocaine. He's madly in love with the dope. I gave him the dope four hours ago, and he has already sold 30 bricks. That's $15,000 in less than four hours. Bang Man!

One hour later

I get a call from Mike's nephew. He tells me to meet him at his house. He must have found out the birds have landed. I meant to call him, but it slipped my mind.

I go to the stash house, grab a quarter of a brick (250 grams), and take off to meet him.

When we arrive at the house, Mike's nephew is pacing back and forth. **"Bang Man, that boy is stressing!"**

When he spots us, he runs to the car and jumps in. **"Damn nigga, you stressing,"** I shout, *in a joking manner.* **"Did you think I wasn't going to bring you no work?"** I ask jokingly. **"Here it is!"** *I pass the work to him. He doesn't look the least bit excited. He slides the work over to the other seat.* **"What's the matter? Look, I know it's only 250 grams, but I can't give you the whole thing. I don't have enough,"** I explain. *Maybe he feels disrespected by me only giving him a quarter. He is a bigger nigga than that.*

I look in the rearview mirror as I explain to him. He has tears rolling down his face. **"What up, baby?"**

He tries to speak, but he can't. He has the frog in his throat from crying. He swallows and then speaks. **"Mike just got shot,"** he mumbles.

"What?"

"He just got shot!" he repeats.

"When?"

"A little while ago."

"Where?"

"On the block."

"Was it a stick up?" I question.

"Nah, it was the goon squad. They came through in that Grand Prix."

"What did they say?" I ask.

"They didn't say shit! They just jumped out and started spraying up the block."

"How many of them was it?"

"It was all of them," he replies.

"The Mayor, too?" I ask. *Damn, that's the first time I ever called him the Mayor.*

"Nah, he came after they finished," he replies. "He pulled up in his Bentley and parked while the ambulance took the people away."

"People? How many people got shot?"

"A lot of people. They shot dope fiends and all."

"Where did Mike get hit?"

"I don't know. He got shot a lot of times. He fell on his face. He didn't look good, him or Rah Rah. Rah Rah was fucked up. Blood was pouring from his mouth. He was over. He could have gotten away. They didn't even see him on the porch. When they jumped out, the kid Spook ran right up on Mike and squeezed close range. Mike tried to run, but he fell on his face. When he fell, Spook caught up with him, stood over him and popped him, again. Rah Rah saved him. After he popped Mike, Rah Rah pulled out two hammers and started letting loose. He hit Spook and knocked him off his feet. But Spook shot once more before he hit the ground. That shot hit Rah Rah in the face. He dropped one of his guns and grabbed his face. Then one of the other goons snuck up the steps and popped him twice in the leg. Then he grabbed Rah Rah's gun, stood over him, and squeezed like eight times. Yo Cash, he wasn't moving. I think they killed him." *My heart drops.*

"Psst! Psst!" *Slim starts picking his teeth.*

"Did the Mayor see you?" I ask. *Damn, I said it again.*

"Nah, he didn't see me," he replies. "I was in Mike's van. The nigga Spook crawled back to the Grand Prix. He jumped in the backseat. One of the others drove them away. Right when the Mayor was pulling up, I was pulling off."

"Here, take this work and put it up. I'll call you later after I get to the bottom of this."

He slowly steps out.

"Bang Man, I knew this shit was going to happen! I told you them boys don't play," says Slim.

"Man, fuck them! They fucking with the right nigga now!"

"Psssttt! Pssttt!" *Slim begins picking his teeth again.*

"Stop making that aggravating ass noise!" I shout. "It's on; I don't give a fuck about them."

"Big Time, think about your wife and your kids. Is it worth it?" he asks.

"Slim, later for the Dr. Martin Luther King, I have a dream shit! I gotta get these niggas."

At this moment, all my common sense and all my goals and dreams just fly right out the window. They want war; they'll get war!

CHAPTER 33

Later that Evening

I stayed at the hospital for hours waiting for Mike to come out of surgery. The surgery was successful. He's in stable condition. He got shot six times. He got shot once in the shoulder, twice in the chest, once in the hip, and twice in the leg. Spook really tried to finish him, but Mike pulled it through.

Rah Rah wasn't as lucky. He died right there on the scene. Nobody knows if Spook killed him or if the other kid did it. Rah Rah was only 18. That's really fucked up, but that's the game.

I didn't speak to Mike. He won't be able to have visitors until tomorrow. Anyway, what can I do for him sitting in the hospital? I'm not a doctor. My business is out here. I have to figure out how I'm going to deal with these guys.

Right now, me and Slim just left my man A.J. He just took 200 bricks.

"**Bang Man, they killed that kid! That's fucked up. I watched that boy grow up. I used to fuck his momma,**" **Slim admits.**

"**Yeah? What kind of woman is she?**" **I ask.**

"**Oh, she's fucked up now,**" **he replies.** "**She's a stone cold dope fiend now, but back in the day she was one of the baddest bitches in this town.**"

Ring! Ring! *My car phone is ringing. I press the intercom button.* "**Hello?**"

"**Cash!**"

"**Yo?**"

"**Cash!**"

This is A.J. What could he want; I just left him not even ten minutes ago. "**A.J., what up?**"

"**Cash, somebody following me,**" **he replies.** "**I think** it's the police. They jumped on me as soon as you turned off! Cash, I ain't trying to get caught with all this shit!"

"Calm down!" *He's scared. I can hear it in his voice. He's talking real fast. I can barely understand him.* "What kind of car are they in?"

"It's a dark-colored car! I can't see what kind it is!"

"A.J., You have to calm down or you will get caught! How close are they following you?"

"Like, like four or five cars behind!"

"Where are you?"

"On Tenth Street! I can see the car now! It's a Grand Prix!" *A Grand Prix? Oh shit!*

"Pssstt! Psstt!" *Slim starts his shit up with his teeth.*

"That ain't the cops! You got a banger on you?" I ask.

"Nah," he replies.

"Yo, you gotta take the chase!"

"Yo, they like two cars behind me now!"

"A.J. go, you gotta get the fuck away from them! What block are you on now? I'm coming to meet you!"

"I'm still on Tenth," he replies.

"Slim, which way should I go?"

"Cut across right here, Big Time!"

"Yo, it's just me and them now," A.J. shouts.

"Just keep driving. I'm coming to meet you."

"Yo, they're close as hell," A.J. shouts hysterically.

"I'm like two minutes away from you! Just keep driving," I shout.

"Yo, they're trying to pull up on the side of me!"

Smack! "They just bumped me."

"A.J. go!"

"They're slowing up," A.J. cries.

"Keep going," I shout.

"I got a little lead on them now," A.J. states.

"Yo, don't slow down, keep going!" I urge.

"They're catching up with me again," he shouts backs.

"I'm a minute away," I shout. "I'm cutting across now."

"Psstt! Psstt!" *Slim picks his teeth.*

"Oh shit! No!" he screams.

"What, what's up?"

"I'm running into a red light and it's mad traffic. I don't think I'm going to be able to cross," says A.J. "Oh shit!"

"Where are they?"

"They're close as hell!" he shouts. "Come on light!"

"Where are you?"

"I'm at the light. Come on light, please change," he begs. "They right here! No!" he screams. Boc! Boc! Boc!

"A.J.?" I scream. Boc! Boc!

"Aghh!" A.J. screams. Boc! Boc! Boc! Boc! Boc!

"A.J.?" Boc! Boc! Crash! "A.J.?"

Seconds later, I can hear fumbling and voices in the background. "AJ?"

"Grab the dope!" shouts the voice.

"I got it," says a different voice. Slam! *There goes the sound of the car door slamming.* Scccuuurrrrrr! *They just peeled off.*

By the time me and Slim arrive at the scene, the Ambulance is trying to revive him. There's no hope. I stand around until the Coroner hauls him away. This shit really hurts me, watching them zip my man up in that bag and drag him away. What really hurts is the fact that he had nothing to do with this beef. He was totally ignorant to all of this. Right now, I feel like I got that man killed. I have to answer to that. How could I put that man's life in jeopardy like that?

I hope this murder doesn't link back to me. I sure hope he didn't discuss his business with his baby's mother. She's the only person who can tell homicide what he was doing here. If she knows, she'll definitely tell them, and when she does, I'm finished. They'll be looking for me for questioning. They might think I set him up. They'll want to know everything. How long have I known him? What was he coming here for? Where was I when this happened? I sure wish I could have gotten there before the police; then I could have taken his phone. My number is the last number on his phone. That's going to lead to a lot of problems. I wonder if they can play our conversation back. If they can, they'll have me on tape saying that's not the police following you. Then they're going to ask how I knew and who they were. I'm in a lot of trouble right now.

I feel fucked up. A.J.'s family doesn't know he's dead. I think about making an anonymous call to inform them, but that might make matters worse.

The only good thing is that the goons took the dope. If the police had found that, they would have put me up under the jail.

How the fuck did I get myself into this situation? Most importantly, how am I going to get myself out of it?

Right now, I'm so scared I don't know what to do. I know what I can't do! That's lay back; I have to handle this situation. Them punk ass goons just killed two kids on my behalf, not to mention the 200 bricks they stole. Half of me is saying stop, but the other half is saying it's too late now.

Right now it's all or nothing. I'm in too deep. It's on now. It's them or me. Whoever gets caught slipping is out of here. I'll be damned if it's going to be me.

CHAPTER 34

Two Hours Later

"Yo, them guys gotta pay!" I shout.

"Easy, Big Time!"

"Easy my ass!" I reply. "They think they can't be touched. I have to show them, if you cross me there will be repercussions. If I don't react I might as well pack the family up and move to another country, I won't be able to live here in peace."

"Bang man, we're outnumbered!" Slim shouts. "It's only you and me! Listen Big Time; we have to be very careful. You see them boys don't care nothing about murder. We have to move wisely," he explains. "It's five of them that we know about. That's not including, his fans that will do anything for him, just to be a part of his team. They'll do it just to be able to say they put in work for the Mayor. Do you know how strong that will make a niggas Resume look?" he asks. "Big Time just keep a cool head. Think about how we are going to handle this. These boys ain't rookies. We have to move with wisdom, not ego. Ego will get us one of two things, a hundred years or an early grave. Me, I don't want either of those choices."

Ring! Ring! *My phone interrupts Slim.* "Pardon me Slim. Hello?"

"Hello, is this Cash?" the caller asks.

"Who is this?" I question.

"The Mayor!" the caller shouts. *My heart starts pounding harder.*

"Listen, motherfucker!" I shout.

"No Cash, you listen," he interrupts.

Slim is looking right in my mouth. He doesn't know who it is, but he knows something isn't right. "Psst! Psst!"

"Do you see what you caused?" Junebug asks. "I asked you to keep that shit out of town. I didn't tell you, I asked you. But you didn't listen. Now two lives are fucked up behind you," he states calmly. *He's speaking so calmly, like this is ordinary. His nonchalant attitude is really pissing me off. Here it is, I'm yelling my head off, and he's interrupting me with the softest voice.*

"Behind me?" I ask.

"Yeah, behind you," he replies. "I could have got straight at you."

"Listen Junebug, it ain't that easy," I interrupt.

"No, you listen Donald. It is that easy," he whispers. "Right before we went to Mike's little block, we saw you and the old fiend riding. My goons wanted you, but I spared you on the strength of my brother. But if you keep on going against the grain, eventually all that, my brother shit, is going to wear out. Oh, and another thing; don't think that was a robbery. I don't need your dope. I let my goons keep that for themselves," he whispers sarcastically. "That wasn't a robbery. That was to show you that I mean what I say."

"You should have came straight at me. I'm the one supplying the dope! My man didn't have shit to do with it. He was innocent."

"He wasn't innocent," Junebug whispers. "He was in the game." *He laughs.*

"Fuck you!" I shout. "Fuck your brother, too! Do whatever you have to do, because I'm going to do me regardless!"

"All right Cash, remember you said this. I'm going to make sure I tell Dre that." Click! *Here goes the dial tone. He hung up on me. I look at the phone and then I slam it onto the floor of the car.*

"Bang Man, why the hell did you just say that? What the fuck did I just tell you?" Slim asks, *with an assertive tone.* "Are you crazy?" *Slim has never talked to me like this. I must*

217

have really pissed him off. "Now you have to do you," he shouts. "You shouldn't have threatened him. Then maybe we could have snuck up on them. But now that you opened up your big ass mouth and warned him, they're going to be on point."

Slim is absolutely right. That's the dumbest shit I could have done. But fuck it! I already said it. I can't take it back.

We ride around for an hour without saying a word. The ringing of my phone breaks the silence.

"Hello?"

"Cash, is my father with you?" *This is Desire.*

"Yeah, hold on!" I snap. *I'm still pissed at Junebug. I pass Slim the phone.*

"Uh huh?" he answers. "Yeah? Is he all right? OK, I'll be there shortly!" *He hangs the phone up, and passes it back to me.* "Psst! Psstt!" *He starts with his teeth.*

"What's up?"

"Bang Man, somebody shot the Doctor's house up!" he shouts, *with a high-pitched, scary voice.*

"Yeah, is he all right?"

"Yeah, luckily he wasn't in there," Slim replies.

We sit in silence.

"You know that was the Mayor's work," Slim assumes.

"You think so?" I ask. *I knew it from the beginning. I just didn't want to say it first.*

"Yeah, I told you everybody knows about him cutting the dope for you. Damn!"

All kinds of thoughts start running through my head. He knows where my kids live. Will he go there next? Maybe he will; maybe he won't. I have to get them out of there! I can't take a chance like that.

"Listen Slim, ya'll gotta leave the house."

"Leave the house?" he asks, *with a clueless look on his face.*

"Yeah, at least until this shit blows over. They might go there next."

"Bang Man, where the hell are we going to go?"

"Ya'll can stay at the stash house. I'll move the work to the basement of my sister's house. No one knows about that spot." *Slim doesn't respond.*

The stash house is on a secluded block in a middle-class area. No one in their right mind will come there shooting.

"So, what do you think?" I ask.

"I don't know. I just wish this shit could have been avoided," he replies.

After that, me and Slim go to get Desire and the three kids. They grab up a few items, and we're out the door.

After I get the kids into the apartment, I explain everything to Desire. She's angry at first, but she understands. Desire is gangster. She's been around this street shit all her life, plus I schooled her back in the day. My kids, on the other hand, can not understand why they have to leave their house.

CHAPTER 35

It's now 3:30 in the morning. Me and Slim are on a mission. Slim informed me that every morning one of the goons opens up the block at 4:30A.M. sharp. He remembers that from when he used to work for Junebug.

We pull up in front of the abandoned building. It's 4'o clock on the dot. It's still pitch black out here. The block is empty. This doesn't even seem like the same block. During the day, you can't even drive through here due to the heavy drug trafficking.

We're sitting patiently, waiting for someone to arrive. The windows are so dark, no one will ever know we're in here. We're in my wife's old car. I'm sure no one will recognize it because I had it painted black and tinted the windows just for occasions like this. My wife doesn't even know about the car. She thinks I sold it.

We're sitting quietly. **"Psstt! Psstt!"** *Besides the irritating noise of Slim picking his teeth, everything is quiet. The radio isn't even playing. Slim is in a daze. I can tell he's nervous. He hasn't stopped picking his teeth since I picked him up a half hour ago. He has butterflies, but he's trying to act like everything is fine. I'm not going to lie, I'm a bit nervous myself. The closer it gets to 4:30, the harder my heart pounds.*

Twenty minutes have passed. It's 4:20. I see headlights approaching. **"Bingo!" Slim shouts.** *My heart starts racing. I pull the gun from my waist and I exhale. I must admit, I'm a little more than nervous right now. The lights are getting closer.* **"Yep, that's them."**

The Grand Prix pulls up slowly and parks diagonally from us. Only one person is in there. Yes! That makes me feel a little more at ease. Now this should be easy.

"That's Sean right there," says Slim. "He's the youngest one out of all of them. I don't even think he's 17."

Seventeen? He's nothing but a baby. I feel bad doing this, but I have to. This little boy is playing a grown man's game. If I let him slide, this will be the same motherfucker who will put one in my head.

Sean still hasn't gotten out of the car yet. He's busy talking on the phone. I wonder if he sees us sitting here. Maybe that's why he hasn't gotten out yet.

I constantly look around to see if anyone else is pulling up. Finally, the interior light comes on. He's getting out.

After stepping out of the car, he slams the door behind him. He has a shopping bag in his left hand, and he's holding his cellular phone to his ear with his right hand. He glances around before crossing the street. He's having a good conversation. He's smiling and everything.

As he approaches our car, I slump back in the seat just in case he can see my image through the tints. **Beep! Beep!** *The loud sound of a horn breaks my concentration.*

Double-parked right next to me is a Jeep Cherokee. I sit up attentively. A pretty white woman rolls down her window and screams, "Baby! Baby!" *Sean turns around.* "Let me get two," she demands.

Sean covers the phone and yells, "It's not 4:30 yet!"

"Come on, please, I have to get to work," she begs. "I have a patient going into labor as we speak." *Sean hesitantly digs his hand into the shopping bag while walking back to her truck. He then reaches into the truck, passes her the dope, and takes the money from her. As he starts back through the alleyway, the woman is still sitting there.*

"Damn bitch, pull off!" *Sean is almost halfway through the alleyway.*

"Bang Man, we can't let him get to the back. They have guns stashed back there," Slim reveals.

I'm so anxious right now. I look at the woman in the truck. She's tearing the bag open. She takes a big sniff and then another. She then takes a third one; this one is the biggest of them all.

Finally, she reseals the bag. After placing the bag into her pocketbook, she immediately pulls her visor down and checks herself in the mirror to make sure there is no sign of residue still on her nose. After wiping her nose off, she slowly pulls off.

As she cruises away, I can't help but notice her license plates. They read MD 1234. This bitch really is a doctor. Ain't that something, your precious little baby being delivered by a dope fiend!

The light at the corner is in the process of changing from green to yellow. She speeds right through the red light. I crack the door open and quietly step out. Sean is so busy yelling on the phone that he doesn't even hear me. I slowly tiptoe behind him. I'm gripping my gun in my hand. My heart is banging through my chest.

"Bye!" he yells, *as he hangs up the phone and puts it in his pocket.* **Clink!** *I accidentally step on a can. He quickly turns around. Damn! We lock eyes, and he takes off. He's quickly approaching the backyard. I'm right behind him, but his youth is taking over on me. He stretches on me. He has a big lead on me now. This kid is fast as hell. Oh shit. Slim said they have guns in the backyard!*

He runs up the steps and reaches for the doorknob. I can't let him get inside. I aim and squeeze. **Boc! Boc! Boc! Boc!** **"Aghh!" he cries,** *as he falls to his knees. He tumbles down the steps. I aim my gun at him and ease my way over to him. I don't know if he has a gun on him. He tries to get up, but he falls back down. As he reaches for the banister, I clunk him across the head with my gun.* **"Aghh, please!" he begs.** *He rolls over onto his back. He puts his hands in the air and curls his knees up to his chest. He looks me in the eyes.* **"Please don't kill me! Please!" he begs.** *I clunk him again.* **"Aghh, please!" he cries.**

"Shut the fuck up, punk," I shout. *I can see the fear in* *his eyes. He's terrified.*

As I stare into his eyes, my nephew's face flashes in the place of his. I have a nephew close to his age. My mind is playing tricks on me. **"Please don't kill me," he begs.** *My nephew's image disappears. I slowly put the gun to his head. He opens his mouth to scream, but he's so scared nothing comes out. The tears are rapidly dripping down his face. I squeeze.* **Click!** *I squeeze again.* **Click!** *And again.* **Click!** *My gun is jammed. The kid is laying there with his eyes wide open. I smack him with the barrel of the gun.* **Smack!** *A speed knot swells instantly on his forehead. I smack him again.* **Smack!** *And again.* **Smack!** *He begs me to stop, but I continuously pistol-whip him until blood has covered his entire face. He's a bloody mess. Besides his face, his jeans are also bloody from the gunshot wound. He lays there barely conscious. I grab his head and slam it onto the concrete twice.* **Thump! Thump!** *He doesn't respond; not a cry or anything. I stand up and kick him in the face one last time before running out of the backyard.*

I jump in the car. Slim already has the car started up. Before I can fully get my entire body inside, he peels off. **Sccuurr!**

"Damn, my fucking gun jammed on me."

"Did you finish him?"

"Nah, I hit him from a distance, and then when he fell, I ran up on him and the gun jammed."

"Shit!"

"I fucked him up though. I pistol-whipped him something terrible."

Slim looks over at me. **"Bang Man, you got blood all over you!"** *I look down. I'm covered with blood.*

"Big Time, you might have made a big mistake by not killing him."

"Slim, it wasn't my fault. I tried to kill him, but the fucking gun jammed. I guess it wasn't his time to go."

I replay the scene in my head. Maybe I should have

kidnapped him, killed him, and dumped his body somewhere. That kid saw my face. Slim is right; this could be dangerous. **"Psst! Psst!"** *Here he goes with his teeth.*

Even though I didn't kill him, Sean knows I tried, so basically I still proved my point to them. Now they know I don't give a fuck about them, and I'm ready to take it to the limit just like they are.

CHAPTER 36

Two weeks later

I know, I know, my 90 days are almost up, I'm supposed to be finishing up.

I haven't seen or heard from Junebug or his goons since the last incident. I guess they're laying low like I am.

Little Rah Rah's funeral was last week. Me and Slim didn't make it. I paid for the entire funeral. The total cost was about $9,000. It was the least I could do, I feel so guilty about his death. I sent Slim over to Rah Rah's house with the dough. Slim said his mom was so high, he doesn't think she even realizes he's dead. Before he left, she begged him for some Bang Man. Isn't that crazy? Her son lost his life behind that dope, and that's still her main concern.

As far as A.J.'s murder, I haven't heard a word about it. Maybe his girl knew less than I thought. It's a shame I couldn't make it to his funeral, but I just couldn't show up knowing that it was my fault. This is something that I'll have to live with forever.

Businesswise things have slowed up drastically. The other day, Juan only had two birds for me. And as for the dope, I haven't taken any from Juan since the incident with Mike. The Doctor refuses to cut the dope for me. He's scared Junebug will kill him. There's no need for me to take it. I can't cut it, and I don't know anyone who can.

This beefing shit is really getting to me. I can barely make any money.

Right now, me and Slim are on our way to drop the kids off at school.

"Daddy, when can we go back to our house?" Ahmir asks.

"Soon," I reply.

"Why do we have to stay at the other house?" Ahmad asks. "Is someone going to shoot at our house like they shot at Pop Pop friend's house?" *Here goes Ahmad with one of his famous questions.* "Daddy, is someone trying to get you?"

"Ahmad, why do you ask these crazy questions?"

"I don't know," he replies.

"Why do you think someone is trying to get me?"

"Because you carry that gun everywhere," he replies. *His answer shocks the life out of me.* "What gun?"

"That gun under your shirt!"

"What gun? I don't have a gun!"

"Uh huh, I saw it! It's silver!"

"No, you didn't!"

"Uh huh, yes I did," he insists.

"Ahmad, you didn't see a gun, and you better not tell anybody that! Do you hear me?"

"Yes," he whispers.

"Listen, nobody is out to hurt me, OK? If anyone ever hurts Daddy, ya'll will have to hold it down. Can ya'll do that?"

"I don't know," Ahmir whispers.

"You don't know! What do you mean, you don't know? You'll be able to hold it down. Do you know why?"

"Why?"

"Because you're the man!" I shout. "Both of ya'll repeat after me. Say, I AM THE MAN!"

"I AM THE MAN!" they repeat.

"Say it again."

"I AM THE MAN!" they both shout.

"That's right! Give me a high five." Clap! Clap! "I'll see ya'll after school. Remember…," *Ahmir cuts me off.*

"I know, I know, after basketball practice, wait for you at the security guard's desk, and don't come outside until you get there," he says sarcastically.

"Right!" I confirm. *They're tired of me drilling them over and over, but I have to. I don't know what Junebug will do next.*

226

After I escort them into the building, me and Slim ride around making our daily drop-offs and pickups. There isn't much to pick up, being that I only have a little bit of work.

Hours Pass

At 1:30, my phone rings. "Hello?" **I answer.** *No one responds.* "Hello!" **I repeat.**

"Yo, Cash!" **the caller shouts.** *It's Junebug.* "Are you there?" **he asks.**

"Yeah, I'm here."

"That's fucked up what you did to my little man," **he whispers.** "I didn't expect that from you. You crossed the line. We could have handled this like family. You know, we could have went in the backyard, just me and you, put the boxing gloves, on and did about three or four rounds, shook hands, and it would have been over. But now we have to get into some gangster shit. Cash, I didn't want to do this, but you made me. I sat back and thought about it. You really disrespected me. At first, I was going to let you slide, but my pride won't let me do that. For the past two weeks, I've thought about it over and over again. This issue has to be dealt with."

"Oh, I almost forgot!" **he shouts.** "Your little man got a hell of a handle, and he can shoot from anywhere. I sat in at one of his practices last week. I was really impressed." *He sat in at a practice?* "It'll be a shame if he can't make it to the championship game. The whole team is depending on him."

"Listen motherfucker, don't threaten my kids! They don't have shit to do with this!"

"Yes they do, they're your sons," **he replies.** "They're your sons just like little Sean is my son."

"Listen!" **I shout. Click!** *The sound of the dial tone*

227

interrupts me.

"Slim, we have to deal with this nigga! He just threatened Ahmir! He said he watched Ahmir at a basketball practice," I shout hysterically.

"Bang Man, this is what I was worried about," Slim yells, *as he punches the dashboard.*

"Slim, we gotta get this nigga!" Ring! Ring! *My phone rings again.* "Hold on Slim, this is probably him again. Hello!" I scream. *No one responds.* "Hello," I repeat.

"Is this Cash?" the caller asks. *This isn't Junebug. I don't recognize the voice.*

"Yeah, this Cash. Who is this?"

"This Ricky," the caller replies.

"Ricky who?"

"Pretty Ricky!" the caller shouts.

"Pretty Ricky? Oh, what up baby?" *This is my man Ricky. I haven't heard from him ever since I went away. I wonder what he's calling me for? This is one of the most dangerous old motherfuckers on the planet. He's what you call a born killer. He's somewhere in his mid 40s. They call him Pretty Ricky because every time you see him, he's dressed up with a trench coat and alligator shoes. He keeps a sawed-off shotgun underneath his trench coat. This motherfucker isn't to be played with.*

"Nothing much," Ricky answers.

"Long time no hear from Rick. How you been?"

"I've been all right. You know me, just trying to lay low, trying to stay out of the way," Ricky claims.

"I hear that."

"Cash, I heard about that shit that happened to Mike."

"Yeah, he all right now. He's still in the hospital though."

"Check it out," says Ricky. "I got the drop on the kid Spook. I know everything, where he lives, where his momma lives, and where each of his little bitches live. I even know what barbershop, and what carwash he goes to. I even know what church his grandmother goes to. He picks her up every Sunday at 2 o'clock."

"Oh yeah?" I question.

"Yeah. How much is it worth to you?"

"Huh?" I question.

"How much is he worth?" he asks. *That's what he's calling me for. He wants me to pay him to take the kid Spook out.*

Umm, I debate with myself before speaking. Should I or should I not? I really don't want to bring Ricky in on this. I want to handle it myself. But Slim did make a good point; we are outnumbered. I don't know. If I let him handle this beef for me, he might think I'm scared to put in my own work. It won't be long after that before he tests me. I've seen it done a million times before. You pay a guy to do your dirty work, and then eventually he starts extorting you; making you pay for protection. I can't go out like that! But if Ricky handles Spook, that should about even everything out. Fuck it. I'm going to let him handle it. I'll deal with that other shit later. If he tries to play me later on down the line, I'll have to bust his head wide open

"I got a dime ($10,000) on it."

"A dime?" he questions. "I was expecting a little more, but I guess that's cool. I already did all the homework on him. It'll be easy. It'll be over before the weekend. All right Cash, I'll holler at you later!"

"Later," I reply. Click!

How the hell did he get my number? Oh well, it really doesn't matter.

I'm not going to tell Slim. It's not that I don't trust him; I just don't want to put too much pressure on the old man. I would hate for us to get caught up and have the old man crack.

At 2:30, I go to pick up the kids from school. I didn't let them go to practice. I don't know if Junebug will pop up there. I don't know how I'm going to get him, but I will get him! I'm totally in the dark. I don't know where he lives or anything. Somehow, some way, I have to catch him slipping.

CHAPTER 37

Later that night

*It's 3:30 in the morning. Me and Love are having it out.
She hasn't let me get a wink of sleep.*

"Listen Donald, all I asked you was when you're going to get fitted for your tuxedo?"

"I told you this weekend!"

"You told me that last weekend and the weekend before that."

"I've been busy as hell!"

"Don't scream at me!"

"I'll do whatever the fuck I want to do," I reply.

"Not to me you won't!" Love shouts.

"Yes the fuck, I will," I challenge.

"No the fuck you won't!"

"Love, stop cursing at me!"

"Motherfucker, you cursing at me,"she replies. "Who the fuck do you think you are? You can curse at me, but I can't curse at you. I'm a grown ass woman!"

"Love, if you keep popping shit, I'm going to slap the shit out of you."

"You're not going to slap nobody!"

"Love, please," I beg.

"I wish you would slap me!"

"Love, I'm begging you. Stop running your motherfucking mouth!"

"I wish you would slap me," she mumbles. "You gone slap me cause I asked you when are you going to get fitted. That will be the last time you slap anybody. As a matter of fact, you don't have to get fitted!"

"**Fuck it then!**" **I reply.** *Her smart mouth is really starting to get under my skin.* "**It doesn't matter to me. I'm doing this for you.**"

"**You don't have to do shit for me,**" **she replies.** *I just fucked up.*

Love stomps out of the room. At first my pride won't let me run behind her. But I know I'm wrong. Ever since I've been beefing with Junebug, I've been real snappy. I know it's not her fault, but I can't help it.

I walk out into the living room. Love is laid out on the couch with a pillow covering her face. I can hear the muffled sound of her sniffling. She's crying.

"**Love, I'm sorry.**" *As I try to grab her hand, she snatches it away.* "**Love, you don't understand. I'm under a lot of pressure.**"

"**You brought this pressure upon yourself. Don't take it out on me,**" *she blurts out, but she still doesn't look my way.*

"**I don't mean to take it out on you,**" **I whisper.**

"**Then why do you do it?**"

"**It's the pressure.**"

"**What pressure?**"

"**Love, you don't know.**"

"**No, I don't. That's why I want you to tell me right now.**"

"**I can't,**" **I reply.**

"**Tell me what it is that's causing us to fight like this. Donald, lately I've been regretting being with you,**" **she admits.** "**Your attitude stinks.**"

I know my attitude isn't the best, but I didn't know she's been living with regrets. I don't want to tell her what's going on, but I can't watch our relationship go down the drain. "**Baby, what is it?**" **she asks.** "**Is it anything I can help you with?**"

"**The only thing you can do is bear with me,**" **I reply.** "**I'm going through a lot right now.**"

"**What is it? Stop beating around the bush,**" **she**

whispers.

"All right listen. I got into a little conflict with a young joker," I mumble.

"Conflict?"

"Yeah, it's not really my beef; it's my man's beef."

"Well, let your man handle it!"

"Love, it's not that easy. He's my man."

"Donald, you are too old for this dumb kiddy shit! You sound stupid as hell, almost 38 years old talking out some beef! Anyway, your time has run out. You told me in 90 days you'd be done."

"I know, but you told me I have until March."

"No, I said you have two months to get it out of your system."

"Love, March and I'm done for real. Word is bond!"

"Yeah, all right," she challenges. "So, who is it?"

"Who is what?"

"Who is it that your man had the conflict with?"

Damn, I don't know if I should tell her this. Maybe I should tell her so she can watch herself. "Junebug."

"Who?"

"Junebug, the tall Philippine-looking kid from the old block."

"Oh, the Mayor," she shouts. *I hate the way that word rolled off her lips.*

"Yeah, Junebug!" *Her face goes blank. She knows all the crazy things him and his goons have done on the block. She's witnessed the majority of it from the window. She's even told me stories that I didn't know about.*

"Those boys are crazy," she says.

"Them motherfuckers ain't crazy! They want people to think they crazy!"

"Baby, you have to be careful," she whispers.

"I'm going to be careful. I'm not worried about myself; I need you to be careful!" I explain.

"On your way to work, circle the block twice before you park and get out. Do the same thing before you come home at night. Watch your rearview mirror carefully. If you see the same car twice, get the plate number. Don't come out for lunch. I'll bring you lunch if you want me to. Right now, Junebug drives a green Bentley. His man drives a black Benz, and they also have a black Grand Prix." *As I updat her she doesn't say a word. She just listens attentively. I can sense fear and confusion in her.*

"Donald, when is all this going to be over? When will we be able to live a regular life? You're stressing me out. Why are you putting me through this? Why are you putting yourself through this? When was the last time you had a good night sleep? You jump in your sleep all night long. What is it that causes you to fight in your sleep? This lifestyle is driving you crazy!" *I didn't answer any of her questions. I can't argue with her because she's totally right. I didn't realize she was aware of me jumping in my sleep. Every night I wake up in a cold sweat. I guess that's my conscience. I've seen too much in my life. This shit is starting to have a big effect on both of us.*

"So now, I have to be out here in fear? I keep telling you, you're the drug dealer, not me. I didn't do all these years of schooling to live like this," she whines. "Now I can't come out for lunch! What am I, a prisoner?"

"Love, please just do what I asked you and everything will be all right. I told you, it's not me they're after."

"So why do I have to hide?"

"I just want to keep you out of the spotlight. You never know how these guys are thinking. If them niggas even look at you wrong, I'll kill all of them! Shit, they better not fuck with my baby!" I scream, *in a laughing manner.*

She laughs. I then give her the tightest, most reassuring hug I can give her, followed by a deep, passionate kiss. That one kiss leads to several other kisses. Those other kisses lead to one hour of meaningful lovemaking. The lovemaking leads to total exhaustion.

CHAPTER 38

Ring! Ring! Ring! *My cell phone interrupts my sleep. I reach for the phone, but my eyes are still closed. As I'm fumbling around on the nightstand, I slowly open my eyes. The clock reads 7:30. I look over at Love. There she is completely nude in a fetal position, the exact same way she was when I fell asleep.* **"Hello?" I answer,** *with a dry, groggy voice.*

"Cash!"

"Yeah."

"This Ricky. Are you up?"

"I am now!"

"Sorry for waking you. Go get the newspaper."

"Huh?"

"Get the paper, there's something in there you need to see. Call me when you wake up."

"No, call me back in a half an hour. I'm going to the store right now," I reply. Click!

I lean over and kiss Love. I then drag myself out of the bed. It's so hard leaving this warm bed, especially with Love laying here like this.

After slipping on my clothes, I brush my teeth. I then grab my dogs' leashes. They're out back, but when they hear these chains, they start barking like crazy. **Woof! Woof! Woof!**

They drag me all the way to the store. They're so big and strong now that my sons aren't able to walk them. I can barely walk them. It takes me a matter of minutes to get to the store.

I'm in total shock as I open the paper and read the headline: **"City Man and Juvenile Are Murdered At Doorstep"** *The article reads like this:*

Late last night, one man and a teenage acquaintance were

found dead. Resident Jermaine Jones, a.k.a. Spook, and Brian
Jackson, a.k.a. Jr., members of the notorious street gang known
as the Goon Squad, were found dead just steps away from
Jones's residence. The shooter remains at large. Also at large
is the leader of the notorious gang, Christopher Blackhead,
a.k.a. "The Mayor." Blackhead controls the drug market in
this city. He's known for distributing the heroin stamped Block
Party. Their sales are estimated at 5,000 bags per day. His
Goon Squad regulates that only their heroin is sold. He remains
at large, for the shooting death of a teenager on a city street a
few weeks ago. He's also wanted for questioning regarding a
murder of an out-of-town man, who was brutally murdered in
his car days ago. He was shot several times in the head. Anyone
with information about either of these incidents is urged to
contact us.

*I'm nervous from just reading the article. Damn! They
know everything about this motherfucker. They even know about
A.J.! I hope this doesn't lead back to me!*

Ring! Ring! Ring! "Hello?" I answer.

"Yeah, this Ricky," the caller states.

"Hey, what up baby? Where are you going to be in one
hour?"

"Wherever you want me to be," he replies.

*After setting up the meeting place, I drop the dogs off at
home, and jump in Love's old car. I'm on my way to meet Ricky.*

*As I'm pulling up, I spot Ricky across the street. As I'm
sitting at the traffic light, I look at Ricky. For the life of me, I can't
figure out why they call him Pretty Ricky. There's nothing pretty
about him. Besides his humongous head, he has the biggest, ashiest
lips I ever saw. Not to mention he only stands 5 feet 2 inches tall.
But at 5 feet 2 inches, he's more dangerous than any gorilla. If
you don't know him, you would probably underestimate him and
disrespect him. He looks like the average nerd. Disrespecting him
would be the mistake of a lifetime. His body count nobody exactly
knows, but it's rumored to be well above the 30s. Murder has been*

his occupation ever since he turned 18 years old. They say all through his childhood he was a bookworm, a straight nerd. He was real quiet. He stayed to himself. No one knows when or why he snapped.

The amazing thing is he's never been convicted of murder. They tried to charge him a few times, but never did it stick. I heard he's real sharp when it comes to law. He knows his shit. When he's in the joint, other inmates pay him to help them with their cases. If you ask me, that's wasted talent. He could be a top-notch lawyer in some big firm, but instead he lives the life of a hit man.

He stands at the corner with a newspaper folded under his arm and a briefcase in his hand. You would think he was on his way to his office somewhere. He has on his famous beige trench coat and his black alligator shoes. I think he's been wearing that same coat ever since I was a kid.

When the light changes, I pull over to him and roll down the window. He jumps right in. He shakes my hand, and I pull off. I have my left hand on the handle of my gun, which is tucked up under my thigh. I don't trust him a bit. Murder is his occupation. He has no loyalty. He rolls with whoever will pay him the most money. For all I know, Junebug could have paid him to kill me right now.

"**I told you it would be easy,**" he states. "**I sat out front all day waiting for him to hop his ass out the house.**" *Spook was on crutches. Little Rah Rah shot him right before they killed him. The impact of the forty-five shattered the bone in his leg.*

"**I didn't plan on doing the other kid, but I couldn't leave a witness. You came off. You got two for the price of one,**" he **says,** *with a goofy-looking smile on his face.*

I hand him the money. I give him $10,000 in $100 bills. "**Where do you want me to drop you off?**" *I have to get him out of the car. His presence makes me feel uneasy. Not one time have I let my banger loose.*

"**Pull over, you can let me out right here.**"
"**Are you sure?**"

"Yeah," he answers.

I pull over and he begins to get out. "Cash, if you need me again, just call me."

My mind starts to wonder. "As a matter of fact, do you have any information on the kid Junebug?"

"Who?"

"Junebug, the Mayor."

"Nah, but I can get some. It might take me a little longer, but I'm sure I can get it. I can't do it for the same price though. He is the Mayor."

"I know, I know, I got 25 cent ($25,000) on him."

"All right, I'll get on it. I'll hit you in a couple of days to let you know if I have something on him."

"Bet!"

"I'll get with you later," he shouts, *as he gets out of the car.*

He cuts through the gas station, and I drive off.

That's two down and three to go. I really don't think the kid Sean wants any more trouble. Him and the other little guys are nothing but babies, nothing but little ass punks. Spook and Jr. were the ones who really made all the moves. I'm glad they're out of the way. That's a big load off me! Look what all that tough shit got Spook, a face full of dirt! Ha, ha, ha!

Ricky is a lifesaver. Not only are Spook and Jr. out of the way, he's going to handle Junebug for me too. You should have seen the look on his face when I said I have a quarter on him. With that kind of price on his head, Ricky is sure to find some information on him.

Shit, I hope he gets to him before this week is out. I'm missing a lot of money.

CHAPTER 39

Two weeks have flown by, and I haven't heard from Ricky. I thought Junebug would have been handled by now.

By the way, the drought is officially over. Last week Juan hit me with 20 joints. We're back rolling. I still can't fully move the way I want. You know I have to watch my back. I don't know when Junebug is going to make another move. No one has seen him. He's been real quiet ever since they put his picture in the newspaper. The less visible he is, the more threatened I feel. I haven't been able to sleep in weeks.

Two weeks from now is my sons' championship game. They made it. I'm hoping Junebug is outta here by then.

For some strange reason, I think that's what he's waiting for. He knows I can't do too much with my boys with me. I think he'll be there waiting for me the day of the game. I might have to pull them from the game. I would hate to do that, the team needs them, but it's safety first.

At this moment, me and Slim are coming back from making a move. My man just bought two joints. He gave me $56,000 cash money. The price has decreased, but it's still not down to the regular price yet. Right now I'm charging $28,000 a joint. I'm only paying $22,000 per kilo. That's $6,000 profit off of each one. That's beautiful. No one can complain, because I'm still $3,000 cheaper than anyone else.

I would be eating hard if I had the dope. Juan keeps asking me when I'm going to get some more of it. He's stuck with it. None of his other plugs can move it like me. I wish I could take it, but there's nothing I can do with it. I begged the Doctor over and over, but he won't touch that shit. They really shook him up.

"Slim, after I put this cash up, I'm going to pick up the boys, so we can all go get fitted for the tuxedos."

Slim and my sons are in my wedding.

"I'm with you Big Time."

As I turn the corner, I have to do a double take. I can't believe my eyes. There's Sal walking down the block. "Yo, there goes that snitch ass nigga who tried to set me up! I'm about to bust his motherfucking head!" *I snatch my gun from my waist.*

"Bang Man, you can't do that right here. The police precinct is right around the corner. Once they hear that gun go off, they gone be on our ass. Let me handle it," he suggests. *Let him handle it? What can his old ass do? Slim pulls his razor from his pocket.* "Circle the block and let me out," he instructs. "Don't let him see the car."

I circle the block like he instructed me to do. I'm still not sure if I want him to handle this. "Right here," he shouts.

I stop and he jumps out. I pull into the parking space just three feet away. Sal doesn't see me. He's walking, eating a slice of pizza. Slim walks toward him. As Slim gets closer to him, he turns his head as if he's looking behind him. They collide into each other. All of a sudden Sal slumps over, holding his stomach like he's in pain.

Sal grabs Slim and they begin to tussle. Slim can't get loose. I run over to rescue him. Sal sees me. His eyes stretch wide open as if he just saw a ghost. He lets Slim loose, and he tries to back away. He's still holding his stomach. Blood is soaking through his goose down jacket. Slim must have cut him with his razor when they bumped into each other. I told you Slim is good with that razor!

Sal backs up against a house. I walk up to him. He doesn't say a word; he just puts his hand up to block me. I swing with all my might. **Crack!** *I nail him right on the chin. I knock him senseless. His knees buckle. If it weren't for the wall he's leaning against, he would have fallen face first.* **Crack!** *I swing again and he stumbles. Then he shakes his head like he's trying to shake it off.*

239

I can tell his vision is blurry. His eyes are googly looking. He can't even focus on me. He reaches for me, but he's off by about a foot or so. **Crack!** *I swing again. Timber! He falls to his knees. He tries to hold onto my legs but,* **Crack!** *I uppercut him. The impact of the punch lifts his head up. His neck snaps back, and he falls onto his back. He rolls over into the alleyway. He clumsily tries to stand up, but I kick him dead in the eye.* **Thump!** *He stumbles backwards. Finally, he lands on his back. Slim runs over and swings his razor.* **Zip!** *The blood instantly pours from his face. It's terrible. Sal's face is open to the white meat from his ear on down to his bottom lip.*

It's happening so fast I don't think Sal even realizes it until he sees the blood dripping. **"Aghh! Aghh!"** *he screams, as he holds his face. I stand over him. I draw my gun and aim at his head. I'm furious. This nigga tried to get me knocked off.*

"Please Cash, they made me call you," he cries.

"They made you?" I ask. "Motherfucker, you lying! They didn't know shit about me! I heard you caught a case right before you set me up! Nigga, I'm going to kill you right here!" *I grab the handle tighter and I inhale while locking my arm. I got my left eye closed while my right eye is squinted, staring down the nose of the cannon. The middle of his forehead is my target. I slightly touch the trigger.* **"Bang Man, not right here, not right now," Slim begs.**

The blood from his cut is dripping rapidly. Damn, I want to do him so bad right now, but I know I won't get away with it. **"You better keep your mouth shut," I whisper. "I swear to God, I'm going to kill you. You over right now, but I'm telling you to your face, I am going to kill you!"**

"Big Time, somebody looking out of the window up there." *I slowly peek up at the window and quickly tuck my gun away. We walk toward the car, leaving Sal leaking blood. We jump in the car and peel off.*

"I should have killed him right there!"

"Nah, Big Time, you did the right thing. If you had

killed him, homicide would have been at the house by the time you got there. They protect their snitches. See, that's the problem with young niggas, they don't respect code and honor. As soon as they get caught up, they start singing like canaries. It wasn't like that in my day. If you got caught, you wore it.

"You see, you got these young niggas riding around here in Mercedes Benzes, they got every color fur and the baddest wife a man could possibly want. I mean bitches so bad, they look like someone tore them straight from a magazine. Ask yourself, Big Time, do you think they ready to give all that up? Do you really think they're willing to leave their pretty young girlfriends out here in the world and risk another dude fucking her and sleeping in his bed? She sucking his dick better than she used to suck her old man's dick, and on top of that he driving the brand new Benz dude left back home. Nah, Big Time, don't think for one minute that these niggas ain't gone tell. They gone tell before they get in the holding cell. You can bet your bottom dollar on that. They ain't ready to give this life up," Slim explains. "But as far as Sal goes, I bet you he'll keep his mouth shut now. Now he's marked for life. Everyone will know he's a snitch."

Slim hit him with the squealers cut. That's how the old heads from back in the day marked the snitches. That's where the saying 'snitches get stitches' came from.

"That'll teach him to keep that hole in between his ears and his chin closed," Slim shouts. "Snitch ass bastard! I hate snitches! I don't understand it; it's like there ain't nothing wrong with snitching now. Back in the day if you snitched, nobody fucked with you. Now if you snitch, motherfuckers will still get money with you and everything. These young motherfuckers got the game fucked up!"

CHAPTER 40

Two days later

So far this has been a hell of a week. It's only two days later and who do I run into at the traffic light?

"Bang Man, ain't that the Mayor?"

"Where?"

"Up the street!" Slim shouts anxiously. *It sure is. He's two blocks up, sitting at the red light.*

It's broad daylight, 2 in the afternoon. The streets are crowded as can be. Should I get at him? Or should I wait until Ricky gets him? What if Ricky can't get him? My sons' game is less than two weeks away. This might be a once-in-a-lifetime thing. What if I let him slide and he makes a move? Then I'll regret it! I can't gamble like that. If I start shooting, someone is liable to see my car and tell on me. Damn, what should I do? I'm sweating. My mouth is dry. Right now, I'm more nervous, than I've ever been. I exhale. **"Slim, I gotta do him!"**

"Big Time, are you crazy? You kill him out here, we are going to jail!"

"If I don't kill him, he'll kill us!"

"Bang Man, you can't do it! Do you see all these people out here?"

"I have to. I let you talk me out of killing Sal, but I have to do this."

The light changes, and I drive off slowly. I can still see him. He's two blocks away, but he's cruising.

"Think about what you doing, Big Time!"

"I don't have time to think," I shout.

Red light! Damn, I'm caught at the light, but Junebug is

still riding. He's going to get away. Damn! Oh no, he isn't. He gets caught at the next light. He's about three lights away.

"Slim, switch seats. You drive!"

"Psst! Psstt!"

"Slim, just slide the fuck over!" *I jump out and run to the passenger's side. He slides over.*

Our light changes first.

"Step on it!" *Slim gasses up. We're getting closer. We're only one light away.*

The light catches Junebug. We're inching up on him. We're three cars away.

The car in front of us turns off. Now, we only have two cars between us.

"What do you want me to do?" **Slim asks.**

"Just follow him."

There's another head in the car besides his. I can't tell who it is.

Another car turns off, leaving only one car between us. The light changes. **"Can you see who he's in there with?"** **I ask.**

"Nah, I can't see them," **Slim replies.** *I wait impatiently for the light to change.* **"Psstt! Psstt!"** *Damn light, hurry up! I look at the gun in my lap. This is a big motherfucker; it's a chrome 11 shot forty- five. I have 11 shots, but I hope I can get the job done using no more than two. I have to finish the passenger too. I can't afford to leave a witness.*

The light changes. Junebug turns on his right blinker. He turns slowly. The car in front of us hasn't moved yet. The car has out of state plates. The driver is an old man. He's looking around as if he's lost. I reach over and mash the horn. **Beep! Beep! Beep!** *He still doesn't budge.* **"Slim, go around this motherfucker!"**

Now Junebug is halfway down the block.

"Catch him!"

"Calm down," **Slim shouts.** *For some reason, something* *tells me Slim is purposely letting him get away.*

Junebug gets caught at another light. We pull up right behind him. He's so busy running his mouth, he doesn't even notice us.

"You see that cop car over there, right?" Slim asks.

While waiting at the light, the passenger door opens slowly. It's a woman. I can see her stilettos coming from the door. It's the Chinese girl. What is she doing? The trunk pops open. She quickly runs to the trunk and grabs a shopping bag. She looks at us as she closes the trunk, but she can't see through the dark windows.

"What do you think is in that bag?" I ask. "Do you think he knows it's us?"

"I don't know, Big Time," Slim replies. *The light changes. The cop car turns down the block. Junebug pulls off and we follow.*

Inhale! **"Here we go!" I shout,** *trying to soup myself up. The light turns red. I glance around quickly.* **"Pull up on the side of him!"** *Slim quickly dips around him as I roll the window down.* **"Cut him off!"** *We have him blocked in. The nose of our car is directly in front of his. Junebug quickly turns his head to face us, but it's already too late. He looks me dead in the eyes as I squeeze the trigger.* **Boc! Boc! Boc!** *He peels off, banging into our car, but that doesn't slow him down.*

"Stay on him!" I shout.

Slim catches up with him. Junebug is driving recklessly. He's swerving from side to side. We finally ease up on the side of him. We're on the wrong side of the street, we're riding side by side with him. Luckily there isn't any oncoming traffic.

I squeeze again. **Boc! Boc!** *I can hear the bullets ricochet. He steps on it. A big truck is coming our way.* **"Cut over! Cut over!" I shout.** *We're on his tail. I lean out the window and squeeze six times.* **Boc! Boc! Boc! Boc! Boc! Boc!** *No penetration. The last bullet ricochets off his rear window and crashes into our windshield.* **Crack!** *Our windshield shatters. Glass disperses everywhere. I cover my face.*

"Aghh!" Slim screams. "I got glass in my eye!" he cries out. *I look at Slim. His face has trickles of blood covering it.*

Junebug is hauling ass down the block. He's gone. Apparently, his car has bulletproof windows.

Damn, now we really fucked up!

CHAPTER 41

Only two days left before the championship game, and I still haven't heard a word from Pretty Ricky. I called him yesterday and left my number so he could contact me.

The other day as Love was leaving the school, she spotted the Grand Prix, parked right next to her car in the parking lot. Instead of calling me, she called the police and told them someone was trying to steal her car. They pulled off before the Police got there. Luckily, she spotted them. There's no telling what those clowns may have done to my baby. I wish I could have caught them. I would have left them stinking right there in the school parking lot. Love knew; that's why she didn't call me. She told me she didn't want me to cause a scene at her job. Plus, she doesn't want me to get into any trouble.

She's terrified now; she won't even go to the store. I feel terrible that I've put her in this situation. I'm ready to handle this kid Junebug. I need him out of the way. He's causing too much tension. He's gotta go. Every time I picture them in that lot parked next to Love's car, I get furious. The thought of what they might have done to her if she didn't see them. Who knows, they might have kidnapped her or killed her. I don't know what their intentions were, but I'll tell you what mines are; I have to finish him. Wherever I see him, I'm going to finish him right there. I don't care where he's at, who he's with, or what time of the day it is. It's wherever and whenever.

Today is the first day I let my boys practice since Junebug called me with the threat. I've been sitting here watching them do drills for almost two hours now. I'm by myself today. Slim isn't feeling well. He couldn't manage to drag himself out of the bed this

246

morning. His doctor was right. Some days he's up, and others he's barely alive.

While watching them practice free throws, my phone rings. **Ring! Ring! "Hello?"**

"Cash?" the caller asks.

"Yeah, this me. Who is this?"

"This is Ricky," the caller answers.

Yes, he has something! Please let him tell me he's got something. **"What up, Rick? Please tell me you got good news."**

"Shit, I wish," he whispers. "Cash, I can't find out shit about him."

Damn! My hopes are crushed. I can't have him running around here like that, especially after I just blazed at him. Even if he didn't want to get at me, he will now knowing that I'm trying to get at him, even if he's only doing it out of fear. **"Nothing?" I ask.**

"Nothing," he confirms. "His shit is tight as hell. He's one of the best that I've ever ran into. He doesn't leave a trace. No one knows any of his bitches, and his mother doesn't live around here. I don't know where to start looking for him. Do you have any leads on him?"

"Nope, all I know is he fucks with a white bitch and a Chinese bitch. I never saw him with a local hood rat. All his bitches are from out of town. As for his mother, his brother Dre bought her a house down south somewhere before he went away."

"Shit! I don't know what to tell you, Cash. I'm going to stay on it," he claims. "I'll call you if I find out anything. Meanwhile, see if you can find out anything."

"True," I answer.

"Later Cash!"

"Later!" Click! *Now what the fuck am I going to do? I was banking on him, but he's clueless. I have to find out something. Somebody, somewhere knows something.*

After the practice is over, I take the kids to the mall to buy them new sweat suits to wear to the game. I buy them matching

247

velour sweat suits and matching sneakers. I couldn't take them to the local Mall, because I couldn't risk anyone seeing us. We're at a mall in the suburbs almost an hour away.

After shopping, we sit and eat ice cream at the ice cream parlor inside the mall.

We're sitting at a booth in the corner. From my seat, I have a view of the entire parking lot.

Ahmad's ice cream melts before he can eat it. He has been asking question, after question, ever since we got in here. **"Daddy, when I make it to the NBA, you ain't going to have nothing to worry about," says Ahmad.**

"You're not," I correct. "There's no such word as ain't!"

"Oh, when I make it to the NBA, you're not going to have anything to worry about. I'm going to buy you another house. It's going to be way bigger than the old one."

The thought is good, but his chances of making it to the NBA are as slim as a dwarf getting drafted. I don't mean to down him, but I don't think he has what it takes to be a pro ball player. I would never discourage him though. I'll just keep motivating him until he finds what his inner talent is. Right now, he's chasing Ahmir's dream. He only loves basketball because Ahmir loves it.

"Daddy, do you think I'll make it to the NBA?"

"Sure you will! Do you know why?"

"No, why?"

"Because you are the man!"

"That's right Daddy, I'm the man!" he replies. "When I make it, I'm going to buy you a Bentley, too. Do you know why Daddy?"

"No, why?"

"Because you are the man!" he replies.

"Ha, Ha, Ha." *We both laugh.*

"I'm going to buy you a Bentley just like that one over there."

"Bentley where?" I question.

"Over there," he says, *pointing across the parking lot.*

"Where?"

"Over there, the green one." *Oh shit! It sure is. It's* Junebug's car.

I get nervous. I start peeking around. Did this motherfucker follow us here? What the fuck am I going to do? I dial Ricky's phone number. The answering machine picks up on the first ring. He must be on the phone. I dial him again, but still no answer. Then I dial again. His answering service picks up both times.
"Shit!" **I blurt out.**

"What's the matter, Daddy?" **Ahmad asks.**

"Nothing Ahmad. Here goes $10. Ya'll go order some more ice cream."

"Yeah!" **they cheer.**

As they walk to the counter, I dial Ricky again; still no answer. I'm scared as hell. For some reason, I feel like I'm being watched. I peek around the store. I walk to the doorway and look out the store into the lobby area. I take notice of a tall, long-legged blond walking through the lobby area. She looks like a famous model walking the runway. She has at least five shopping bags in each hand. As she gets closer, I realize who she is. She's Junebug's girl.

Oh shit, let me hide over here. I know he isn't far behind. As she passes the ice cream Parlor, I hide behind the statue of a gigantic ice cream cone. I stand there for a second, waiting to see if he's following her.

She prances into the ladies room. Still no Junebug. Minutes pass. She's taking forever in the rest room.

She must be in there for at least 15 minutes before she steps out and goes directly into Victoria's Secret. I still don't see any sign of Junebug.

I have to get out of here. I know we can make it to the car, because I'm parked directly in front of the exit.

"Come on, let's go," **I yell to the boys.**

"Daddy, we're not finished!"

"Come on, we have to go. Eat in the car!"

They get up hesitantly. **"The last one in the car is a rotten egg!" I shout.** *Everyone takes off at full speed. I'm the last one, of course.*

After starting the car, I just sit for a moment. From the angle I'm sitting, I can see everyone who walks in and out of the mall. I decide to sit here to see who the white girl is with.

Approximately ten minutes later, she comes out. She has added two more shopping bags to her collection. Before she steps out, she pauses in the doorway and places all ten of her bags on the floor. She begins to button her full-length, white and black chinchilla. After that, she walks right past me and crosses the lot in the direction of the Bentley.

When she gets in, she doesn't pull right off. First, she puts on her sunglasses, then she slips on her leather driving gloves. Immediately after that, she cruises through the parking lot.

"Daddy, why are we still sitting here?" Ahmad asks. *I ignore him.* **"Huh Daddy?"**

When she gets to the exit, I pull off.

I follow her out of the parking lot. After driving about two blocks, she pulls over and parks. I park about seven cars behind her.

"Daddy, where are we going?" Ahmad questions.

"Shhh, cool out Mod," I whisper. *She walks into a bakery. Just seconds later, she comes back out and jumps back in the car. She pulls off, and I pull off. Before she gets to the traffic light, she puts on her left blinker. After the oncoming traffic passes her, she turns into a driveway between two big, beautiful white houses.*

I pull over and watch her get out. She doesn't even notice me sitting here. Not once has she looked in her mirror. Now do you see why I drill Love so much about that?

She grabs her bags and walks up the steps of the bigger house. After she goes inside, I pull up directly across from the house. **"Bingo!" I blurt out.** *What do I see in the backyard? I see the black 500 and I see the Harley parked in the garage with the doors wide open. I peel off.* **Sccuuurr!** *I can't let anyone see* *me and blow my chances of getting him. Besides, I've already seen enough.*

No wonder we can't find him. He's nowhere in the hood. He's deep in the suburbs. No one would think of coming way up here.

I pull out a pen and a pad from my glove box. I scribble down the street and house number.

From there I drop the kids off, and I immediately call Ricky again. This time he answers. We meet up and I give him the information. I give him $10,000 up front and tell him I'll give him the other $15,000 when the job is done.

CHAPTER 42

Two days later

Today is the day of the big game. I haven't heard from Ricky since I gave him the information. I wonder what's taking him so long. He should have handled that already. All yesterday I checked my phone continuously just to make sure it was working.

This morning, I woke up bright and early. I'm just arriving at the building to pick up Slim and my sons. Slim looks different compared to the way he's been looking the past two days. Today he looks bright and cheerful. As he walks to the car, he smiles from ear to ear. I haven't seen him this happy in a while. He's whistling a tune as he gets in the car. **"What's up, Daddy?" the boys shout.** *Slap! Slap! They both give me a high five.*

"Damn Slim, you look happier than a fag with a bag of dicks," **I whisper.** *He chuckles.*

"You're going to be happy too when you see the surprise I got for you!"

"What is it?" **I ask.**

"Hold up, hold up," **he insists.** *He then digs in his inside pocket, pulls out a newspaper clipping, and tosses it onto my lap.* **"Bang Man!"** *I quickly fix my eyes on the clipping. I can't wait to read how Ricky executed Junebug. I already know what's going on, but I don't want Slim to know that I'm in on it. I never told him about the order I put in.*

I slowly read the entire article, reading every small detail twice. No! This is not what I expected to read! Hell no! This is how the article reads:

KILLER OF TWO CITY MEN SOUGHT
The notorious Mayor, leader of the Goon Squad, known for his famous heroin labeled Block Party, was taken into custody

yesterday evening. He was apprehended after federal officials raided his suburban home. Federal agents confiscated a 9mm. handgun, two .40 calibers, three 44 magnums, two machine guns, an assault rifle, more than 25,000 bags of heroin, and a total of $2,300,400 in cash.

Taken into custody with him were his two female acquaintances, Liu Ching and Megan Bess. Officials also confiscated a Bentley Azure, a Harley Davidson, and a Mercedes Benz that are all registered to Liu Ching. Megan Bess holds the deed to the $500,000 home. If convicted, Liu Ching and Megan Bess will face up to 25 years for conspiracy.

Blackhead (the Mayor) not only has been indicted for numerous drug charges, officials have evidence leading to murders dating back five years ago. If convicted Blackhead could face multiple life sentences.

Officials escorted him from his home wearing only a white, hooded, terry cloth Polo robe, and Gucci slippers. As he was dragged across his lawn, he spit into the face of an official and sang the words "Every dog will have his day. I guess it's my turn now. What goes up must come down."

"Bang Man, it's over. They ain't never coming home."

"Damn, I didn't want it to go like this. I wanted his ass dead!"

"Who do you want dead Daddy?" Ahmad asks. *I totally forgot they were in the car.*

"Nobody, Ahmad. That's not what I said."

"Uh huh, I heard you."

"No, you didn't hear that. Phew." *I exhale.*

"Big Time, look at the bright side. He's out of the way, and you didn't have to do it. He self-destructed. You're out here as free as a bird. Now you can do whatever you want to do."

"I was going to do whatever I wanted one way or the other!" I shout. "This just feels like the sucker way out."

Hours later

I sit carefree, and watch our team blow the other team out. The score is 76 to 40. The first quarter doesn't look too good at first when the off guard gets stripped of the ball seven times back to back. The coach then pulls him out and puts Ahmad in. To my surprise, my sons run the court like two professional guards. I've never seen Ahmad play like this. He shoots from everywhere and scores. He finishes off with more points than Ahmir. He has 34 points, and Ahmir only has twelve. Together they scored over half of the team's total points. If Ahmad keeps playing like this, I might get that house and that Bentley he promised me! I'll never forget the look on Ahmad's face when they handed him the MVP trophy. I could see jealousy all over Ahmir's face, as Ahmad looked up at me, and said 'I'M THE MAN!' Ahmir hates to be second; especially to Ahmad. He thinks he's supposed to better than Ahmad in everything, they do. This is good medicine for him. This way he'll learn to never take anything for granted. He just knew that MVP trophy was his. He already had a spot cleaned up for it, on the mantle. I'm so glad it went that way.

CHAPTER 43

One month later

Things are going terrific. The cocaine price is back down. I'm paying $16,000 a joint and selling it for $19,000. I even talked the Doctor into teaching me how to cut the dope. He charged me $10,000 for the recipe. He refuses to be my chemist because of all the madness his mix started.

Oh, even Mike is back rolling. He hasn't fully healed up yet, but he's killing them. He has the block banging with the blow and the dope. He moves 25 bricks (1,250 bags) and a quarter of a kilo (250 grams) a day. In total, that's over $19,000 a day. After paying his soldiers and getting me out of the way, he walks away with about $6,000 profit a day, which equals out to over $40,000 a week. That's not bad for a 40-year-old dude who never did anything but extort guys for little pennies all his life.

I took over Junebug's old block. Bang Man is moving. I can't keep enough of it. I move about 75 bricks a day out there. I also opened my old block back up. I sell nothing but dimes of cocaine out there. My crew bumps two and a half kilos every week.

Even Slim is eating heavy. I gave him a raise. He no longer makes $1,000 a week. Now he makes $2,500 a week just to ride with me while I'm making moves. Every now and then, he makes a drop-off or a pickup, but most of the time he just rides shotgun.

Oh, I almost forgot. I did have a small problem when I first got the dope back. I couldn't get in touch with my main man Bilal. He's one of my plugs from out of town. After trying over and over to contact him, I called some of his plugs to let them know Bang Man was back. I thought maybe he had got locked up or something. Come to find out, they never stopped getting Bang Man. Bilal didn't go one single week without it. Through all the beefing and everything, Bilal copied my stamp and continued to sell it as if it were mines.

I put Pretty Ricky on him. I gave him all the information he needed. I gave him a picture of Bilal, his baby momma's address, and his new girl's address.

It only took Ricky two days to find him. Let's just say that $10,000 I gave Ricky to handle Junebug he no longer owes me, we're even!

As for Junebug's two little men, no one has seen them. I don't think they come around here anymore.

I love it when a plan comes together. Cashmere is back! If only Jake and Ab could see me now. Not even a year after coming home and I'm in charge of everything, just like I told you I would be. A motherfucker can't sneeze without asking me first! And guess what! I did it without Jake and Ab. I did it by myself!

CHAPTER 44

Today is the big day, finally. Today is my wedding day. I haven't seen Love since we went to pick up the tuxedos. That was two days ago. Boy, do I miss her! In less than one hour, I'll be standing in front of 350 people. I'm nervous as hell.

My left eye has been jumping since this morning when I woke up. I'm not superstitious, but if Big Ma were alive, she would be like, "Boy that's a sign of bad luck. If you gotta go outside, you better be careful."

I don't believe in luck or none of that dumb shit. I believe whatever is meant to be will be.

Right now, I'm fully dressed. Fuck one million bucks; I look like three million bucks! This tux is fitting me perfectly. Black as I am, I got the nerve to have on a black tux. That was all Love's idea. We're going to look so good standing in front of all those people. The bridesmaids are wearing wine-colored dresses; the same color as my car.

I got the car detailed yesterday. She's ready to go. My man did his thing. She looks like she just left the showroom.

I got one move to make. I know, I'm supposed to be done, but I'm making so much money it's hard to walk away. Love doesn't know I'm still hustling.

I have a loyal team with me, so I really don't have to go out unless I want to. They handle everything.

My man wants a bird. The only reason I'm delivering it myself is he came all the way from North Carolina, and he doesn't have time to wait. It's going to be simple though, because where I have to meet him is in the direction of Desire's house. By the way, they moved back in last month.

After I drop the bird off, I'll go straight to the house and scoop my best men up and we're out. Slim and my sons will be standing next to me at the altar. When we get to the park, a horse and carriage will bring us in.

As I pull into the mini mall, something doesn't feel right. I feel like someone is watching me. I glance around, but I don't see anything out of the ordinary. I don't see my man either. I'm not going to park. I can't trap myself off like I did with Sal.

I circle the lot twice, then I exit. I slowly drive around the block trying to give him time to get here.

He's still not here.

As I pull into the parking lot, I notice a cherry top approaching. He slows down as he gets closer to me. He stops. We lock eyes. Oh shit! Here we go!

I continue to ride. Through my rearview mirror, I see him busting a U-turn. He quickly pulls behind me. I'm driving regular, as if I don't know he's behind me. Then, **Whoop! Whoop!** *He hits his siren. Damn!* **"Pull over!"** *he instructs over the loudspeaker. I pull over, like he told me to.*

I'm shaking like a leaf. The officer slowly walks over to my car. **Sniff!** *I take a sniff of the air just to see if you can smell the loud aroma of the cocaine. I sniff again.* **Sniff!** *Without a doubt, you can definitely smell it. I'm in trouble.*

"Hey son, is there a problem?"

"No sir," I answer confidently. **"Why do you ask that?"**

"Uh, I noticed you riding around the parking lot three or four times. Is everything all right?"

"Uh, yes Sir!"

"Are you waiting for someone?" he asks. *Before I can answer, he says,* **"Can I see your license, insurance, and your registration son? Turn the car off son!"**

"Yes sir!" I shout, *as confidently as I can.*

I pat my pockets before realizing that due to me rushing, I left my wallet in my other pants pockets. I then reach in the glove box for the other paperwork. **"Officer, I'm sorry, I left my wallet** at home with my license in it, but I have everything else," I explain.

"Let me see it," he orders.

I hand it over and he reviews the paperwork.

"Sir, step out of the car please."

"Huh?" I question. "My name is Donald Pierce! You can record check my name. I have a license, I just forgot it sir, honest."

"Step out of the fucking car, sir," he yells.

Oh shit, it's going down! What can I say? He's not trying to hear anything. I have the bird laying right on the front seat in a brown paper bag. I know he sees it. I'm going to jail forever.

As I step out of the car, he looks me up and down. "Why are you all dressed up, boy?"

"I'm getting married in less than one hour."

He pats my waist as if he's checking for something. He cracks a smile. "Get back in your car, boy. Congratulations!"

"Exhale! *What a relief!*

As I'm getting back into my car, I notice my man pulling into the parking lot. As he pulls toward me, I shake my head no. The officer is in the car sitting in the cut. He's watching everything. I pull out of the parking lot. My man comes behind me shortly after. He follows me to a dead-end block. We park, he jumps in, and I serve him. We make the move successfully. That was a close call.

Minutes later

As soon as I turn onto Desire's block, I begin dialing the number. "Hello?" Ahmir answers.

"Ya'll ready?" I ask.

"Yeah, we ready, but Pop Pop is still in the bathroom," he replies. "Mommy is helping him get dressed."

"All right, I'll be in front waiting for ya'll."

Slim is doing terrible. I told him he could stay home, I would understand. But he told me he wouldn't miss the wedding for the world. Desire had to bathe and dress him. I hate to see him like this. From the looks of things, these might be his last days. I can't even picture standing over him in a casket. The thought of it stresses me out.

When I pull up to the house, I notice someone going up the steps. I can't make out who it is. The squeaking of my brakes startles him. He quickly turns around. It's Ice. He starts to come back down the stairs.

Never once does he look me in the eyes. As he's crossing the street to get to his truck, I get out of my car. **"Yo! What's up?"** I ask.

"What's up Cash? What's going on?" *I can tell he's scared. He didn't expect to see me here.*

"Didn't Desire ask you to stay from around here?" I ask.

"I, I, I," he stutters.

"I, what?" I ask sarcastically.

"Cash, you don't understand. I love Desire! She's playing with my heart. I love that girl. I'll do anything for her. I want to be with her. I can't live without her." *His eyes start to water. He starts pacing around in little circles.*

"You played me," he mumbles. **"That's fucked up. You played me,"** he whispers.

"What?" I ask.

"You heard me, I said you played me."

"I played you?" I question. **"How did I play you?"**

"You know what the fuck I'm talking about," he shouts aggressively.

"Hold up youngen. Who the fuck are you talking to?"

That really makes him go crazy. **"I'm talking to you motherfucker!"** he cries. *Foam drips from the corner of his lips. I walk toward him. I've been waiting for this.*

I reach out for him. He quickly draws a gun from under his white, oversized T-shirt. I slowly back away from him.

"What the fuck are you doing?" I ask.

"You know what this is about," he shouts. "Stop acting stupid!"

I'm watching him carefully. He's acting like a madman. He backs me up all the way to my car. I'm towering over him. His face only comes to my chest. He's looking up at me as he talks. Everytime he yells, slob drips from his mouth. Tears are pouring down his face. He's mad about me taking all his customers.

He comes at me. "I thought you didn't want Desire no more!" he shouts.

"What the fuck are you talking about?"

"I'm talking about you and Desire! You said you were happily married! Why are you trying to fuck us up? It's your fault she don't want me no more! We was fine until you came home popping that dumb shit, whispering in her ear!"

"You got the game fucked up. I don't want Desire!"

"Then why are you playing with her then? You leading her on!"

"I ain't leading her on.

"Motherfucker, I saw you!"

"You saw me what?" I ask.

Now he's furious. He aims his gun at my head. "Get that gun out my face!"

"Motherfucker, I saw ya'll in the house that morning; hugging and shit!" he cries. "She was butt ass naked!"

I replay that day in my head. He saw us hugging and then he ran off the porch. "Ice, it wasn't what you thought," I explain.

"So, now I'm stupid! You saying, she wasn't naked?"

"Y, yeah," I stutter. "She was naked, but we weren't doing anything. We were just talking."

"Stop lying motherfucker!"

"I ain't lying," I mumble.

"Ooh! Stop lying!" *He covers his ears like he doesn't want to hear anymore.*

Of all the days to be without my gun. Please Slim, please come out and stop him.

I turn my head slightly toward the porch and, **Boom!** *My ears start to ring.* **"Aghh!"** *The impact of the bullet caves my chest in.* **Boom!**

He fires again. This one crashes into my forehead, causing the back of my head to bang into the roof of the car. I tumble over face first onto the concrete.

As I peek up, I see him jumping in his truck. He speeds off recklessly. Aghh! The pain is unbearable. The blood is pouring down my face. I can barely see. My chest is pounding.

"Daddy!" **Ahmad cries.**

"No! No!" **Desire screams,** *at the top of her lungs. She takes off up the stairs.*

Suddenly, there's no more pain. Everything is dark now. I can't see shit. I can hear everything, but I can't see. **Inhale, exhale.** *I can barely breathe. It feels like my chest is closing up on me.*

"Wake up, Big Time!" *That's Slim.* **"Wake up baby!"** **Slap!** *He's slapping my face.* **"Big Time, who did this to you?"** *I can't answer him. I feel both of my sons holding each of my hands.*

"Breathe, Big Time!" **Slim shouts.** **"You gotta breathe."** **Inhale, exhale.........inhale, exhale.**

"Breathe!" **Slim shouts.** **"Big Time, give me a sign. Tell me who did this to you!"**

"I, I," **I stutter.** *I can't manage to tell him.*

"Who?" **he asks.**

The words are on the tip of my tongue, but they won't come out. Please don't let this motherfucker get away. I can't believe this punk motherfucker shot me.

"Breathe, Big Time!"

Inhale, exhale. *I'm fading in and out.*

"Wake up, Big Time, wake up! The ambulance is on their way."

I feel like I'm about to die. Please, I can't go out like this. Please don't let this punk get this off on me.

"Big Time, please! Wake up! Tell me who did this to

you," he cries.

Inhale, exhale.

"Cash, you have to breathe!"

Inhale, exhale. *I'm fading out again.*

"Breathe!"

"I can't." *I manage to mumble.*

"You have to!" he shouts. "Big Time, you can't die! You have too much to live for! You got a beautiful wife and two boys who need you! Breathe!"

Inhale, exhale.

"Love is at the altar waiting for you! You can't die, she waiting for you!" he shouts. "Breathe baby!"

Inhale, exhale. *I can't die. Love is at the altar waiting for me. I have to prove her sister and her mother wrong.* Inhale, exhale. *My sons need me. Without me, they're headed for destruction.*

"Breathe, Big Time! You're fading out on me! You gotta breathe," he shouts.

"I, I." *I don't have any breath left.*

"Big Time, wake up! Please don't die on me like this," he cries.

I shake my head to tell him I can't breathe.

"Daddy, you have to breathe!" Ahmad screams.

I shake my head no.

"Daddy, you can do it!" he shouts. "You can do it!"

I can't let my boys see me go out like this. I'm going out like a sucker.

"Daddy, you the man!" they both scream.

Inhale, exhale.

"You the man," they repeat.

I have to pull this through.

"Breathe, Big Time!"

Inhale, exhale.

DONALD? DONALD?

Someone is calling me.

263

DONALD?

Oh no, it's the Angel of Death. Go away! I'm not answering! Go away! Please God, don't let him take me. Love is waiting for me. **Inhale, exhale.** *My boys need me. They can't grow up without a father. They'll turn out just like me.*

DONALD? DONALD?

Go away! Please God, if you get me out of this one, I swear I'll change my life around.

DONALD?

"Bang Man, you gotta breathe!" Slim shouts.

"Daddy, you the man! You the man, Daddy!"

Inhale, exhale.

DONALD?

I envision my first day of school.

DONALD?

Go away! Please God!

"Big Time, breathe!"

Inhale, exhale. *I remember sitting on my grandpa's lap.*

DONALD?

"Breathe, Big Time!"

"Come on Daddy! Please, Daddy! Don't die," Ahmad

begs.

I envision my first day of high school.

"Daddy, we need you! Breathe!"

Inhale, exhale.

"Where the fuck is the ambulance?" Slim screams.

I remember holding my first gun.

"Breathe! You gotta breathe!"

DONALD?

Inhale, exhale. *My 21st birthday.*

DONALD?

Big Ma just baked me a cake.

"Breathe!"

Inhale, exhale. *I'm at the Benz dealer with Desire.*

Inhale, exhale. *I'm riding with Love.* **Inhale, exhale.** *I just witnessed Ahmir being born.*

    DONALD?

    Ahmad is just born.

    "Breathe!"

    DONALD?

    Please God, don't let him take me. I promise I'll change. *Please!*

    "Breathe!"

    Inhale, exhale.

    "Daddy, you the man!"

    Me and Love just got married.

    DONALD?

    They're letting me out of the gates of prison.

    DONALD? DONALD?

    I'm not answering you! Go away!

    "Come on, Big Time, you're fading on me."

    Inhale, exhale. *I just met Juan.* **Inhale, exhale.** *I'm at the Benz dealer again.*

    "Come on, Daddy!"

    Latif just killed the young kid.

    "Breathe!"

    Me and Love are at the caterer.

    DONALD?

    "Breathe, Big Time! Breathe!"

    Inhale, exhale. *We're getting fitted for the tuxedos.* **Inhale, exhale.** *I'm shooting at Junebug's car.*

    "Come on Daddy!" **Whoop! Whoop!**

    Here comes the ambulance. I gotta make it! **Inhale, exhale.**

    "Come on Big Time, don't give up now."

    DONALD?

    Get out of here! **Inhale, exhale.** *I'm watching my son's championship game.*

    "Daddy, you the man!"

    "Come on, Big Time!"

The cop just asked me to step out of the car. **Inhale, exhale.**
I just served my man. **Inhale, exhale.**

DONALD?

"Come on, Big Time!" Slim begs. "Tell him ya'll love
him! Tell him how much ya'll need him! Tell him to breathe!"

"Daddy breathe," Ahmir cries. "We love you Daddy, you
can't die."

Inhale, exhale. *There's Ice.* **Inhale, exhale.** *He just
squeezed.*

"Breathe!" Slim shouts. "These boys need a father. You
can't die on them like this!"

DONALD?

"Daddy, please don't die!" Ahmad begs. "We need you
Daddy! Please don't die!" Ahmir begs.

Inhale, exhale.

"Daddy, you the man! Say it Daddy! Say I'm the man!"
Inhale, "I, I, I'm the………….

DEDICATION

I dedicate this book to all my brothers just coming home or on their way home from doing multiple-year sentences.

It's a new day. The young jacks have taken over. The same young jacks that used to admire you as their mothers escorted them to the corner store ten years ago.

Some you may have acknowledged; some you may have overlooked. But now the tables have turned. Now they control the streets. It's their turn! Let them do them. Don't stand in the way.

You may feel that you've paid your dues. You may feel the hood owes you something, and your pride won't let you get out of the way. But guess what. They have their pride too. But what's scarier is they have the same cold heart and the same I-don't-care attitude you had 20 years ago.

The only difference is they aren't playing by the same rules you used to play by. The old rule book you live your life by has been discarded and rewritten. The new rule book doesn't teach code or honor. There's no more loyalty.

Don't come home trying to change the game. Either you learn how to play by their rules, or don't play the game at all!

Peace, and stay up!!!!!!

Acknowledgements

    First and foremost, I have to thank God for keeping me focused long enough to produce another book.

    Second, I would like to thank my entire hood for supporting me. I can't go into a list of names, because I'll be writing forever, but if you have supported me in any way, I'm thanking you. Whether you have purchased a book, read someone else's book, recommended the book to someone, or even hated on the book, it's all-good. Thank you!!!

    I also would like to thank my friends and my family for keeping me motivated. Big shot out to TLE Variety on Central Avenue and Keystone Variety on South Orange Avenue. Thank you for introducing "No Exit" to the hood.

    Big up to Friend or Foe Entertainment, thanks for the help. This ya'll year. Take that label to the next level.

    Special shot out to Maria Holloway. Thanks for the information you gave me to get this whole ordeal started. Mikell Davis (author of Black Mafia) may God continue to reward you, As Salaamu Alaikum!!!!

    In addition, I would like to thank all of my readers. If I could thank each of you one by one, trust me I would. I'm glad you're feeling me!

    Danny, what up? Raul, it's been a few years now and I still haven't received my 36 team jersey. You and Rally have to talk to them cats ya'll need to change 36 to 37, you feel me?

    Fajr, look at Daddy, I'm doing it! I love you!
    XOXOXO

Author's Comments

Way too many prisoners of war doing lifetime bids.

Way too many fallen soldiers, killed on front line.

Way too many brokenhearted mothers mourning over the loss of their children.

Way too many widows holding onto memories of their husbands.

Way too many bastards left after the tragedy, left to defend themselves in this cold world.

Wake up people. We gotta do something different!!!!!

R.I.P. SHELDON DEAS
November 20, 1972 – October 24, 2003

On October 24, 2003 I lost a very dear friend of mine to a tragic accident. I'm asking all my readers to keep the Deas family in your prayers.

Sha- Sheldon, this tragedy caught us all by surprise. In between the short time span from <u>No Exit</u>- <u>Block Party</u>, we lost a member of the squad. I never got a chance to thank you for your support in this book venture. I took you for granted. I thought I would be able to show you my gratitude once the project developed and became a success. No matter where I needed to be, all I had to do was pick up the phone, and you would be there almost instantly. We would pile up in the truck, pack the boxes in the back, and we were on the road. You knew the roads like the back of your hand. I never heard you say, 'You didn't know how to get to a particular place.'

I just want to say thank you.

You hold it down up there and we'll hold it down on this end, then when it's all over and we all meet up again, we'll put everything in one pot; just like we used to, back in the day.

Rest in Peace my nigga.

P.S. I know you're in Paradise. You knew how to get every place else. I know you had to find your way there. Just make sure you hold us some seats. We'd hate to get all the way there and get turned around at the gate because it's too crowded, and there aren't any more seats. Hide a few chairs somewhere!

One Love!!!!!

TRUE 2 LIFE PRODUCTIONS
Order Form

True 2 Life Productions
P.O.BOX 8722
Newark, N.J. 07108

E-mail: true2lifeproductions@verizon.net
Website: www.true2lifeproductions.com

SINCERELY YOURS ?
ISBN # 0-974-0610-2-6 $13.95
Sales Tax (6% NJ)   .83
Shipping/ Handling
Via U.S. Priority Mail $ 3.85
Total $18.63

Also by the Author:
Block Party
ISBN # 0-974-0610-1-8 $14.95
Sales Tax (6% NJ)   .89
Shipping/Handling
Via U.S. Priority Mail $3.85
Total $19.69

No Exit
ISBN # 0-974-0610-0-X $13.95
Sales Tax (6% NJ)   .83
Shipping/ Handling
Via U.S. Priority Mail $ 3.85
Total $18.63

PURCHASER INFORMATION

Name: _____

Address: _____

City: _____ State: _____ Zip Code: _____

Sincerely Yours? ____

Block Party ____

No Exit ____

HOW MANY BOOKS? _____

Make checks/money orders payable to:
True 2 Life Productions